"I was on the lake this morning taking samples," Tilson said, a grimness in his tone.

"Samples?" asked Grissom.

Tilson shrugged. "Testing chemical pollution in the lake, at various depths. It's an ongoing USFW concern. Anyway, I bring up my container, then start hauling up the anchor to move to another spot. Well, the damn anchor snags on something." Another shrug. "Happens once in a while. Lotta shit's ended up in this lake over the years."

"I can imagine," Brass said, just moving it along.

"So," the wildlife man said, "I start pullin' the anchor chain back in, and damn, it's heavy as hell." Tilson moved close to the boat, then glanced up toward the parking lot—to make sure they were undisturbed—and pulled back the tarp. "And this is what I found."

Nick winced. "That's one hell of a catch of the day," he said.

Original novels in the CSI series

CSI: Crime Scene Investigation

Double Dealer

Sin City

Cold Burn

Body of Evidence

Grave Matters

Binding Ties

Serial (graphic novel)

Killing Game

CSI: Miami

Florida Getaway

Heat Wave

Cult Following

CSI: NY

Dead of Winter

CSI:

CRIME SCENE INVESTIGATION

SIN CITY

a novel

Max Allan Collins

Based on the hit CBS television series
"CSI: Crime Scene Investigation"
produced by Alliance Atlantis in
association with CBS Productions.
Executive Producers: Jerry Bruckheimer,
Carol Mendelsohn, Ann Donahue,
Anthony E. Zuiker
Co-Executive Producers: Sam Strangis, Jonathan Littman
Producers: Danny Cannon, Cynthia Chvatal &
William Petersen
Series created by Anthony E. Zuiker

POCKET **STAR** BOOKS
New York London Toronto Sydney

An *Original* Publication of POCKET BOOKS

A Pocket Star Book published by
POCKET BOOKS, a division of Simon & Schuster, Inc.
1230 Avenue of the Americas, New York, NY 10020

For information address Pocket Books, 1230 Avenue of the Americas, New York, NY 10020
ISBN 13: 978-0-7434-4405-7
ISBN 10: 0-7434-4405-1
First Pocket Books printing October 2002

19 18 17 16 15 14 13 12 11 10 9

POCKET and colophon are registered trademarks of Simon & Schuster, Inc.

For information regarding special discounts for bulk purchases, please contact Simon & Schuster Special Sales at 1-800-456-6798 or business@simonandschuster.com

Front cover illustration by Patrick Kang

Manufactured in the United States of America

For Chris Kaufmann—
the CSI who saw the body

M.A.C. and M.V.C.

When two objects come into contact,
there is a material exchange,
from each to the other.

—Edmund Locard, 1910
Father of Forensic Science

Las Vegas—like New York and rust—never sleeps. From dusk till dawn, the sprawl of the city and its glittering neon jewelery enliven the desert landscape, competing with a million stars, all of them so tiny compared to Siegfried and Roy. From the fabled "Strip" of Las Vegas Boulevard to the world's tallest eyesore—the Stratosphere—Vegas throbs to its own 24/7 pulse, hammering into the wee-est of wee hours.

If such modern monuments as the Luxor and Bellagio indicate a certain triumph of man over nature, this shimmer of wholesome sin is nonetheless contained by a desert landscape, including mountains (almost) as green as money, as peaceful as the Strip is not. And a slumbering city—as normal as any urban sprawl, people living, working, loving, dying—exists in the reality of Vegas off the Strip, away from Fremont Street, a world where couples occasionally marry in a real chapel, as opposed to a neon-trimmed storefront where the pastor is Elvis, and "gambling" means getting to work five minutes late, or eating fried food, or cheating on your wife, or maybe trying to get away with murder, figurative or literal.

Nonetheless, as Sinatra said of New York, New York (the town, not the resort), Las Vegas, Nevada, indeed does not sleep. This is a city where, for many a citizen, working nights is the norm, from a pit boss at the Flamingo to a counter clerk at a convenience store, from an exotic dancer in a live nude girls club to a criminalist working the graveyard shift.

1

Millie Blair hated spending nights alone. She had always been anxious, and even being reborn in the blood of Christ hadn't helped. Nor did the nature of her husband Arthur's job, which sometimes meant long evenings waiting for him to get home.

Tonight, Millie couldn't seem to stop wringing her hands. Her collar-length brunette hair, now graying in streaks, framed a pleasant, almost pretty oval face tanned by days of outdoor sports—playing golf or tennis with friends from the church—and she looked young for forty. A petite five-four and still fit, she knew her husband continued to find her attractive, due in part to her rejection of the frumpy attire many of her friends had descended to in middle age. Tonight she wore navy slacks with a white silk blouse and an understated string of pearls.

Millie was glad Arthur still found her desirable—there was no sin in marital sex, after all, and love was a blessed thing between husband and wife—

but she was less than pleased with her appearance, noting unmistakable signs of aging in her unforgiving makeup mirror, of late. Frown lines were digging tiny trenches at the corners of her mouth—the anxiety, again—and although she tried to compensate with lipstick, her lips seemed thinner, and her dark blue eyes could take on a glittering, glazed hardness when she was upset . . . like now.

Moving to the window, she nervously pulled back the curtains, peered out into the purple night like a pioneer woman checking for Indians, saw nothing moving, then resumed her pacing. Tonight her anxiety had a rational basis—Millie had heard something terribly disturbing yesterday . . . an audiotape of an argument between a certain married couple.

It was as if some desert creature had curled up in her stomach and died there—or rather refused to die, writhing spasmodically in the pit of her belly. Millie knew something was wrong, dreadfully wrong, with her best friend Lynn Pierce. A member of Millie's church, Lynn seemed to have fallen off the planet since the two women had spoken, at around four P.M. this afternoon.

"Mil," Lynn had said, something ragged in her voice, "I need to see you . . . I need to see you right away."

"Is it Owen again?" Millie asked, the words tumbling out. "Another argument? Has he threatened you? Has he—"

"I can't talk right now."

Something in Lynn's throat caught—a sob? A

gasp? How strange the way fear and sadness could blur.

Millie had clutched the phone as if hauling her drowning friend up out of treacherous waters. "Oh, Lynn, what is it? How can I help?"

"I . . . I'll tell you in person. When I see you."

"Well that's fine, dear. Don't you worry—Art and I are here for you. You just come right over."

"Is Arthur there now?"

"No, I meant . . . moral support. Is it that bad, that Arthur isn't here? Are you . . . frightened? Should I call Art and have him—"

"No! No. It'll be fine. I'll be right over."

"Good. Good girl."

"On my way. Fifteen minutes tops."

Those had been Lynn's last words before the women hung up.

Lynn Pierce—the most reliable, responsible person Millie knew—had not kept her word; she had not come "right over." Fifteen minutes passed, half an hour, an hour, and more.

Millie called the Pierce house and got only the answering machine.

Okay, maybe Millie *was* an anxious, excitable woman; all right, maybe she *did* have a melodramatic streak. Pastor Dan said Millie just had a good heart, that she truly cared about people, that her worry came from a good place.

This worry for Lynn may have come from a good place, but Millie feared Lynn had gone to a very bad place. She had a sick, sick feeling she would never see her best friend again.

As such troubled, troublesome thoughts roiled in her mind like a gathering thunderstorm, Millie paced and fretted and wrung her hands and waited for her husband Arthur to get home. Art would know what to do—he always did. In the meantime, Millie fiddled with her wedding ring, and concocted tragic scenarios in her mind, periodically chiding herself that Lynn had only been missing a few hours, after all.

But that tape.

That terrible tape she and Arthur had heard last night. . . .

Millie perked up momentarily when Gary, their son, came home. Seventeen, a senior, Gary—a slender boy with Arthur's black hair and her oval face—had his own car and more and more now, his own life.

Their son kept to himself and barely spoke to them—though he was not sullen, really. He attended church with them willingly, always ready to raise his hands to the Lord. That told Millie he must still be a good boy.

For a time she and Arthur had been worried about their son, when Gary was dating that wild Karlson girl with her nose rings and pierced tongue and tattooed ankle and cigarettes. Lately he'd started dating Lori—Lynn's daughter, a good girl, active in the church like her mom.

He was shuffling up the stairs—his bedroom was on the second floor— when she paused in her pacing to ask, "And how was school?"

He had his backpack on as he stood there, dutifully, answering with a shrug.

From the bottom of the stairs, she asked, "Didn't you have a test today? Biology, wasn't it?"

Another shrug.

"Did you do well?"

One more shrug.

"Your father's going to be late tonight. You want to wait to eat with us, or . . . ?"

Now he was starting up the stairs again. "I'll nuke something."

"I can make you macaroni, or—"

"Nuke is fine."

"All right."

He flicked a smile at her, before disappearing around the hallway, going toward his bedroom, the door of which was always closed, lately.

Growing up seemed to be hard on Gary, and she wished that she and Arthur could help; but this afternoon's taciturn behavior was all too typical of late. Gary barely seemed to acknowledge them, bestowing occasional cursory words and a multitude of shrugs. Still, his grades remained good, so maybe this was just part of growing up. A child slipping away from his parents into his own life was apparently part of God's plan.

But the problem of coping with Gary, Millie realized, was something to be worried about after this mess with Lynn got cleared up. The woman let out a long breath of relief as she peeked through the drapes and watched Arthur's Lexus ease into the driveway.

Finally.

A moment later she heard the bang of the car

door, the hum of the garage door opener, and—at last!—Arthur stepped into the kitchen.

Stocky, only a couple of inches taller than his wife, a black-haired fire hydrant of a man, Arthur Blair—like Millie—had retained a youthful demeanor. Even though he was older than his wife (forty-four), his hair stayed free of gray; God had blessed him with good genes and without his wife's anxious streak. Black-framed Coke-bottle glasses turned his brown eyes buggy, but Millie's husband remained a handsome man.

Arthur had first met coed Millie ("Never call me Mildred!") Evans at a frat party back in their undergraduate days. A sorority sister and a little wild, she had dressed like, and looked like, that sexy slender Pat Benatar, all curly black hair and spandex, and she took his breath away. Immediately recognizing that she was out of his league, the bookish Arthur wouldn't have said a word to her if she hadn't struck up a conversation at the keg. Throughout the course of the evening they'd exchanged glances, but no further words. He could tell she was disappointed in him, but he'd been just too shy to do anything about it, at first; and then, pretty soon, he'd been too drunk. . . .

The next semester they'd had an Econ class together and she had recognized a familiar face and sat down next to him. Now, twenty years later, she still hadn't left his side.

Walking through the kitchen, Arthur moved into the dining room, set his briefcase on the table, tossed his suit jacket onto a chair and passed straight into the living room to find Millie standing in the middle of the room, holding herself as if she were freezing. Her face seemed drained of color, her eyes filigreed red. She'd clearly been crying. . . .

"Baby, what's wrong?" he asked, moving to her, taking her into his arms.

Arthur knew his anxious wife might have been upset about anything or nothing; but he always took her distress seriously. He loved her.

"It . . . it's Lynn," she said, sobs breaking loose as he hugged and patted her.

It was as if his arms had broken some sort of dam and she cried uncontrollably for a very long time before she finally reined in her emotions enough to speak coherently.

Arthur held her at arm's length. "What's wrong, baby? *What* about Lynn? Has that tape got you going . . . ?"

"Not the tape . . . I mean, *yes* the tape, but no . . ." Gulping back a last sob, Millie said, "She phoned this afternoon, about four—real upset. Said she had to see me, talk to me. Said she was on her way over."

"Well, what did she have to say, once she got here?"

"Arthur, that's just it—she never showed up!"

She told him about trying to call, getting the machine, and how she just *knew* Lynn had "disappeared."

Her husband shook his head, dismissive of the problem but not of her. "Honey, it could be anything. There's no point in getting all worked up . . . at least, not until we know what happened."

She stepped out of his embrace. Her eyes moved to the drawer handle of the end table across the room. His gaze followed hers—they both knew what lay in that shallow drawer: the tape. That awful audiotape that they had played last night. . . .

"Just because . . ." He stopped. ". . . this doesn't mean . . . necessarily . . ."

She drew in a deep breath, calming herself, or trying to. "I know, I know . . . It's just that . . . well, you know if she'd been delayed, she would have called, Arthur. Certainly by now she would have called."

He knew she was right. After a sigh and a nod, he asked, "Is Gary home?"

She nodded back. "In his room, of course. Behind the closed door."

"It's normal."

"He . . . sort of gave me the silent treatment again."

"Really?"

"Well. No. He was polite . . . I guess."

Arthur walked to the foot of the stairs and called up. "Gary!"

Silence.

A curtness came into Arthur's voice, now: "Gary!"

The clean-cut young man peeked around the hallway corner, as if he'd been hiding there all the while. "Yes, sir?"

"Your mother and I are going out. You okay with getting your own dinner?"

"Yes, sir. Already told mom I would microwave something. Anyway, I have to go into work for a couple of hours. Maybe I'll just grab something on the way."

"Well, that'll be fine, son. . . . We'll see you later."

"Yes, sir."

The boy disappeared again.

Millie, shaking her head, said, "All I get are shrugs. I can't believe how he opens up to you. He really respects you, Art."

Arthur said nothing, still staring up the stairs at where his boy had been. He wondered if his son's respect was real or just for show—assuming the kid even knew the difference. Arthur had had the same kind of relationship with his own father, always "yes sirring" and "no sirring," thinking he was doing it just to stay on the old man's good side, then eventually finding out that he really did respect his father. He hoped Gary would some day feel that way about him . . . even if the boy didn't do so now.

He turned to his wife. "Come on, sweetie," he said. "And get your coat. Some bite in the air, tonight."

"Where are we going?" she asked, even as she followed his directions, pulling a light jacket from the front closet. Also navy blue, the jacket didn't quite match her slacks and she hoped at night no one would notice.

"I think we'll drop by at our good friends, the Pierce's."

She didn't argue. For a woman with an anxious streak, Millie could be strong, even fearless, particularly when the two of them were together. Arthur realized going over to the Pierces was the course of action she'd wanted all along, she just hadn't wanted to be the one to suggest it.

Her respect for him was real, Arthur knew. Anyway, their church taught a strict, biblical adherence to the husband's role as the head of the household.

They moved to the door, but—at the last second—Millie hurried back to the living room, grabbed the small package out of the end table and tucked the audiotape into her purse.

The drive to the Pierce home took only about twelve minutes. Traffic had thinned out and the cooler autumn temperatures had settled in, apparently convincing many a Las Vegan to stay inside for the evening. Millie wondered aloud if they should listen to the tape again, in the car's cassette player, as they drove over.

"No thanks," Arthur said, distastefully. "I remember it all too well." Then he shook his head and added, "I don't think I'll ever forget the . . . thing," almost swearing.

Though Owen and Lynn Pierce were supposed to be their best friends, Arthur and Millie Blair both loved her, and barely tolerated him. Arthur found Pierce to be a vulgar, cruel, Godless man, an opinion with which Millie agreed wholeheartedly. Arthur also believed that Owen dabbled in drugs, or so the rumors said; but he had no proof and kept that thought to himself. He feared that Millie wouldn't allow Gary to continue dating Lori Pierce if she thought there were drugs anywhere near the Pierce home—even if Lynn *was* her best friend.

The Pierce house looked like a tan-brick fortress, a turret dominating the left side of a two-story structure that presided over a sloping, well-landscaped lawn, sans moat however. Inside the turret, a spiral staircase led to the second floor (the Blairs had been guests at the Pierces' home, many times). The front door sat in the center of this mini-Camelot with a three-car garage on the right end. With just the one turret, the house seemed to lean slightly in that direction, giving the place an off-kilter feel.

When the Lexus pulled into the castle's driveway, Arthur said, "Now let me handle this."

Again, no argument from Millie on that score. She just nodded, then—almost hiding behind him—she followed her husband up the curving walk to the front door.

Arthur rang the bell and they waited. After thirty seconds or so, he rang it again, three times in rapid insistent succession. Again they waited almost a half a minute, an endless span to spend standing on a front porch; but this time as Arthur reached for the button, the door jerked open and they found themselves face-to-face with Lynn's husband—Owen Pierce himself.

Muscular in his gray Nike sweats, with silver glints in his dark hair, Pierce had striking blue eyes, and a ready, winning smile that displayed many white, straight teeth. Pierce's face seemed to explode in delight. "Well, Art! Millie! What a nice surprise—what are you doing here? I mean . . ." He chuckled, apparently embarrassed that that might have sound ungracious. "How are you? We didn't have plans for dinner or something tonight, did we? Lynn didn't say anything . . ."

The therapist's grin seemed forced, and his words came too fast and were delivered too loudly. Arthur again considered those drug rumors. "No, no plans tonight, Owen. We were hoping to speak to Lynn."

"Lynn?" Pierce frowned in confusion, as if this were a name he'd never heard before.

"Yes," Arthur said. "Lynn. You remember, Owen—your wife?"

An uncomfortable silence followed, as Pierce apparently tried to read Arthur's words and tone.

Finally, Millie stepped forward. "Owen, Lynn called me earlier, and said she was coming to see me . . . then she never showed up."

"Oh!" He smiled again, less dazzlingly. "Is *that* what this is about. . . ."

Millie said, "It's just not *like* her, Owen. She would have called me, if she had a change in plans."

Pierce's smile finally faded and his eyes tightened. "Her brother called. She barely took time to tell me! Something about an illness, and how they needed her there. You know how she jumps to, when her family's involved. Anyway, she packed a few things and left, lickety split."

What a load of bull, Arthur thought. He knew

Lynn Pierce wouldn't leave the city without telling Millie where she was headed, and how long she'd be gone—particularly when Lynn had told Millie she was coming "right over"! Something was definitely not right here.

Arthur considered the tape in Millie's purse. Should he confront Pierce about it?

As Arthur was mulling this, his wife took a step nearer to Pierce, saying, "I'm sorry, but I don't believe you, Owen. Lynn would never . . ."

A frown crossed Pierce's face and Millie fell silent. The expression replacing the phony smile was all too sincere: as if a rock had been lifted and the real Owen had been glimpsed wriggling there in the dirt.

Over the years, the Blairs had both seen Pierce lose his temper, and it was never a pleasant sight—like a boiler exploding. Arthur took Millie gently if firmly by the arm and turned her toward the car. "Excuse us, Owen. Millie's just concerned about Lynn, you know how women are."

Pierce twitched a sort of grin.

As the couple moved away, Arthur said, "Hope Lynn has a good trip, Owen. Have her give us a call when she gets back, would you? . . . Thanks."

And all the time he spoke, Arthur steered Millie toward the car at the curb. She did not protest—she knew her place—but when he finally got her in the car, backed out of the driveway, and drove away from Owen Pierce and the castle house, she demanded an explanation.

"Don't you worry, darling," Arthur said. "We'll do something about that evil bastard."

Sometimes, when a swear word slipped out of him, she would scold him. He almost looked forward to the familiarity of it.

But tonight, she said only, "Good. Good. Good."

And she sat beside him in the vehicle, with her fists clenched, the purse in her lap . . . and that tape, that terrible tape, in the purse.

2

Captain Jim Brass ambled down the hall toward the washed-out aqua warren of offices that served as headquarters for the Las Vegas Criminalistics Bureau, a coldly modern institutional setting for the number-two crime lab in the country. The sad-eyed detective was sharply attired—gray sports coat over a blue shirt, darker blue tie with gray diagonal stripes, and navy slacks—and his low-key demeanor masked a dogged professionalism.

A cellophane bag dangled from the detective's right hand, an audiotape within. Slowing to peer through various half-windowed walls, Brass passed several rooms before he found the CSI graveyard-shift supervisor, Gil Grissom, in the break room at a small table, hunkered over a cup of coffee and a pile of papers. Dressed in black and wearing his wire-framed reading glasses, the CSI chief looked like a cross between a gunfighter and a science geek, Brass thought, then realized that that was a pretty accurate mix.

Grissom—one of the top forensic entomologists in the country, among other things—was in his mid-forties, with his boyishly handsome features seemingly set in a state of perpetual preoccupation. Brass liked Gil, and felt that what some considered coldness in the man was really a self-imposed coolness, a detachment designed to keep the CSI chief's eye on facts and his emotions in check.

Brass pulled up a chair. "Latest issue of *Cockroach Racing Monthly?*"

Grissom shook his head, and responded as if the detective's question had been serious. "Staffing reports. Scuttlebutt is the County Board wants to cut the budget for next year."

"I heard that, too." Brass sighed. "Doesn't election time just bring out the best in people?"

Grissom gave him a pursed-lipped look that had nothing to do with blowing a kiss.

"Maybe you need something to put you in a better mood, Gil—like threats of dismemberment."

Grissom offered Brass another look, this one piqued with interest.

Brass held up the plastic baggie and waved it like a hypnotist's watch, Grissom's eyes following accordingly. "Among your state-of-the-art, cutting-edge equipment . . . you got a cassette player?"

Nodding, rising, removing his glasses, Grissom said, "In my office. What have you got?" He gathered up the pile of papers, the cup of coffee, and led Brass out into the hall.

The detective fell in alongside Grissom as they

moved down the corridor. "Interesting turn of events, just now, out at the front desk."

"Really?"

They moved into Grissom's office.

"Really."

Brass had only lately ceased to be creeped out by Grissom's inner sanctum, with its shelves of such jarred oddities as a pickled piglet and various embalmed animal and human organs, and assorted living, crawling creatures—a tarantula, a two-headed scorpion—in glassed-in homes. At least the batteries had finally worn down on the Big Mouth Billy Bass just above Grissom's office door.

A desk sat in the middle of the methodically cluttered office, canted at a forty-five-degree angle, two vinyl-covered metal frame chairs in front of it. Brass handed the bag over to Grissom, then plopped into a chair. Behind his desk, Grissom sat and placed the bag on his blotter like a jeweler mounting a stone. From the top righthand drawer, he withdrew a pair of latex gloves and placed them next to the bag.

"Is this all tease," Grissom said, hands folded, "or do you plan to put out?"

Brass sat back, crossed his legs, twitched a non-smile. "This couple comes in tonight, to the front desk. Nice people, late thirties, early forties—straight as they come. He's in the finance department at UNLV."

Grissom nodded.

"Arthur and Millie Blair. They say their friend, woman named Lynn Pierce, has disappeared . . .

and they think something 'bad' has happened to her."

Grissom's eyes tightened, just a little. "How long has Lynn Pierce been missing?"

Checking his watch, Brass said, "About seven hours."

Grissom's eyes relaxed. "That's not twenty-four. She may be gone, but she's not 'missing,' yet."

Brass shrugged. "Officer at the desk told 'em the same thing. That's when they pulled out this tape."

Grissom glanced at the bag. "Which is a tape of what?"

Brass had to smile—Grissom was like a kid waiting to tear into a Christmas present. "Supposedly an argument between Lynn Pierce and her husband."

"Husband?"

Brass pulled a notebook from his jacket pocket and flipped it open, filling Grissom in on the particulars—Owen Pierce, successful physical therapist, married eighteen years to the missing woman.

"Clinic—'Therapeutic Body Works'—in a strip mall out on Hidden Well Road. East of the Callaway Golf Center."

One of Grissom's eyebrows arched in skeptical curiosity. "And the Blairs are in possession of this tape because . . . ?"

"This is where it gets good," Brass said, shifting in the chair. "The Blairs say Mrs. Pierce showed up on their doorstep last night—with this tape in her hot little hand. Mrs. Pierce told her friends the

Blairs that she'd hidden a voice-activated tape player in the kitchen. Wanted to prove what kind of verbal abuse she'd been suffering, of late."

"I like a victim who provides evidence for us," Grissom said.

"Well, then you'll love Lynn Pierce. Her hidden microphone caught a doozy of an argument, it seems. Anyway, the Blairs said that Mrs. Pierce gave them the tape for safe keeping, then she sat with them and talked and talked about her marital problems, and trouble with their daughter, Lori . . ."

"Lori is whose daughter?"

"The Pierces. But most of all, Lynn was tired of the constant threats of violence her husband had been making."

"Let's hear the tape."

Brass held up a palm. "You still haven't heard the best part."

The detective told Grissom about the Blairs going to the Pierce home, where Owen Pierce claimed his wife had gone to visit a sick brother.

"Is that the best part?" Grissom asked, unimpressed.

"No—the best part is, while the Blairs are talking to one officer at the front desk, the other officer is taking a phone call from guess who."

"Owen Pierce."

"Owen Pierce. Calling to report his wife missing. He now claims that she got pissed off after a 'misunderstanding,' and he figures she left him, and he doesn't know where the hell she went."

Grissom was sitting forward now. "Did the wife take anything with her?"

"A couple of uniforms went to the house," Brass said. "Pierce told them he didn't see her go. But she took her own car—a '95 Avalon—also a suitcase, some clothes."

"Let's listen to the tape."

Brass raised both eyebrows. "Why don't we?"

Slipping on the latex gloves, Grissom removed the tape from the bag. He rose, moved to a small boombox behind the desk, and slid the tape into the holder. After closing the door, he pushed PLAY with a latexed fingertip—Brass noted that Grissom brought the same anal-retentive precision to the simple procedure of playing an audiotape cassette as he would to one of his bizarre experiments involving blood-spatter spray patterns or insect eating patterns.

The sound was somewhat muffled; apparently the couple had been standing across the room from the secreted tape recorder. But the words soon became clear enough, as the Pierces raised their voices in anger.

"If you don't stop it, just stop it, I swear I'll do it! I'll divorce you!"

That had been the woman's voice.

Now the man's: *"Stop it? Stop* what? *What the fuck are you talking about?"*

"I'm talking about the cocaine, Owen—and your slutty women! I've already talked to a lawyer—"

"You bitch—lousy rotten bitch . . . go ahead, go ahead and file for divorce. I'll make sure you don't get a goddamned thing—including Lori!"

Brass glanced at Grissom, but the criminalist's face was blank, his focus complete.

"Owen . . ." The woman's voice had turned pleading. *"I just want us to be a . . . family, again. Do you think what I really want is a divorce?"*

The man's reply was mostly inaudible, but they heard three words clearly: *". . . give a fuck."*

The woman spoke again, and she too was inaudible, but then her voice rose, not in anger, but as a conclusion to a speech: *"I just want you and Lori to find the peace that I've found serving our Lord!"*

"Oh, Christ! Not that Jesus crap again. I've told you a thousand fucking times, Lynn—I believe what I believe."

"You don't believe in anything.*"*

"That's my choice. That's America. That's what your forefathers died for, you dumb . . ."

At the next word, Grissom shot a look at Brass.

The man was saying, *"You need to give Lori the same space, too, Lynn. She's a young adult. She deserves a little respect."*

"She's a child."

"She's sixteen! Hell, in half the world she'd be married already! Old enough to bleed, old enough to breed!"

"Owen!"

"I'm just telling you what I *do, what our grown* daughter *does, is none of your goddamned Bible-beating business."*

"Maybe . . . maybe I should *get a divorce then."*

"Knock yourself out. . . . But remember, you don't get one dime, not one fucking thing."

"Is that right? I hired the best divorce lawyer in town,

Owen—and when I get around to telling him about the drugs and the women and you screwing the IRS by skimming off the top of the 'Body Works'? Well, then *we'll just* see *who gets custody of Lori!"*

The woman sounded triumphant, Brass thought, and for a moment the husband had no response. The woman's time on top of the argument didn't last long.

"You do," Pierce said, *"and I'll kill your holier-than-thou ass . . ."*

"Owen! No! Don't say—"

"And then I'll cut you up in little pieces, my darling bride. I will scatter your parts to the four winds, and they will never *put Humpty Dumpty back together!"*

The argument lasted only a couple of more minutes, none of it coherently audible—the couple had apparently moved farther away from the hidden machine—before the detective and the criminalist heard the sound of a door slam and then the tape clicked off.

"What do you think?" Brass asked. "We got enough to go out there? Or is that just the road company of *Who's Afraid of Virginia Woolf?"*

Grissom stood. "I think we need to go out there. Everybody's in-house, at the moment—let's take the whole crew."

Brass winced. "Don't you think we should try for a warrant, first?"

Grissom gave Brass that familiar mock-innocent smile. "Why? Mr. Pierce called the police. He's concerned about his missing wife. We should help the poor guy, don't you think?"

"Yeah, who needs a warrant to do that?" Brass said, grinning, climbing out of the chair. "What about the tape?"

"What tape?"

"Yeah," Brass said, eyes narrowing. "Obviously Pierce doesn't know it exists. No need to tell him that we do."

"I don't know what you're talking about," Grissom said. "Let's go see what there is to see."

Ten minutes later, six colleagues—all but Brass in dark FORENSICS windbreakers—met in the under-lit parking lot.

Lanky, loose-limbed, African-American Warrick Brown stood a few inches taller than the athletically brawny Nick Stokes; both men were in their very early thirties.

Off to one side were the two women on the team, Grissom's second-in-command, Catherine Willows, and the relatively recent addition, Sara Sidle.

The Willows woman had a checkered past, Brass knew, but her experience had made her a valuable counterbalance to the overly cool Grissom. Brass had less confidence in Sara Sidle, despite her status as a former Grissom pupil handpicked by Gil for the job. Sidle seemed to be a Grissom-in-the-making, similarly obsessed with work—and with people skills rivaling those of her tactless mentor.

Grissom filled his people in, quickly, on the contents of the tape and the potentially missing woman.

"So we have a verbally abusive husband," Grissom said, tone as tight as his eyes, "who threatened his wife with dismemberment."

"But we're pretending to help him out," Warrick said.

"I didn't hear that," Grissom said, sweetly.

Warrick, Nick, Catherine, and Sara rode in the Tahoe, Grissom rode with Brass in the detective's Taurus. Just before midnight, they arrived at the castle-like house on the impressive sloping lawn, lights shining out downstairs windows, sending sword-like shafts of light into the dark.

Brass and Grissom led the way to the front door. The detective rang the bell and had to wait only a moment before the door opened to reveal a muscular man in dark slacks, black T-shirt, and black loafers, dark hair peppered with gray. The man stood before Grissom like a mirror reflection—only, Brass thought, this was Gil Grissom on steroids.

Brass smiled, mildly. "Mr. Pierce?"

The man nodded. He seemed anxious. "You're the police?"

Touching the badge on his breast pocket, Brass affirmed, "We're the police—sorry it took us so long to respond to your call. . . . We had to round our people up."

Grissom flicked Pierce an insincere smile. "We're a full-service operation, Mr. . . . Pierce, I assume?"

Still not inviting them in, Pierce nodded.

Grissom lifted the necklace I.D. "Gil Grissom, Las Vegas Criminalistics. This is Captain Jim Brass, and this is our Criminalistics crew."

Pierce regarded the considerable assembly overflowing his front stoop. "Then . . . you haven't found my wife?"

"No, sir," Grissom said, "I'm sorry, as yet we haven't."

Pierce shook his head. "I don't understand what you're doing here. I gave all the information to the officer, on the phone. Shouldn't you be out looking for Lynn, Detective . . . Griswald, is it?"

"It's Grissom, Mr. Pierce, only I'm not a detective. I'm a supervisor of Criminalistics." He flashed another empty smile. "And we *are* out looking for your wife. That's why we're here. You see, we handle crime scene investigation."

A puzzled look tightened Pierce's face. "Crime scene? I don't understand. This isn't a crime scene—my wife walked out on me."

"Sir, my understanding is, you don't know that for sure. She might well have been abducted."

"Well . . . that's possible. Maybe I hadn't wanted to . . . admit that to myself."

Grissom nodded in supposed sympathy. "Also, there's the matter of the Blairs."

"The Blairs."

"Yes. Your wife called them in the afternoon . . . said she would come by, never materialized. They said they spoke to you."

Pierce sucked in air, his expression turning sheepish. "Oh. I see . . . look, when they came by, I was embarrassed. I told them that Lynn went to visit her brother to, you know, get rid of them."

Frowning, Brass asked, "You wanted to get rid of them?"

"They mean well, Detective . . . Brass?"

"Yes. Brass."

"They're kind of busybodies, Detective Brass. Judgmental types—Bible beaters? And the wound was fresh, Det . . . uh . . . Mr. Grissom. I needed to be alone while I sorted some things out."

Grissom shrugged one shoulder. "Then why did you telephone the police?"

He shrugged both his. "I wanted someone to help me find her. I thought maybe Lynn and I could find a way to work out our problems."

"So, then, you really don't know where she is?"

Pierce shook his head. "Nope, no idea."

"And you weren't here when she left?"

"No. I was at my office . . . my clinic."

"That makes abduction a real possibility, Mr. Pierce. And that's why we're here."

He frowned. "Just because I have no idea where Lynn is? And because she made a phone call?"

"Yes, sir." Grissom's expression turned almost angelic. "We want to help you. Maybe we can find a clue as to what happened to your wife."

"But," Brass said, with half a smile, "we can't help you out here on the stoop."

Pierce sighed again, shrugged with his eyebrows this time. "Well—if it'll help find Lynn . . . of course, come in."

The response surprised Brass a little, and he exchanged glances with Grissom, who the detective figured had also been expecting objections from Pierce, not cooperation—particularly if a crime had gone down within these castle walls, earlier today.

Pierce stepped back inside and held the door as

the group trooped in, moving through a small entryway into a larger anteroom of a home whose walls were cream-color stucco with dark woodwork. A winding staircase disappeared up a landing at left, and a hallway was at left also, with the dining room visible through one arched doorless doorway, in the facing wall, and, to the right, a living room yawned through another archway. The furnishings were colonial, tasteful enough, but a bit at odds with the castle-like architecture.

Brass asked, "Is there anyone else in the house, sir?"

"Just my daughter."

Grissom asked, "Was she here when your wife left?"

"No. I'm afraid not."

A teenage girl stepped down the winding stairs into view. She wore Nikes, nice new jeans, a big white sweatshirt, with her long blonde hair pulled back and held in place with a blue scrunchy. Her pretty face—she resembled her father, though the eyes were wider set—was well scrubbed and her bright blue eyes were rimmed red. She glanced down at the contingency in the anteroom, and froze on the landing.

"This is my daughter," Pierce said, "Lori."

The girl gave a barely perceptible nod, then turned and disappeared back upstairs.

Pierce sighed again and said, "You'll have to forgive her, please. This has been hard for both of us, but especially for Lori. She's taken it pretty hard, the idea of her mother . . . abandoning us."

Brass nodded. Grissom was looking around, taking in the framed wildlife artwork.

"Will you have to . . ." Pierce looked for the words. ". . . disturb Lori, when you make your search?"

Brass glanced at Grissom, who gave a little shrug.

"I don't think so, sir," the detective said. "We'll leave her alone for now . . . though it's possible we might have some questions later."

"I understand."

Grissom approached Pierce, standing a little too close, as if having a better look at an insect specimen, and said, "Mr. Pierce, if you and Captain Brass will wait in the living room, we'll get to work. Then we'll talk to you when we're finished."

"All right."

For the next two hours, the CSI crew—in latex gloves but wielding little else of their elaborate equipment—crawled over every inch of the house, examining everything from the basement to the garage, speaking to the teenage girl only to ask her to step out of her bedroom for a few minutes. When they had finished, they conferred in the kitchen, careful to keep their voices down as they discussed what they'd found, and hadn't found.

An eyebrow arched, Catherine said to Grissom, "There are gaps in the closet. Some clothes and shoes gone, apparently."

"Consistent with Lynn Pierce packing up and leaving," Grissom said.

Catherine smiled humorlessly, nodded.

Sara was nodding, too. "Yeah, and there's a row of suitcases in the basement, with a space in it—so maybe one of them is gone. Space on the shelf above, where a train case could've been."

Warrick piped in: "Only one toothbrush in the master bathroom. Some empty spaces on her makeup table, like she took perfume, makeup, stuff like that."

"No sign of her purse," Nick said. "And there was no blood in the drains, no knives missing that I could tell, no sign anyone did . . . what he said he would . . . on the tape."

"I'd sure like to bring a RUVIS in here," Catherine said, referring to the ultraviolet device that would show up blood stains.

"I don't think we can justify that," Grissom said. "If there *is* a crime here, we don't want to do anything that would be thrown out of court. . . . So what does this house tell us?"

"She may have gone," Catherine said.

Sara's eyebrows were up. "Or somebody may have made it look like she left."

"Gris," Warrick said, "I did find one thing that could be significant." He showed them a clear evidence bag with a hairbrush in the bottom.

Grissom took the bag, held it up and looked at it as if it held the secrets of the universe; several blonde hairs dangled from the brush. He asked, "Does a woman pack up and go, and leave her hairbrush behind?"

"Maybe Sara," Nick said with a grin, and Sara grinned back and elbowed him, a little.

Grissom focused on the hairbrush in the bag. "Why don't we ask Mr. Pierce about this?"

They followed their supervisor into the living room where Pierce and Brass (his notepad out) sat on a couch in front of a thirty-six inch Toshiba in an early-American entertainment hutch (just like George and Martha Washington used to have); CNN was going, with the mute on.

"Anything you'd like to share?" Brass asked Grissom.

"You'll be relieved to know," Grissom said, "that there are no signs of a struggle anywhere in the house."

"I could have told you that," Pierce said.

Catherine said, "We don't see any overt indications of abduction."

"That's a relief, anyway," Pierce said, letting out a big sigh—too big, maybe.

Grissom offered up his patented smile. "What can you tell me about this, Mr. Pierce?"

And he held up the bag with the brush.

"Well . . . that's Lynn's," Pierce said.

Catherine asked, "Would you say your wife is well-groomed, Mr. Pierce? Takes pride in her appearance?"

Pierce bristled. "She's a beautiful woman. Of course she's . . . well-groomed."

Catherine's smile was utterly charming, her words casually heartless. "Does she usually go off without her hairbrush?"

"Maybe she has more than one." Pierce held his hands out, palms open. "How should I know? . . .

Anyway, she only uses a brush when her hair is long. Lynn had her hair cut recently—it's barely over her ears. I've seen her combing it, but not brushing."

Sara said, "I noticed three computers in the house, Mr. Pierce."

He nodded. "Yes. Lori's is in her bedroom, mine is in the basement—I have my business programs on that—and in the spare bedroom, Lynn has her own for e-mailing her friends and, I don't know, whatever else she does."

Grissom said, "We'd like to take Lynn's computer with us, if you don't mind."

Pierce winced at that one. "You want her *computer?*"

With a brief nod, Grissom said, "May help us track her movements. See if your wife e-mailed someone to notify them that she'd be coming for a visit. Can you access her account?"

"Afraid I can't. She has her own password. . . . Even the closest couples have privacy issues—who doesn't want to have a few secrets?"

Grissom said, "Secrets don't stay secret long, in my world, Mr. Pierce."

Catherine asked, "How about a cell phone? Does Mrs. Pierce have one?"

"Why, yes—she carries it in her purse, all the time."

"Have you tried to call her since she turned up missing?"

"Of course!"

"And?"

A shrug. "And it comes back 'out of service.' "

Catherine thought about that, then asked, "May we see last month's bill?"

Starting to look mildly put-out, Pierce said, "Well . . . all right."

"And her credit cards and bank statements?"

Pierce gave Grissom a sharp look, as if to say, *Can't you keep this underling in check?*

Grissom turned on the angelic smile again. "It's an old, old theory, Mr. Pierce—follow the money. Wherever Mrs. Pierce is, she's spending money, somehow or other . . . and unless she left carrying a massive amount of cash, there should be a credit-card trail to follow."

The color had drained from Pierce's face. "Well . . . Now, she could have taken cash with her, quite a bit of it. But I wouldn't know."

"You had separate accounts?"

"Yes."

Catherine said, "Privacy issues?"

Pierce ignored that, looking instead at the CSI chief. "Lynn's from a wealthy family, Mr. Grissom. She has a considerable amount of money beyond what I earn. . . . There's her money, my money, and our money—lots of couples are that way." With yet another sigh, he rose. "I understand you're just trying to help. . . . I'll get you the papers you need."

Brass, still seated, asked, "Do you have a recent photo of your wife we could take?"

"Yes. Of course. I'll get one for you." Pierce left the room, and they could see him going up the stairs; in a few minutes he was back, handing Brass a five-by-seven snapshot. "This was taken at her birthday party, just two months ago."

Grissom took the photo away from Brass and looked at the casual image of a haggard, haunted-eyed blonde standing rather somberly next to several laughing female friends, a HAPPY BIRTHDAY banner in the background. In her late thirties, early forties, with short hair that flirted with the collar of a blue silk blouse, Lynn Pierce had blue eyes that matched her daughter's, high cheekbones with a touch too much blush, a long but graceful nose, nicely full lips, and a stubby flat chin. She was neither beautiful nor unattractive—a "handsome" woman, as they used to say. As she stared up at him with clear, piercing eyes, Grissom got the impression that she was a no-nonsense, down-to-earth person.

The somberness of her expression, however, seemed almost to speak to him, as though there were something she needed to say.

Fifteen minutes later, after forced-friendly handshakes and good-byes with their host, the group trooped back out of the Pierce home, Catherine's arms piled with papers, Nick lugging Mrs. Pierce's computer.

As the rest of the CSI team loaded what they'd taken into the Tahoe, Catherine, with arms folded like a Sioux chief, faced Grissom. "Your tape not withstanding . . . the evidence shows no signs that any crime has been committed on those premises."

Nearby Brass was rocking on his heels. To no one in particular, he said, "You really think Owen Pierce is the distressed husband he claims to be?"

"You looking for an opinion?" Grissom asked. "I don't do opinions."

Catherine was smiling, though, regarding her boss with cat's eyes. "You don't fool me."

Grissom's brows rose. "I don't?"

"Something's wrong in that house, and you know it."

Grissom frowned at her. "I *don't* know it," he said.

And he stalked back toward the Taurus, Brass following him, throwing a shrug back at the quietly amused Catherine.

"Retaining water," Catherine said to Sara.

"And me fresh out of Midol," Sara said.

Grissom got in on the rider's side and sat and brooded. He *didn't* know that something was wrong in that house—but he *felt* it.

And he hated when that happened.

For now, he had nothing to go on. Nothing to do but return to HQ and wait for a real crime to come in.

And hope it wasn't a murder, and the victim: Lynn Pierce.

3

A DAY LATER, AND LYNN PIERCE REMAINED AMONG THE missing—the only change in status was that she was now officially listed as such.

Grissom was seated at his desk in his office, dealing with paperwork. The CSI supervisor would not have admitted it under torture, but the face of the sad-eyed blonde in that snapshot haunted him.

Still, at this stage, little remained appropriate for his CSI team's attention: no sign of foul play had been found. There was only the husband's threat to kill his wife to go on . . . and how many husbands and wives, in the heat and hyperbole of an argument, had threatened as much?

He had assigned Sara to the case, and she had drawn upon her considerable computer expertise to track the woman's credit cards; but none of the cards had been used since Lynn Pierce's disappearance, and the woman hadn't been to an ATM or used a phone card either. E-mails from friends were piling up unanswered and none of her recent cyber-correspondence mentioned a trip or hinted that she might be preparing to run away.

If she was alive, she would leave a trail—this Grissom knew to a certainty; the absence of such, so far, only substantiated his conviction that she had been killed. This was not a hunch, rather a belief built on the circumstantial evidence thus far.

Sara, sitting at her computer, had looked up at him with eyebrows high, and said, "She could be paying her way with cash—she does have money of her own."

"Check for withdrawals, then."

"Maybe she kept a stash of cash, somewhere."

"What, under a mattress? No, if that's the case, it'll be in a safety deposit box—check with her bank on that, as well."

Sara smirked at him. "But that's the point of safety deposit boxes—nobody knows what goes in and out, banks included."

Grissom lifted a finger. "Ah, but the banks record *who* goes in and out, to have a look at their safety deposit boxes. . . . See if Lynn Pierce has done that, lately."

Sara, nodding, went back to work.

Even as he sent Sara scurrying to check, Grissom didn't hold much stock in the notion that Lynn Pierce was funding her disappearance, paying as she went. From what he had gathered thus far, this was a woman of faith and family who spent little money on herself.

The phone rang. Grissom, who hated having his thoughts interrupted, looked at it like the object had just flipped him off. It rang a second time, and finally, he reached for the receiver.

He identified himself, listened for several moments, writing down the information, and then told Jim Brass, "I'll have a team there in under fifteen minutes, and see you in five."

Grissom glanced at his own notes.

A dead woman—not Lynn Pierce—needed their attention.

Catherine Willows—typically stylish in a formfitting green V-neck ribbed sweater, tailored black slacks and ankle-high black leather boots—was peeling an orange when Grissom walked into the break room and handed her his notes.

"Dream Dolls?" she asked, peering over the edge of the note at Grissom. Her expression split the difference between a smile and a frown. "You're kidding, right?"

Grissom risked just the hint of a smile. "You know the place better than anybody else on staff."

"What's that, another excerpt from *The Wit and Wisdom of Gil Grissom?*" She tossed the scrap of paper on the table next to the orange peels. "A very slender volume, I might add."

He took a seat beside her. "You *can* handle this? It's not a problem, is it? Is this . . . a sensitive issue with you?"

Her eyes were wide and unblinking as she said, "You'd know this, why? Sensitivity being your long suit and all." She sighed, nibbled an orange slice. "A dead stripper, and you immediately think of me—should I be complimented?"

Grissom thought about that for a moment. "You may have my job one day, you know."

"It's been offered to me before," she reminded him, adding wryly, "Sometimes I wonder why I didn't take it."

"Me too," Grissom admitted. "If you were supervisor, and one of your CSIs was a former stock-car racer, and you had a case turn up at a speedway . . . who would you send?"

She sighed. "Point well taken." She glanced at the notes again. "How did the woman die?"

"That's what the coroner will tell us . . . Looks like strangulation."

"All right," she said. "You're not coming?"

He shook his head. "I'm meeting Brass in five minutes. He's invited me along—interviewing the Blairs, the friends who reported the Lynn Pierce disappearance . . . now that it's official."

Catherine was cleaning up her trash, depositing the peels and her Evian bottle in a bin, when he told her, "I said a CSI team'd be right out."

She bestowed him her most beautiful sarcastic smile. "I'll shake a tailfeather."

On her way out of the break room, he called, "And take Sara!"

Catherine nodded, threw him a wave over her shoulder, and strode down the hall.

Catherine found Sara Sidle huddled over her computer monitor, her mouse racing around the pad as she studied something on the Internet. Wearing dark bell-bottom jeans and a dark blue scoop-neck top under her baby-blue lab coat, she looked more like a clerk at Tower Records than a dedicated scientist. Her dark curly hair bounced as she bobbed in time to some internal rhythm.

"Sorry to interrupt," Catherine said, "but we've got a call."

Sara barely glanced at her. "Uh, Grissom assigned me to this Pierce disappearance."

"Well, he wants you to accompany me on this one. We've got a live one."

"You mean a dead one."

Catherine shrugged.

"Just give me another minute," Sara said, her gaze glued to the monitor.

Catherine leaned in for a look.

"I've been checking hotel reservations and check-ins for the last two days," Sara said, "and nothing."

"We'll find her," Catherine said, "or she'll turn up on her own. Nobody disappears 'without a trace,' no matter what you hear."

They gathered their equipment, jumped in one of the department's black Tahoes—Catherine tossing the keys to Sara—and strapped themselves in for the short drive to Dream Dolls.

"So," Sara said, with a sideways glance, "this is one of the older, uh, clubs in town, isn't it?"

"That's right. And yes, Dream Dolls *is* one of the clubs I worked at."

"Oh. Really. Interesting."

"Is it?" Catherine turned and folded her arms and faced the windshield. "Grissom assigned me to this, he says, because I worked there, and have an advance knowledge of the place."

"Makes sense. But . . . why'd he send me?"

"Probably because he figured it would be less awkward for me, than taking Nicky or Warrick . . . assuming Grissom could be that sensitive."

Sara mulled that a moment or two. "Maybe he figures, since we'll have to deal with a lot of women, you know, at the club . . . sending two women kinda makes sense."

"Maybe."

The club sat in the older part of downtown, blocks away from the renovation of Fremont Street. Though it wasn't that far from headquarters, and she had passed the place numerous times, Dream Dolls—and that life—seemed to Catherine worlds away from where she was now. She wondered if Ty Kapelos still ran the show there. He'd always seemed just one brick short of a pimp; but he had, at least, always been fair.

"Even *your* looks won't last forever," he'd told her. "Start saving. Think up a future for yourself."

In a way, that had been an important point on the winding road to the straight life she now lived.

Sara pulled the SUV into a parking space beside two squad cars, whose rollers painted the night alternately blue and red. The two women climbed out of the Tahoe, gathered their equipment, and turned toward the club, a one-story faded bunker of a redbrick building.

Catherine looked up at the garish glowing neon

sign on a pole looming over the sidewalk, featuring a red outline that suggested an overly endowed woman, sliding down a blue neon firepole; when the neon stripper reached the bottom, giant green letters . . . one at a time . . . spelled out DREAM DOLLS, then held and pulsed . . . before the sequence started again.

Smirking, shaking her head, Catherine figured Ty must have finally decided to spend a few bucks on the business. Hearing footsteps on the cement, she looked toward a young male uniformed officer coming their way from where he'd been positioned at the front door.

"CSI?" the officer asked.

She read his nameplate: JOHNSTON. A newbie, right out of the academy she'd bet, all wavy blond hair and blue-eyed, vacant stare—was this his first crime scene?

"Catherine Willows and Sara Sidle," she said with a nod toward her partner. "Pardon the expression, but it's kinda dead out here."

His voice was a breathy tenor. "I was told not to let anyone in or out, 'cept you guys and the detectives."

She nodded and strode past him.

"Real mess," he said, hollowly.

Spinning to face him, Catherine demanded, "You were in there?" All she needed was for some rookie to contaminate her evidence. "You saw the scene?"

Eyes bright and glistening, he nodded. "Just for a second—from out in the hall." He swallowed. "Never seen anything like that."

"But you didn't go near the body?"

"No."

She studied his face for a second, then—satisfied he'd been frank with her—said, "Good," turned back to the club and pulled open the front door. Behind her, Sara tossed a hip to hold the door open. They entered a small alcove with still another door between them and the bar; already the smoky, spilled-beer-stench atmosphere assailed them. To their right, behind a small table, sat a good-looking if steroidally burly doorman in a white shirt, red bow tie and black jeans.

"You ladies . . ." He seemed to have been about to say one thing, in his pleasant baritone, then—perhaps noting Sara's silver flight-case field kit—finished by saying something else. ". . . are with the cops?"

Catherine said, "Crime scene investigators."

He nodded, gesturing toward the club, as if there were anywhere else to go.

Catherine opened the inner door and the blare of amplified rock almost knocked her back into the entryway. The music hadn't been this loud back in her day—or at least she didn't remember it that way. Stepping inside, the two women let the door swing shut behind them.

The stage was where it had always been, still about the size of Wayne Newton's yacht, filling the center of the room, a brass pole anchoring either end. No dancers were on stage at the moment, though the lights continued to blink to the beat of the music. A few customers dotted the chairs near the stage and most of the girls huddled in a faraway corner with two uniformed officers. In the corner to the left an elevated DJ booth oversaw the room like a prison tower, the sentry a scrawny guy in headphones, a scruffy beard, short blond hair and a fluorescent DREAM DOLLS T-shirt. His head moved to the music like a head-bobbing toy. He seemed oblivious to the fact that another employee was dead and the stage was empty.

Detective Erin Conroy stood at the long bar at the right, a notepad in hand, talking to someone Catherine couldn't see.

Still moving slowly, Catherine and Sara made their way to the bar and Conroy looked up, her green eyes tight, whether from the situation or the smoke, who could say? On the other side of the bar stood a short, bald, fat man, the sleeves of his white shirt rolled up, the top three buttons left open to reveal the sort of gold chains it takes hours to win at a carnival.

Catherine had to yell to be heard. "Hey, Ty!" She jerked a thumb toward the DJ, then slashed her throat with a finger.

His mouth dropped open, as he recognized her, but he obeyed. Tyler Kapelos looked over at the DJ's corner and yelled. *"Worm!"*

The DJ glanced up—the club owner, too, dragged a finger across his throat, the DJ nodded and the sound system went quiet, though Catherine figured she'd be hearing the echo for hours. Minus the blare of music, the club's essential seediness seemed to assert itself.

"Cath," Kapelos said, a smile spreading like a rash over his ample face. "Jeez, it's good to see you.

What's it been . . . ten, fifteen years? I was starting to think you didn't love me no more. I heard you were with the cops, but still . . . never expected to see you in my place. You know me, I run a clean shop—no drugs, no hooking."

"I'm not a cop, Ty—I'm a scientist."

His dark eyes danced; he was in a good mood, considering. "You *did* make good!"

Sara—apparently feeling left out—said, "Crime scene investigators—my name is Sidle."

Kapelos acknowledged Sara with a nod, then turned his sweaty grinning countenance back on Catherine. "I just knew you'd make something of yourself." He gestured with a wag of his head to the squalid world around them. "You were always too good for this place."

"Okay," Catherine said, all business, "we're officially all caught up—now, what happened here?"

Kapelos began to speak, but Detective Conroy stepped in, glancing occasionally at her notepad. "We have a dead dancer in the back, in one of the private rooms. Goes by 'Jenna Patrick'—don't know if that's her real name or not. Late twenties, strangled—apparently by a john."

"Excuse me," Kapelos said, mildly indignant, "but they're not 'johns.' This is not the Mustang Ranch, y'know. They're customers. Patrons."

"Speaking of which," Catherine said to Conroy, "if you don't mind a suggestion—we could use a couple more detectives to question those customers. We can't release them without preliminary statements, at least."

But Conroy was ahead of her. "I have a call in. O'Riley and Vega are on the way. . . . Crime scene?"

The detective led the way, Catherine and Sara falling in line behind her as they moved to the back. With the music off and the echo subsiding, the customers and dancers corralled out there were talking too loud, yelling to be heard over music that had gone away.

As the trio of female investigators edged into the cramped hallway in back, Catherine noticed a small video camera overhead. She paused and pointed it out to Sara, who had seen it, too.

"We'll get the tapes before we go," Sara said.

The hallway contained six doors, three on each side, all standing open; this area was not part of the building's original design, and had not been here during Catherine's tenure—strictly contrived out of sheetrock, cheap trim and black paint, to accomplish a specific purpose.

Looking through the first door on the left, Catherine saw a room the size of a good-sized closet with a metal frame chair facing the door. The walls back here were black, too, and the carpeting looked like some cheap junk maybe picked up at a yard sale. Each cubicle had a mounted speaker to feed in the DJ's tunes.

"Private dance rooms," Conroy said. "Lap dances, they call 'em."

Table dances—where a dancer, between sets, would work the room, squeezing dollars out of patrons for up-close-and-slightly-more-personal glimpses at a girl—were as far as things had ever gone, in Catherine's day. Nothing to compare with the likes of "lap" dances and the stuff that went on in these private rooms, on the current scene.

"There are doors on the rooms," Conroy pointed out, "but no locks."

"If a customer gets out of line," Sara said, thinking it through aloud, "a bouncer can respond to a shout or a scream, and put a stop to it."

"In theory," Catherine said. "But that doesn't seem to have helped, here. . . ."

Peeking over Sara's shoulder, Catherine got her first look at the body. Nude except for a lavender thong, Jenna Patrick lay in a fetal position, her long blonde hair splayed away from her face and bare back, something thin and black tight around her throat. Her head faced left, one sightless brown orb staring at the place where the wall and floor met. Full dark lips were frozen in a parody of a kiss and a tiny mole punctuated the corner of her mouth. She had full, heavy breasts and the strong, muscular legs of a dancer. She wore black patent-leather spike heels that would have been a bitch to walk, let alone dance, in.

"That looks like an electrical tie," Catherine said.

"Looks like it," Conroy said.

The women remained in the hallway, huddled around the doorway, maneuvering around each other for a better view.

Sara said, "Cut off the carotids—she was out in seconds . . . and dead in under a minute."

Catherine said to Conroy, "How many men was she in here with tonight?"

The detective shook her head, ponytail swinging. "Kapelos said they never settled up till the end of the night—he and the dancers split the take, back here . . . twenty-five dollars a dance."

"Plus tips," Catherine said, "which the girls wouldn't share, even if they were supposed to."

Conroy went on: "Jenna came in at five and was scheduled until twelve—only a couple of bathroom, cigarette breaks. No lunch break."

Catherine nodded; she knew the drill.

"That normal?" Sara asked, wincing.

"Yeah," Catherine said. "Most of the girls don't eat much anyway, gotta stay in shape. If they want a meal, they brown-bag it in the dressing room. . . . Jenna here would've worked straight through till midnight, getting out before the crowd got too out of hand. . . . Those last hours of the night are the worst."

Sara was doing a lousy job of hiding how fascinated she was, hearing Catherine's inside scoop on the skin business.

"Or," Catherine went on, "if there were some high-rollers and she thought she could make some real bucks, maybe she'd stick around another hour or so. That's pretty typical."

Sara asked, "When did you quit doing this . . . yesterday?"

Conroy piped in: "Am I catching the drift of this, correctly? You used to dance for Kapelos? *Here?*"

"About a hundred years ago, I did. Got my degree, and got out—any other questions?"

"No," Conroy said. "None. Glad to have your, uh, insights."

The two CSIs unpacked their tools in the tiny hallway and went to work. First, Catherine used an electrostatic print lifter to get footprints off the floor of the room, and then the hallway. She'd have to take shoe prints from the cops, Sara and herself, to eliminate them, but she still had hope of getting something. They photographed everything, dusted the chair and the door knobs for prints; then Catherine bent close to the victim's neck for a better look at the weapon that had taken Jenna Patrick's life.

"About three-eighths of an inch in diameter," Catherine reported. "Standard black electrical tie, available in every hardware store in the free world."

Picking a spot that looked clean, she used a small pair of wire cutters to snip the tie, which she then bagged. It wasn't very wide, but even if they snagged a partial print, that'd be useful.

Over the course of the next two hours, they lifted hairs, samples of stains, fibers, dirt, anything that might help them identify who had killed Jenna Patrick in that room. Using the RUVIS—a sort of pistol-gripped telephoto lens—they turned up occasional white splotches on the carpet, indicating probable semen spills from happy customers.

"Greg's going to love us," Sara said sarcastically, referring to their resident lab rat, Greg Sanders, whose job it would be to wade nose deep in the DNA cesspool they uncovered tonight.

"This cubicle could be a career for him,"

Catherine said with a smile. "But oddly . . . there's not as much as I thought there would be. Place like this should be wall-to-wall DNA."

Sara nodded, shrugged. "Yeah. What's up, y'suppose?"

Catherine thought Sara's question over for a few seconds, then said, "I'll be back."

Walking across the club—the lights on now, exposing Dream Dolls as the dingy nightmare it was—she saw that the place had emptied out except for cops and employees. She nodded to Detectives O'Riley and Vega, who were interviewing a waitress and the red-bow-tied bouncer. The dancers were in the dressing room in back where Conroy would be questioning them; the DJ in his corner was covering his equipment under tarps. Catherine moved to the bar, behind which Tyler Kapelos moped with a cup of coffee.

"How long am I gonna be closed down, Cath?" he asked as he poured her a cup, too.

"You can probably reopen tomorrow if you want. We'll be done soon."

"That's a relief, anyway." He nodded and sipped from his cup.

"Pretty ugly in there."

"Shame. She was a nice kid."

Catherine knew that whichever one of his dancers had died, Kapelos would likely have said the same thing.

"But, y'know, funny thing," she said casually, "it's not as bad as it could have been." She sipped her coffee, hot, bitter, but better than the break room swill. "You got a cleaning woman coming in daily or something?"

He smiled a little, shrugged. "Spent some money, fixed stuff up, some. How d'you like the new sign?"

"Class," she said, only half-sarcastic. "What did you do in the back? And when?"

"Fresh paint, new carpet." He rubbed a palm over his forehead, then back over his balding scalp, distributing the sweat. "Maybe a month ago, two no more'n that."

"I should thank you. You're making our job a little easier."

"Yeah? How so?"

Now she shrugged. "Normally, a place like this—we'd be sifting through DNA until we all retired."

A defensive frown formed on his Greek Lou Grant face. "I told ya, Cath, this is no hooker haven. With these lap dances, guy makes a mess, it's in his pants."

"Even so—there'd be some of that on the floor, and hairs and sweat and . . . well, the general residue that follows a good time being had by all."

"That wicked sense of humor." His smile was feeble but sincere. "Almost wish you was still here, kid."

"That makes one of us, Ty."

"Seriously. You still got the looks, and Lord knows you got style."

Interrogation was Conroy's job, but the detective was busy, and Catherine knew her familiarity with Kapelos might make him more open with her. "Any idea who would do this to her, Ty?"

He sucked in a breath. "Probably that son of a bitch Ray Lipton. . . . I guess I shoulda thought to tell that female detective about that prick. Nice looking woman, that detective." He glanced back toward the hallway. "And you know that kid you come in with, what's her name? Siddon?"

"Sidle."

"She could make a few bucks here, too. What's the PD policy on a little innocent moonlighting?"

Catherine ignored that. "Who is this Ray Lipton?"

"Jenna's boyfriend. He hated her workin' here." He shrugged. "Old story."

Very old story, Catherine knew. Half the guys dating dancers hated what their women did for a living; the other half only dated the women *because* they danced. Sometimes the first group had started out in the second. "Ray and Jenna, they fight?"

Kapelos snorted a laugh. "Cats and dogs. It got so bad I had to get a damn restraining order against the guy."

Catherine frowned. "Did he hit her?"

"Well . . . not exactly—he would kinda manhandle her, sometimes. Anyway, he kept coming in here, making scenes, causin' trouble. Hell, Lipton practically choked one of my regulars here, once."

The image of the strangled woman leapt into Catherine's mind. "You call the police on him?"

"Naw. You remember how it is, Cath—like I said, the guy Lipton got into it with, he was a regular. Didn't want no trouble, either. After that, I got the restraining order to keep Lipton out."

"Could we talk to this regular?"

Kapelos found a glass to dry with a dirty towel and considered that. "You ain't gonna make no trouble for him, Cath, right? I mean, he's a right guy."

In other words, married.

"No trouble, Ty," Catherine said. "The detectives'll just want to ask a couple questions."

Kapelos shrugged again and said, "Guy's name is Marty Fleming."

"Know where we can find him?"

The bar owner thought about that and dried two more glasses. "He ain't been in for a while. Last I heard, he was dealing over at Circus Circus."

"When did this run-in with Jenna's boyfriend happen?"

"Oh, three . . . maybe four months ago."

She patted the man's hand, where it rested on the counter. "Thanks, Ty. By the way, restraining order or not—you didn't happen to see Lipton in here tonight?"

Kapelos shook his head. "Nope; but I was in the back, in the office, most of the time. Ask the girls, or maybe Worm."

"The DJ?"

"Yeah. He knows Lipton. Anyway, I've seen 'em sit and chew the fat, before."

"Thanks for the coffee," Catherine said, and had a final sip.

The CSI was starting away when Kapelos said, "She was a nice girl, Cath—like you. Mighta got outa the business one day. . . . Do me a favor?"

"Try to."

"Catch the son of a bitch?"

She grinned at him. "That's why they pay me the medium-sized bucks."

Catherine crossed the room to the opposite corner where the DJ was just pulling on his jacket. "You speak to a detective yet?"

He shook his head. Worm was maybe twenty-five, his black satin jacket bearing a Gibson guitar logo on the left breast. He wore black jeans, Reeboks, and a black T-shirt with a Music Go Round logo stenciled across the front. "That lady cop, she told me to wait around for her."

Catherine nodded. "Detective Conroy. Shouldn't be long. As soon as she's done in the dressing room, she'll be out here."

"It's all right," he said, with a good-natured shrug. "I've got nothin' better to do anyway. Still on the clock."

"So they call you Worm?"

He flashed an easy smile. "Name's Chris Ermey. Why they call me Worm's a long story—let's just say it involves a tequila bottle."

"I'll take your word for it," Catherine said, with a little smile. "Ty mentioned you know a guy named Ray Lipton."

"Yeah, sure, I know Ray."

"See him in here tonight?"

Worm thought about that for a long moment. "I might have."

Catherine cocked an eyebrow. "*Might* have?"

"Gets pretty smoky in here, but I thought I saw him, across the room—see, Ray usually wears that one jacket of his."

She nodded, letting him tell it in his own way, his own time.

"It's kinda like a letter jacket, 'cept it's denim with, like, tan cotton sleeves. Has the name of his company—Lipton Construction? On the back."

"And you saw him tonight."

"I saw a jacket like that, across the bar tonight—near the private dancer rooms? Guy had a cap on and dark glasses, coulda been Ray—only I think he had a beard."

"Does Ray have a beard?"

"When I first met him he did. Then he didn't. And I haven't seen him for a while, so he coulda grown it back. Hell, come to think of it, it probably *was* Ray. He hated Jenna working here, y'know."

"Thanks, Mr. Ermey," Catherine said.

"Am I done now?"

"No—I was just getting a little background. The detective will be with you soon, and go over all of this again."

The DJ nodded, said, "Fine with me, still on the clock," plopped on a chair, fished a pack of cigarettes out of somewhere and lit up.

Catherine went back down the hall, where she found Sara packing up the last of their gear. Conroy, moving briskly, came down the hall from the dressing room end.

"Get anything?" Catherine asked.

"Her boyfriend seems prime." She glanced at her notepad. "One Ray Lipton—lot of the girls mentioned him. Said he had an attitude about Jenna dancing here."

"Yeah, I heard that story too," Catherine said, and quickly filled the detective in on what Ty had told her.

"Doin' my job again, Catherine?" Conroy asked, kidding.

"I figured Ty might open up to me," Catherine said, lifting her shoulders and putting them down again. "For old time's sake."

"Well, evidently the Patrick woman lived with another dancer, a . . ." Conroy checked her notes. ". . . Tera Jameson. They say Jameson used to work here, too, but took a job at another club, Showgirl World, about three months ago."

"Movin' on up," Catherine said.

"I'm going to talk to the DJ," Conroy said, "then follow up with Kapelos—half an hour, I'll be done here."

"We're wrapping up now," Sara said.

"If I can find Ray Lipton tonight," Conroy said, moving off, "I'll be bringing him in for questioning—you two want a piece?"

Sara and Catherine traded looks, then both gave Conroy nods.

Catherine said, "Let us know when you get back to HQ. In the meantime, we'll run our findings over to the lab and get the DNA tests started."

The two CSIs had the SUV loaded up when Sara remembered the videotapes; Catherine went back inside to talk to Ty Kapelos one last time.

"Ty," Catherine said, "we're going to need tonight's security tapes."

Kapelos was seated on a bar stool now, on the

customer side of the counter; he was smoking the stubby remains of a foul cigar. "No problem, Cath. Got 'em in back."

Five minutes later he handed her a grocery bag brimming with videotapes.

Her eyebrows rose. "These are all from *tonight?*"

"Yeah, sure," Ty said, as he swept his hand around the bar, a king gesturing to his kingdom. "Eight cameras—can't be too careful, in this business. One over the door, one on each corner of the stage, two behind the bar, and that one at the end of the hallway. Seems like every other asshole who walks in the place is lookin' to sue me over some goddamn thing or another. Tapes don't lie."

"Thanks, Ty," Catherine said, arms filled with the bag, the heft of it reassuring. "We'll get these back to you."

"Keep 'em till ten years from Christmas," he said, "if it'll help get that son of a bitch."

Catherine glanced around, to make sure no one was looking, and gave the bar owner a kiss on the stubbly cheek.

Then—once again—she was out of there.

4

ARTHUR AND MILLIE BLAIR LIVED IN AN ANONYMOUS, cookie-cutter white-frame two-story with a well-tended barely sloping lawn on a quiet street in a fairly well-to-do neighborhood not far from the UNLV campus, where Mr. Blair worked. The effect of the Lynn Pierce disappearance on the Blairs was at once apparent, when Brass and Grissom rolled up in the unmarked car: every light in the house was on, lighting the grounds like a prison yard.

To Brass, the Blairs seemed like nice people, salt-of-the-earth church-goers who kept to themselves mostly, worked hard, saved money, raised their only son the best way they knew how. Then, one day, their lives had changed forever—just because of who they were acquainted with.

Happened every day. Somebody had to live next door to JonBenet and her parents; someone had to take the apartment next to Jeffrey Dahmer; John Wayne Gacy had nextdoor neighbors on his quiet street; O.J.'s wife Nicole had girl friends close to her.

Lynn Pierce was Millie's friend, Arthur's too, and had trusted them with the tape that might now be the only link to what Brass still hoped was just a missing persons case, and not a murder. Even though the disappearance was in no way the fault of this nice couple, Brass could see the guilt there on their faces.

He could tell they felt they should *know* where she'd gone, even though they couldn't possibly have that information. Like most people caught up in a tragedy, the Blairs battled the feeling that somehow, some way, they should have done something, anything, to prevent this terrible situation . . . and they hadn't.

Yes, they could have come to the authorities with the tape right after Lynn brought it to them; but the Pierce woman had asked them to hold onto it for her. They couldn't have realized she might have anticipated her own murder, and was leaving a smoking gun behind, to identify her killer.

Only right now Brass did not have a murder—just a missing person. Nonetheless, he had brought Gil Grissom along, since at present the criminalist and his people were the only ones really, truly looking for Lynn Pierce.

The couple sat on their tasteful beige couch across from Brass and Grissom. Mr. Blair was in the white shirt, striped tie and gray slacks he'd probably worn to work that day. Nervously, the man pushed his dark-rimmed glasses back up his nose, so thick-lensed they exaggerated his eyes—to comic effect in other circumstances. Next to him, his wife Millie had on black slacks and a black-and-white striped silk blouse—dignified attire, vaguely suggesting mourning. She kept her arms crossed in front of her, clutched to herself, as if they could somehow keep out the problems that now faced them.

Grissom, like a priest in black but without the collar, perched on the edge of a tan La-Z-Boy, as if afraid to sit lest the thing might swallow him whole. Grissom, it seemed to Brass, seemed uncomfortable with comfort. On the other hand, Grissom surely knew as well as Brass that this was not going to be a pleasant interview.

After clearing his throat, Brass asked, "So, Mrs. Blair, you don't believe that Mrs. Pierce would abandon her husband and daughter?"

"No, I don't." She looked at him curiously. "Do you?"

Brass smiled meaninglessly. "It's not important what I believe, ma'am. What's important is that we find Mrs. Pierce."

Mrs. Blair unfolded herself a little, revealed the tissue in her right hand, and dabbed at her eyes. "Lynn would never run off like that, and not tell anyone where she's going. That's just not her. Not at all."

"Help me get to know her, then."

"She's . . ." Mrs. Blair searched for the word. ". . . sounds corny but . . . she's sweet." The woman glanced toward her husband, who took her hand in his. "We met a year or so ago, when she joined our church . . . then our women's Bible study group."

"You didn't know the Pierces before that?"

"No." She smiled—it was half melancholy, half

nervous. "I think Lynn had a change of heart, a change of . . . spirit . . . direction."

"I see," Brass said, not seeing at all. Grissom was looking at the woman as if she were something on a lab slide.

"Before she met the Lord, Lynn had a different set of values, a different social circle . . . but since she joined our group, she and I became good friends—best friends."

"Would you say Lynn is reliable? Could she ever be . . . flighty?"

Mrs. Blair smiled at the absurdity of the thought. "Oh, Detective Brass, you can always count on Lynn. If she says she's going to do something, she does it."

"I see."

"That's why I was so surprised last night when she phoned to tell me she was on her way over—*right* over—and then never showed up."

"Tell us about that phone call," Brass said. "How did she sound?"

She glanced at her husband; they were holding hands like sweethearts. "I feel so bad about that . . ."

"Darling," Mr. Blair said, "it's all right."

His wife went on: "I've thought and thought about it since last night. I knew at the time she was upset, but I should have heard it then—she sounded distraught. Even terrified, but trying to . . . you know . . . hide it a little."

"You're sure about this?" Brass asked.

She shook her head, sighed. "I'm not sure about anything, anymore. I've replayed it so many times in my mind, I don't know if she *really* sounded distraught or if I'm putting my own feelings into it. . . . I won't lie to you, Detective Brass, I have . . . nervous problems. Sometimes I take medication."

Brass glanced at Grissom, but the criminalist's eyes were fixed upon the woman. The detective said, "Is that right?"

"Yes—Prozac."

Her husband added, "A small dosage."

"Well," she said. "Prozac or no Prozac . . . I think Lynn was distraught. Really and truly."

"Any idea what was troubling her?"

With a tiny edge of impatience, Arthur Blair said, "Maybe it was her husband threatening to cut her up in little pieces."

Brass nodded. "I don't mean to downplay the tape. But remember, some husbands and wives make those kind of idle threats all the time—"

"We don't," Mr. Blair said.

Brass continued: "And, at any rate, that was an argument from the day before. Did you get a sense of what *specifically* was troubling her the afternoon she called?"

Glumly, Mrs. Blair shook her head. "No. She didn't tell me what it was, exactly . . . and I'd have no way of guessing."

"Was she upset with her husband? I mean, this is a woman who went to the trouble of capturing her husband's verbal abuse on tape, after all."

"That was my assumption, but when I asked her, directly, if it was another argument with Owen, she kind of . . . dodged the issue."

Mr. Blair sat forward. "It must have been about

Owen. Lynn calls Millie all the time when Owen becomes . . . uh . . . overbearing."

"That's happened a lot?"

"I don't know if it's fair to say 'a lot,' " Mrs. Blair said, thoughtfully. "She does call other times, though."

"Has she ever called upset about something other than her husband's abusive behavior?"

"Lori," Mr. Blair blurted, before his wife could answer. "Their daughter—she aggravates Lynn almost as much as Owen."

"That's true," Mrs. Blair admitted, shrugging one shoulder, raising one eyebrow. "Lori gave Lynn fits . . . although—and I don't like to brag—they seem to've had a lot less trouble with her, since Lori started dating our Gary."

Brass smiled. "Then Gary's a positive influence on the Pierce girl?"

Mr. Blair smiled and nodded. "He's a good boy—follows the Lord's teachings and studies hard in school."

Brass wondered what planet this was, but said, "That's great. You're very lucky."

"No question," Mr. Blair said. "Gary's helped settle Lori down. She was a little . . . wild, before."

"Wild?" asked Brass. "How so?"

Mr. Blair was searching for the words, so Mrs. Blair answered for him: "Impetuous, I would say. She made some mistakes with boys . . . drugs. It's an evil world out there, Detective Brass."

"I've noticed."

Mrs. Blair went on, in a pleased rush: "But between Gary's good influence, and Lynn's good parenting, they got her straightened out."

"Despite her father," Mr. Blair grumbled.

"Anyway," Mrs. Blair said, "I would say the girl's doing fine now. Better grades, active in church, doesn't try to dress like those . . . slatternly singers that are so popular now—like Lori *used* to."

"Even so," Brass said, "it would seem Lynn's had more than her share of stress in her life—would you agree?"

The Blairs exchanged searching looks.

Then, at the same time, Mr. Blair said, "Yes," as Mrs. Blair said, "No."

The two laughed in awkward embarrassment, and Brass waited for them to sort it out themselves, each saying, "You first," and "No, you." Finally, Mrs. Blair said, "Lynn has stress, but I'm not sure it's any more than anyone else, you know, in these troubled times."

Brass sat forward. "You mean to say, you don't consider her problems with her daughter, and her abusive husband, exceptional?"

Mrs. Blair shrugged with her eyebrows. "Well, I think the trouble with Lori, at least, is behind them."

"But what about with Owen?"

Mrs. Blair turned to her husband. Arthur Blair's lips peeled back and his eyes narrowed. The calm Christian removed his mask to reveal an angry human beneath. "Owen Pierce is a worthless, Godless son of a . . ." Blair's voice trailed off and his knuckles turned white on the arm of the sofa as he struggled to control his emotions. His wife slipped her arm around his shoulder, comfortingly.

Captain Jim Brass had spent enough time with the Blairs, and people like them, to know that for Arthur Blair to come as close as he had to calling that son of a bitch Pierce a son of a bitch indicated an unfathomable depth of anger toward Owen Pierce.

"I take it you listened to the tape?" Blair asked, his voice still edged with an unChristian viciousness.

"Yes, sir." Brass nodded toward Grissom. "We did."

Blair sighed heavily. "Then you know what that monster must be capable of, to threaten his wife with that." He shifted on the couch, sitting forward. "Understand something, Detective—I wouldn't have allowed Gary to get involved with Lori if I didn't think that Lynn was going to . . . divest herself of Owen, and soon."

Millie Blair patted her husband's arm in an effort to calm him.

"Normally," Mrs. Blair said, "our faith discourages divorce. But Pastor Dan says, when a spouse has fallen into satanic ways, a person must protect one's self, and children."

Brass winced. "You don't mean . . . literally . . . that Owen Pierce practiced satanism?"

"Of course not," Mr. Blair said, sitting back, calmer. "But he's a . . . devil . . . a demon himself. Capable of the worst atrocities. . . ."

For the first time, Grissom spoke. "So, then, Mr. Blair—I take it you think Owen Pierce has made good on his threat to cut her into 'little pieces'?"

Arthur Blair's eyes became huge behind the

lenses and his wife's curled-fingered hand went to her mouth, where she bit a knuckle. Grissom might have slapped them, the way his words registered.

"That is what you think, isn't it?" he pressed. "Isn't that why you brought the tape to us?"

Mrs. Blair stared at her lap and covered her face with one hand and began to cry, quietly. Mr. Blair, slipping an arm around his wife's shoulders, gave a tired nod.

Yes, Brass thought, *Gil really has a way with people.*

Grissom pressed on. "Do you think there are any circumstances at all under which Lynn might have just . . . left?"

Trembling with tears, Mrs. Blair shook her head.

Calmly, Grissom said, "Mr. Pierce said his wife had a significant amount of money in her own name and could have used it to disappear."

"She had money," Mrs. Blair conceded, the tears subsiding, "but it was all tied up in investments . . . stocks, bonds, CDs."

Mr. Blair concurred: "None of it was liquid enough for her to get to easily."

Nodding, Mrs. Blair went on. "She complained about that. It was something Owen talked her into. Even though she had her own money, she had little cash. I don't think I ever saw her with more than, say, fifty dollars in her purse. Even though the money was hers, Owen seemed to keep her on a tight leash."

The interview continued for a few minutes, but neither Brass nor Grissom found any new ground to cover. The Blairs had been unfailingly cooperative, but they were weary, and the detective and the criminalist knew nothing more was to be learned here, at least not right now.

On the way back, Grissom rode up front with Brass.

"Do *you* think Owen Pierce is the devil?" Brass said to the CSI, half-kidding.

"No," Grissom said, seeming distant even for him. "But he's a hell of a suspect."

At headquarters, back from the strip club, Catherine sat down in the layout room, with a notepad and pen, the Dream Doll tapes and a VCR. Meanwhile, Sara took their findings to Greg Sanders so he could begin testing.

The tapes weren't labeled, so each one was a new adventure. The first one had been from the back right corner of the stage, the camera farthest from the door, the bar, and far to the left of the hallway. Only the chairs around the stage on the backside were visible from this angle.

No one fitting the description of Ray Lipton came into view. Catherine flew through the tape on fast forward, knowing she would view the tape more carefully later. For now, she just wanted to see what Worm, the cheerful DJ, had seen. Ejecting that tape, she moved on to the next one. This camera hung behind the left side of the bar, nearer the front door.

Halfway through the tape, Catherine was about to give up and move on, when she glimpsed, on the fuzzy black-and-white picture, a two-tone jacket. Stopping, she rewound the tape until the jacket came into view, and went in reverse, then pushed PLAY.

The guy came into view wearing the denim and tan jacket, a ball cap pulled low, dark glasses and jeans. He walked through the shot and out the other side. She rewound it, ran it again. Something on the guy's face . . . a beard? Worm had said Lipton might have grown his beard back; hard to tell with this tape. Popping the cassette out, Catherine went to the next, then the next—one after another, until she finally got through them all.

This Lipton guy, it seemed, had gone out of his way to avoid the camera. He hadn't walked over to the bar, for a drink; and the camera above the door had gotten barely a glimpse of him . . . none of the stage cameras caught more than a snatch of him. Of course, Catherine told herself, with that restraining order, Lipton wasn't supposed to be in there anyway, so maybe he was just being careful.

Only the camera at the head of the hallway got a decent shot of him, and that was of his back as he led busty, leggy Jenna through the door. Even with the poor quality of the tape, Catherine was able to make out the words Lipton Construction on the back of the jacket, as the couple disappeared out of frame.

Catherine sped the tape forward, until the figure in the jacket . . . bearded, all right . . . returned for a quick exit—alone.

"Conroy's back."

Catherine spun to see Sara standing in the doorway.

Sara ambled over to the monitor. "Anything good on?"

Catherine nodded. "Looks like Lipton was there, all right—got a good shot of his jacket going down the hallway with Jenna Patrick."

"Time on those tapes?"

"Yeah . . ." Catherine pointed to her notes. "Time jibes. And Lipton, or anyway a guy in a Lipton Construction jacket, comes back out of the lap-dance cubicle . . . alone."

"Interesting," Sara said. "But why watch TV, when a live performance is available? . . . Come on. Conroy's got the star of your show in interrogation."

They walked quickly down several connecting hallways and ducked into the observation room next to interrogation. Through the two-way mirror, they could see Ray Lipton, directly across from them—sitting alone, eyes cast down, the streaks of tears drying on his cheeks.

"He must've loved her," Sara said. "Crying for her."

"Love's the motive of choice," Catherine said, "of many a murderer."

Lipton's hands were balled into fists and lay on the table like objects, forgotten ones at that. The denim jacket with the tan sleeves hung over the back of the chair. He was thinner and shorter than Catherine would have expected from someone in construction, with hazel eyes, a long, narrow nose and, to her surprise, no beard.

Could she have been mistaken about what she'd seen on the video? He might have shaved, but . . . no, his cheeks were shadowed blue with stubble, indicating Lipton hadn't shaved for many hours.

A moment later, Detective Erin Conroy entered the interrogation room, a Styrofoam cup of water in one hand, notepad in the other. She placed the cup in front of Lipton, said, "There you go," and sat at the end of the table, giving her observers a view of both of them. Lipton picked up the cup, sipped from it, returned it to the table, then leaned his elbows on the wood, running his hands through his longish brown hair.

"I can't *believe* she's dead," he said, his voice quiet and raspy, a rusty tool long out of use.

Catherine looked at Sara as if to say, "What's he trying to pull?"

Lipton looked across at Conroy, his expression pitiful. "We were going to be married, you know."

"Again, Mr. Lipton, I'm sorry for your loss," Conroy said. "But there are some things we need to talk about."

Lipton looked down, shaking his head, tears again trailing slowly down his cheeks. "Can't it . . . can't it *wait?*"

"No. The first hours of a murder investigation are vital. I'm sure you understand that."

"Murder . . . a gentle soul like Jenna . . . murdered. . . ."

"For Jenna being a 'gentle soul,' Mr. Lipton," Conroy said, no inflection in her voice, "you two seemed to fight a great deal . . . especially for a couple about to be married."

"But . . . we didn't fight," he sputtered. Then his eyes moved in thought. "Well . . . no more than anybody else. *All* couples fight."

Conroy shook her head. "All couples don't include a partner with a restraining order on them . . . like the one the court issued on you, to keep you away from where Jenna worked—right?"

"Oh Christ," Lipton said, all the air rushing out of him. Catherine and Sara watched as, before their eyes, sorrow turned to despair. "You . . . you think *I* killed her!"

"I didn't say that, Mr. Lipton."

"Do I . . . need a lawyer?"

Conroy ducked that. "No accusations have been made. I simply asked if there isn't an in-force restraining order against you."

"You must know there is," he said, sullenly. Now his voice grew agitated: "I loved Jenna, but I *hated* her job—everybody knew that. But that doesn't mean I killed her. Jesus, she was going to quit! We were going to be married."

"Where did you meet Jenna?"

"At . . . Dream Dolls."

"You were a customer."

"At first, but. . . ." His look was more pleading than angry now.

"How do you explain being in Dream Dolls tonight?" Conroy asked. "Considering the restraining order."

Now he sat up, alert suddenly. "Dream Dolls? I

wasn't in Dream Dolls! You think I want to go to jail?"

Conroy didn't answer that.

"Lady, I was home all night."

"That's not what everyone at the club says."

"What do you mean by 'everyone'? Who *says* I was there?"

"Just the owner, the girls, and the DJ "

"What the hell . . ." Lipton's voice was incredulous; he shook his head, desperately. "Well, they're mistaken. They're wrong! Or maybe lying!"

"All of them? Wrong? Or lying?"

"That fucking Kapelos, he hates me. He's the one took out the restraining order! He'd say *anything*. Where was he when Jenna was . . . was . . ."

He couldn't seem to say it.

Conroy said, "And the rest of them? Lying? Wrong?"

He sighed, shrugged. "I don't know what else to say—I was home all night. Honest to God. I swear."

"Anybody to verify that?"

"I live alone, except . . . when Jenna stays over."

And he began to cry. To sob, burying his face in his hands.

Catherine left the observation room, circled to the other door, and strode in. Lipton jumped in his seat, looking up, though Conroy didn't even turn.

"Who . . . who are you?" Lipton asked, face a wet smear, eyelashes pearled.

"Crime scene investigator, Mr. Lipton. Catherine

Willows." She came around and sat opposite him. "Would you like to know how I've been spending the night?"

He swallowed thickly, shrugging as if nothing could rock him now—he'd been through it all. But he hadn't.

Catherine said, "I've been watching videotape of you at Dream Dolls—videotape captured on security cameras . . . tonight."

His eyes widened, lashes glistening. "What? But that's . . . that's just not possible." His voice had a tremor, as if he was about to break down, utterly.

Still Catherine pressed, gesturing to his jacket. "I saw Jenna going into one of the back rooms, with a man about your size, wearing your jacket."

"My jacket?"

"The jacket had your Lipton Construction logo on the back. Denim with tan sleeves—just like that one."

Something close to relief softened his face. "Oh, well shit. I had those made up for all my guys, and even a few of our better customers."

Conroy, poised to write in her notepad, asked, "How many jackets like this exist?"

Another shrug. "Twenty-five . . . maybe thirty."

"Could you be more exact?"

"Not off the top of my head. Probably my secretary could. At work."

A bad feeling in the pit of her stomach started to talk to Catherine, and she wished those security cams had caught a better face shot of the person wearing the jacket in the bar. *Was it Lipton or not?*

Catherine asked, "Have you ever worn a beard, Mr. Lipton?"

"What? Yeah . . . yes."

"Recently?"

"No. That was last year."

"You didn't shave off your beard, this evening."

"No! Hell no."

Catherine studied the man. Then she said, "I'll need your jacket, Mr. Lipton."

"Sure. But I'm tellin' you—I wasn't there."

"Jenna was strangled with an electrical tie."

Lipton flinched, then shook his head. He could obviously see where this was going.

She said, "And when I search your truck, I'm going to find electrical ties in the back, aren't I?"

"You . . . you could search a lot of trucks and find that."

Catherine could tell Conroy was starting to have her doubts about the suspect, too, particularly when the detective tried another tack.

"While you were home alone tonight, Mr. Lipton, did you call anybody?" Conroy asked. "Anybody call you?"

He thought for a moment, then shook his head.

"D'you order pizza or something?"

This required no thought: "No."

"What *did* you do this evening?"

Lipton lifted his hands, palms up, and shrugged. "I watched TV—that's it."

"What did you watch?"

"Was it . . . a football game?"

Conroy leaned forward now. "What, you're asking me?"

"No, no, I know! Yeah, I watched a football game."

"What game, what network, what time?"

He collected his thoughts. "I didn't see the whole thing—I came in during the third quarter. Indianapolis Colts against the Kansas City Chiefs."

Conroy was writing that down.

Lipton went on: "Just as I sat down, Peterson kicks a field goal for the Chiefs . . . then on the kickoff, some guy I never heard of ran it back for a touchdown."

"That was the very first thing you saw?" Conroy asked.

"Yeah. Very first. Field goal. Peterson."

"We'll check that out, Mr. Lipton," Catherine said. "If you're innocent, we'll prove it. But if you're guilty . . ."

His eyes met hers.

". . . we'll prove that too."

"I'm not worried," he said.

But he sure as hell looked it.

5

AMID PINE TREES IN A DECEPTIVELY PEACEFUL SETTING, A low-slung nondescript modern building played host to a maze of hallways connecting the conference rooms, labs, offices, locker room and lounge of the Las Vegas Police Department's criminalistics division. A sterile, institutional ambience was to be expected, but the blue-tinged fluorescent lighting and preponderance of mostly glass walls gave CSI HQ an aquarium-like feel that Nick Stokes, at times, felt he was swimming through.

In one of these hallways, Nick rounded a corner and all but bumped into Grissom, who had just returned from the interview with the Blairs.

Grissom paused, as if it took him a moment to register and recognize his colleague, who had also paused, flashing his ready smile.

The CSI supervisor did not smile, nor did he bother with a hello. "Nick, Sara's teamed with Catherine on the stripper case—I need you to take over the search of the Pierce records."

Nick shrugged. "No problem."

"It's all in Sara's office—work there . . . she won't mind. Look at the Pierce woman's computer, her bank accounts, ATM, calling card, the works. Find us something."

"How far has Sara gotten?"

"Start over. Fresh eye."

"Okay." Nick risked half a smirk. "I don't suppose you considered assigning me to that exotic dancer case."

Grissom's bland baby-faced countenance remained expressionless. "No. Not for a second. Warrick, either. He's on the Pierce case, too."

"You gotta admit, this doesn't sound like as much fun as interviewing nude girls."

Now, finally, Grissom smiled a little. "But you're like me, Nick—only interested in truth and justice, right?"

Then Grissom was gone, leaving Nick to wonder if that had been sarcasm. . . . Sometimes it was damn tough to tell, with that guy.

Nick set himself up in Sara's office—she was out in the field with Catherine, but Grissom was probably right, she wouldn't mind. Sara was that rare individualist who relished being a team player. Though his specialty was hair and fiber analysis, Nick—like all the CSIs Grissom had assembled—was versatile enough to step in and take over any other criminalist's job. And a video-game buff like Nick was hardly a stranger to computers.

With a sigh and a mental farewell to his bevy of beautiful dancers, Nick Stokes buried himself in the computer records of Lynn Pierce. E-mails were still coming in, mostly junk, but one from her brother indicated she hadn't gone to visit him . . . unless something really clever was going on—a possibility that, however far-fetched, had to be considered.

Another e-mail, from a Sally G., whose handle was AvonLady, was even less promising. Several mass e-mailings from Lynn Pierce's church indicated a limited and specific social circle. But Nick kept digging and had been at it about an hour when Grissom stuck his head in Sara's office and announced their first real chunk of evidence.

"You coming with?" Nick asked.

"No. Take Warrick."

Less than two minutes later, Nick strode into the locker room, where Warrick sat on the bench in front of his locker, his head hanging down, a jock who just lost the big game.

"Who cleaned your clock?" Nick asked.

Warrick gave him a slow exhausted burn. "Me, myself, and all that overtime."

"Well, guess what—we just bought some more."

Looking up, alert suddenly, Warrick asked, "What gives?"

"Grissom got a call from Brass—Lynn Pierce's Toyota's turned up in long-term parking at McCarran."

Warrick was on his feet. "Yeah, I was hoping to put in a few more hours—let's go before I change my mind."

McCarran International Airport was one of the five busiest airports in the nation, and one of the most efficient. In the wee hours, dawn not yet a threat, airliners still screamed hello and good-bye, and cars made their way in and out of the parking lot.

Twenty-five minutes after leaving HQ—five minutes of which had been taken up dealing with security at the parking-lot entrance—Nick and Warrick's black Tahoe pulled to a halt behind a squad car that blocked in a white 1995 Toyota Avalon. As they climbed down from the Tahoe a uniformed officer got out of his squad and came back to meet them.

"Anybody been near here?" Warrick asked.

The uniformed man, a fair-haired, weathered pro in his forties, shook his head; his nameplate read JENKINS. "Airport security, making the rounds, recognized the car from our wants list and matched the plate, then gave us a call."

"Good catch," Warrick said.

Officer Jenkins nodded. "They've been making more frequent visits out here ever since September eleventh. Security guy stayed by the car until I got here, but he never got out of his Jeep."

"Good," Warrick said.

"You take a look?" Nick asked.

"Yeah," Jenkins said. "Walked around it once, cut it a wide swath, though—looks locked. Didn't touch shit. Didn't smell anything foul comin' from the trunk area, so I just got back in the squad and waited for you."

"Not your first time at the rodeo," Warrick said. "Thanks."

Jenkins liked that. "You fellas need me to stick around?"

"Naw," Warrick said.

Nick asked, "You call for a tow truck?"

Jenkins shook his head. "Should I have?"

"Naw, that's cool," Warrick said. "We'll get it."

"All right then," Jenkins said, and let out some air. "I'm gone."

"Thanks again," Nick called after him.

The officer waved but never turned back. He climbed into the cruiser, fired it up and rolled away—Nick's guess was the officer's shift was also long since over and the guy had likely logged more than his own share of overtime.

Warrick used his cell phone to call for a truck. The parking lot was well lighted and, at first, they didn't need their Maglites for their work, which they began by photographing the car from every angle. Then they dusted the handles, the hood and the trunk for prints.

"Wipe marks on the handles," Nick said.

Warrick smirked humorlessly. "Trunk too."

"Kinda makes you think maybe it wasn't Mrs. Pierce who parked it here."

"Don't let Grissom catch you at that."

Nick frowned. "At what?"

"Thinking."

Nick grinned, and Warrick motioned for them to go back to the Tahoe, and wait, which they did.

"You know, if you're in the trunk of a car," Nick said, "you're doing one of two things."

"Yeah? What's that?"

"You're a corpse waiting to get dumped, or you're sneakin' into a drive-in movie."

Warrick smiled a little. "They still got drive-in movies in Texas?"

"Last time I was home, they did."

It took forty-five minutes for the flatbed truck to arrive and another three or four for Warrick to stop Nick from bitching out the driver for taking so long. In under ten minutes, the driver—a civil servant in coveralls impervious to Nick's complaints—had hooked up the car and dragged it onto the bed.

"Well, that *was* quick," Nick admitted to the guy.

"You made my night," the driver said with no sincerity whatsoever, and disappeared into it.

Once they had the car out of the way, the pair of CSIs got out their flashlights and searched the parking space carefully, even getting down on their hands and knees—but found nothing. Satisfied they hadn't overlooked anything, they drove back to the CSI garage to take a more careful look at the car.

After putting on coveralls, they entered the bay where the Avalon sat like a museum exhibit. Fluorescent lights gave the car a bleached, almost ghostly cast. Warrick used a slim-jim to undo the lock.

"Twelve seconds," Nick said with a chuckle. "Man, you're slippin'."

"Want me to lock it back up, and give you a shot?"

Waving his hands in surrender, Nick said, "No, no, that's okay—if I showed you up, you'd lose the will to live."

"Yeah, well I'm just hangin' on as it is," Warrick

harumphed, and opened the door. He dusted the driver's door handle, the armrest, the steering wheel and the gear shift. Nick did the passenger side handle, armrest, and the glove compartment. Again, they noticed that the car had been wiped.

"Somebody's hiding something," Warrick said.

"Usually are," Nick nodded, "or we wouldn't be involved—we're just going to have to look harder."

"Yeah, well I better start looking with my eyes open, then," Warrick said. He stared down at the armrest of the open driver's door. "You see that funky power-window button?"

Nick glanced down at the passenger arm rest. "Yeah, it's got that weird . . . lip, in the front."

"So . . . how do you suppose one would go about raising the window?"

Nick frowned—was this a trick question? "Well, 'one' would put his finger under the lip . . . and pull up."

"Which should leave the clever team of criminalists with . . . what?"

Nick smiled, wide. "A fingerprint on the underside . . ."

"Very good, class."

So Warrick printed the underside of the power-window button . . . and got a partial. He got another partial off the back of the gear shift lever, and Nick lifted a pretty good print off the passenger-side window button. The prints would go into the computer as soon as they finished with the rest of the vehicle. They would also need to take Owen Pierce's prints, of course, and daughter Lori's.

"You got a preference over the trunk," Nick asked, "or the interior?"

Warrick shrugged. "Whichever."

"I'll take the trunk."

"Go for it, drive-in boy," Warrick said dryly, and opened the passenger-side door. Sinking to his knees, next to the car, he shone his Maglite on the floor and started going over the carpeting, inch by inch. After his inspection he would vacuum the floor as well; but for now, he just wanted to see the car, up close and personal.

The two CSIs worked in church-like silence, each focused on his particular task. Nothing on the passenger-side floor, nothing in the glove compartment, nothing wedged into the seat. Warrick looked in the cup holders, in the console storage area, even ejected the plastic sleeve of the CD player and found nothing.

Moving around to the rear of the vehicle, Warrick stopped for a moment. "Anything?"

Nick was bent over the trunk, his face buried under the spare tire. "Nothing—you?"

"Zip squared. Somebody's cleaned this car within an inch of its life. It's like it just came off the showroom floor. It's got everything but the new car smell."

Nick beamed at him, mockingly. "I know where you can get a little spray can that'll provide that, if you want."

"I'll pass."

"So we keep lookin'?"

"Keep looking," world-weary Warrick said, and moved to the driver's side of the car.

As he went to lean in, the beam of his flashlight swept over the headrest and . . . *something glinted.*

It was there, then it was gone—like the car had winked. Warrick frowned. The Avalon had tan cloth seats . . . what could've glinted?

He swept the flashlight over the headrest a couple of times, but nothing showed up. The car did not wink at him. He leaned in, inspected the headrest, saw nothing. He raised the Maglite so that the beam shone straight down. Leaning in closer, he looked at the seam that ran across the top of the headrest. Then he saw it . . .

. . . gleaming up at him: *a tiny piece of glass.*

After photographing the mini-shard at rest, Warrick tweezered the fragment free. He carefully studied it for a moment, but its miniscule size kept its origin a secret.

After bagging his prize, Warrick went back to the seam. Moving slowly, a stitch at a time, he found first one blonde hair, then another. Both hairs, like those on the brush already in evidence, could easily belong to Lynn Pierce Then he found another hair—shorter, darker.

Bingo, he thought.

He stored all three hairs in separate baggies and went back inside the Avalon for one last look at that helpful headrest—first the side on the right, then the top, and finally down the left side, nearest the door. He shone the light at the underside of the headrest and picked up on a tiny spot on one of the stitches, about the size of a period. His experience told him the answer to a question he didn't bother to ask.

"Found it!" he yelled, but his voice remained cool.

"All right," Nick said, coming around from the back. "Found what?"

"Blood."

Nick leaned in. "Where?"

Warrick showed him.

"I think we have a crime scene," Nick said.

Warrick said, "I think we have a crime scene."

They got a photo of the blood speck, after which Warrick carefully scraped the tiny dot into an evidence bag.

Grissom strolled in and looked through the open driver's door. "Clean car."

"Too clean," Nick said.

"And yet not clean enough," Warrick said.

"Give," Grissom said.

They explained what they had found so far.

"What's next?"

"Luminol," Warrick answered, shrugging as if to say, *What else?*

"If there's one spot of blood in that car," Grissom said, nodding, "there's probably more."

When they sprayed the luminol on, any other blood would fluoresce. No matter how carefully the car had been cleaned, blood would glow blue-green at even one part per million.

"Before you hit that interior with luminol," Grissom said, "are you otherwise through in there? Anything else you found? Noticed?"

Nick could sense they were being sucker-punched, but nonetheless he shrugged and said, "No, that's it."

Warrick, though, said, "Why, Gris? You got something?"

Grissom leaned inside the car for a look of his own; his eyes were everywhere. "How tall was Lynn Pierce?"

Nick thought that over. "Five-four?"

"That's right," Grissom said, withdrawing himself from the vehicle. "And if she was five-four and drove her car to the airport and left it parked there . . . why is the driver's seat all the way back?"

Nick and Warrick traded *how-the-hell-does-he-do-it* looks.

Grissom asked, "Or did you move the seat, Warrick? Going over the interior?"

Warrick shook his head.

Grissom turned to Nick, asking pleasantly, "You?"

Another head shake.

Grissom looked at Warrick. "Thoughts?"

Warrick sighed to his toes, holding up his hands in admission of frailty. "I'll fingerprint the power-seat button . . . *then* we hit the interior with luminol."

"Smart thinking," Grissom said, then he turned and left.

"I hate him," Nick said, admiringly.

"Yeah," Warrick said. "He's good."

The power-seat button stuck out from the side of the seat like a tiny shiny peanut. Warrick dusted it . . . and found out it too had been wiped.

"This is starting to piss me off," Warrick said as

he reached for the luminol. "Every time we get hold of something, it grins and gets away."

Warrick started at the floor and worked his way up, spraying the luminol on the driver's-side floor mat, the seat, and then the headrest. Instantly, the surfaces became dotted with bluish green pinpoints.

"Nick," Warrick said, "you gotta see this."

Nick peered in from the passenger side. "Uh oh . . . I don't think Lynn Pierce caught her flight."

Gravely, Warrick shook his head. "Flew apart, maybe. . . ." He sprayed luminol over the backseat and the passenger side, but all the blood seemed to be concentrated in the driver's seat. "Let's get the seat covers off, and see what's underneath."

The two used utility knives and, whenever possible, followed seams, to cause as little damage as possible, preserving the seat covers. Nick climbed in the back and attacked the driver's seat from the passenger side, while Warrick knelt on the floor next to the car and started cutting the edges on his side. In short order they had the covers off the seat, the back and the headrest.

Then they were staring in disbelief at the foam rubber cushions. Dark stains spread ominously from the headrest down the back to a low spot on the back edge of the seat.

Finally Nick said, "Somebody got shot in the head . . . would be my guess."

"Educated guess," Warrick said, eyebrows lifted. "Damn. . . . Let's find out if it was Lynn Pierce."

"We got hairbrush hairs," Nick said. "But DNA testing is going to take a while."

"Then the sooner we get the ball rolling with Greg, the better. . . . After that, let's talk to Gris—but I think I already know what he's going to say."

Warrick shot Polaroid photos of the interior while Nick took a small scraping from the seat to use in a DNA test. After stopping by Greg Sanders in his lab, they called on Grissom, who was buried in paperwork in his office.

They explained their findings and showed him the photos of the blood-spattered seat. Grissom stared at the photos long enough to make Nick uneasy.

Finally Grissom said, "All right . . . first thing, line up one of the dayshift interns to start calling the glass companies in town."

Warrick nodded. "To see if anybody's replaced the driver's side window of a white '95 Avalon in the last few days."

Nick, nodding, too, said, "On it."

Grissom studied one of the photos again. "It's probable that fragment of glass you found came out of the original window."

"Yeah, that's our take on it," Warrick said.

"But we need to know, don't we?" Grissom tossed the grisly photo on his desk and his grin was a horrible thing. "And now we get a search warrant and go over the Pierce house again. Only this time . . . we do it right."

Nick tilted his head. "But we don't have enough to arrest Pierce—do we?"

The CSI supervisor considered that for a long moment. Then, he rattled off his mental findings, clinically: "There's the tape where he threatened to cut up his wife and there's blood in the car, but there's no body, no weapon, no DNA match for a while—I don't think we can even speculate on a motive, yet."

"In a bad marriage," Warrick said, "you won't have to look very hard."

"But we haven't looked yet," Grissom reminded them. "And the DA isn't going to want to even *talk* to us, if we don't find something better than what we have now."

"That's a crime scene," Nick said, frustrated. "Broken glass, blood spatter . . ."

Warrick was nodding, punctuating his colleague's points. "Nick's right, Gris."

Grissom said, "I'll go along with you on that, Nick—that's a crime scene . . . but what's the crime? Who's the victim? Isn't it also possible that the short dark hair and the fingerprints belong to a victim who isn't Lynn Pierce?"

Warrick rolled his eyes and asked, "Who else *could* it be?"

"Or maybe it's not a victim at all. Maybe it's the daughter—maybe she or her mom had a nosebleed."

"Ah, man," Nick groused, "you don't believe that!"

"I don't believe anything yet, Nick. The evidence will show us the way—we just need more of it."

Warrick leaned a hand on the desk. "Odds are the blood is Mrs. Pierce's, Gris. I mean, we can't find her, she doesn't seem to be using any of her credit cards or her phone card—the blood's in *her* car . . ."

"The odds say it's her," Grissom agreed. "But we

don't play the odds. We put all our money on science. . . . Now, we start with the Pierce house again and find out the truth. You two go on out there. I'll call Brass and meet you there—we don't have enough for an arrest . . . yet . . . but I know just the judge to give us a search warrant."

An hour later, as dawn was breaking, Captain Jim Brass parked his Taurus behind the black Tahoe in the Pierces' driveway. "I don't see your people," Brass said.

"Maybe they're already inside," Grissom said.

"Without a warrant."

Grissom gestured with open palms. "Maybe—Pierce has cooperated so far."

"I don't like him—he's an arrogant prick."

"You have some evidence, Jim, that led you to that conclusion?"

The detective gave the criminalist a tired smile and pointed to his own gut. "Yeah, this—it's my prick detector."

Grissom's smile was skeptical. "A judge and jury may want more."

Brass summoned half a smirk. "That's what's wrong with our judicial system."

The two men climbed out of the car and walked up the sidewalk to the front door. Grissom was about to ring the bell when Warrick pulled the door open.

"He let us in," Warrick whispered, stepping out onto the stoop. "He didn't even bitch about getting woken up."

Grissom asked, also sotto voce, "What have you told him?"

"Nada," Warrick said, doing the umpire "you're out" gesture. "Not even that we found the car. Just that his wife was officially missing now, and we needed to step up the investigation . . . apologized for the early hour."

Brass was impressed. "Nice work, Brown."

Warrick ignored the compliment, saying to Grissom, "You can give him the warrant, though—he's in the living room."

His voice still low, Grissom asked, "Find anything?"

"No. . . . Either this guy is really good, or there's nothing to find."

"Stick with it."

Warrick headed in and disappeared down the hall to the left, as Grissom and Brass walked into the living room where Owen Pierce stood in fresh blue jeans and tasseled loafers, a blue Polo shirt open at the neck; he was unshaven, and sipping a cup of coffee.

"Morning," Pierce said. "Can I get you guys some coffee?"

"No thanks," Brass said, though the smell of it was tempting. He handed Pierce the warrant, who accepted it without looking at it.

"May I ask why you believe you need a search warrant?" He seemed more hurt than indignant. "Haven't I made my home available to you, in every way?"

Brass gave Grissom a look and the CSI supervisor

stepped forward. "We've located your wife's car, Mr. Pierce."

"You . . . the Avalon, you mean?" He sounded genuinely surprised, his expression hopeful.

"Yes, sir," Brass said. "A few hours ago at McCarran."

Pierce tried out a smile, looking from the detective to the criminalist. "Well, that's a break for our side, isn't it?"

Brass wasn't sure who exactly was on "our side," as Pierce defined it. "It's a break in the case, Mr. Pierce. But I'm afraid the situation has taken a serious turn."

Grissom, flatly, declared, "We found blood on the driver's seat of your wife's car."

"The driver's seat was . . . there was blood?" His hopeful expression vanished, but nothing replaced it—an alert sort of blankness remained. He set his cup down on a nearby coffee table.

"Actually, the car was clean, sir." Grissom shrugged. "Well, except for a drop of blood on the headrest."

Pierce's face remained impassive as he stared Grissom down. "One drop?"

"One drop—but that was to enough to indicate we should look . . . closer."

Curiosity filled the void of his expression. "And how did you do that?"

"We peeled off the seat covers. Those can be cleaned, but underneath? Practically impossible. And we discovered a large quantity of blood on the seat's cushions."

Now confusion colored Pierce's face. "Under the seat covers? What the hell does that mean?"

"The amount of blood indicates the probability of something violent happening in the car. . . . The absence of blood on the seat covers indicates someone covering up that violence."

Shaking his head, seemingly feeling helpless, Pierce said, "I don't know what to say, Mr. Grissom . . . Detective Brass. Other than, I hope to God Lynn's all right."

God again, Brass thought. *He's all over this goddamned case.*

Grissom was asking, "Have you had an automobile accident, in the Avalon? Was it necessary to repair the driver's-side window of your wife's car recently?"

"No—why?"

"We also found glass in the car . . . and we believe it came from the driver's-side window."

Pierce began to pace a small area. "I don't know how that could be possible . . ." His eyes were wide, a frown screwing up his face. "That window's never been broken."

Grissom changed direction. "Do you own a gun?"

"What? No. Of course not."

"Never? With all these outdoorsman prints, ducks and geese and deer, I thought maybe you were a hunter."

"No. Not since I was a kid, with my dad. . . . I just like looking at a landscape that isn't desert, once in a while. Where are you going with this, Mr. Grissom?" Then a mental light bulb seemed to go on for Pierce, his eyes flaring. "You're here looking for a gun. . . . You think I killed my wife!"

Brass stepped forward. "We're not making any accusations, Mr. Pierce."

Pierce was shaking his head, his eyes wild now. "There's blood on the seat of my wife's car . . . so that means I *killed* her? This is absurd—you should be out looking for her! She's alive, I'm sure! You don't have any evidence."

Grissom said, pleasantly, "That's why we brought the search warrant, Mr. Pierce."

Warrick stepped into the living room and said, "Gris? A word?"

Grissom turned to Pierce. "May we use your kitchen, to confer?"

"Oh," Pierce said with a sarcastic wave, "be my guest! By all means!"

Other than not bothering the sleeping Lori Pierce, Nick and Warrick had searched the house from top to bottom, giving the home a much more thorough going over than the first time.

"No gun," Nick told Grissom and Brass, leaning against the kitchen counter. "No bullets, either—nothing to indicate that there's ever been a gun in the house."

"No significant new evidence?" Grissom asked glumly.

"Not of murder," Warrick said, and gave them a cat-that-ate-the-canary grin.

Grissom and Brass just looked at him.

Warrick milked it for a few seconds, then he

spilled: "I found this little darling in a vent in the basement . . ."

And he held out a clear plastic bag containing a small amount of white powder. The baggie had a small red triangle stamped in one corner, a dealer's mark.

"Coke?" Grissom asked. "Pierce has cocaine in the house?"

"That's right," Warrick said, pleased to be the man of the hour.

"Not very much, though," Grissom said.

"Misdemeanor," Brass said.

"But enough to book his ass," Warrick pointed out. He held up the baggie. "You recognize this?" He showed Grissom the triangle, Brass too.

"Never seen that mark before," Grissom said.

Neither had Brass.

Grissom asked, "And there's nothing else pertaining to Mrs. Pierce?"

Nick shrugged. "Sorry, Gris. No gun, no bullets, no blood, no nothin'. We went through everything, even the drains . . . zippo."

They followed Brass and Grissom into the living room, the detective heading for Pierce, who was seated on the sofa, sipping his no doubt cold-by-now coffee.

"Mr. Pierce," Brass said, "I'm placing you under arrest."

The therapist's eyes widened, but the hand holding the coffee cup remained steady. "For . . . murder?"

Brass shook his head. "Possession of cocaine."

Grissom held up the evidence bag for Pierce to see.

Pierce made a face, tried to wave this off. "Oh, Jesus, that's *years* old! I forgot it was even in the house."

Brass put on his patented grin. "I know this'll be hard for you to believe, Mr. Pierce, but that's not the first time I've heard that."

"Hey, I used to snort some, but I haven't used since, hell . . . forever. It's an innocent mistake. When I got off it, that's one little stash I missed, when I threw out the rest."

"Interesting defense," Brass said.

Pierce let out a weight-of-the-world sigh. "Fine, fine. . . . Will I need my lawyer?"

"This small amount is just a misdemeanor, Mr. Pierce," Brass said. "Probably not, but of course it is your right to seek counsel."

"No, to hell with it," Pierce said, standing. "Let's just get this over with, so you can get back to the business of finding my wife. . . . Are you going to slap on the cuffs?"

Brass beamed at him. "Not unless you're going to make a break for it."

"I'll try to restrain myself," Pierce said. "My daughter's still in bed . . . I need to leave her a note."

"Go ahead."

"Very generous of you."

Soon the five of them were marching through the front door of the Pierce castle into the sunshine. Brass guided the suspect into the backseat while he and Grissom climbed in front. Nick and Warrick took the Tahoe.

Traffic was already heavy. They were almost halfway back before either of them said a word.

Finally, Nick asked, "There is a crime here, right? Besides misdemeanor controlled-substance possession?"

"What we have here," Warrick said, "is a crime scene . . . in search of a crime."

6

SOMETHING ABOUT RAY LIPTON—HIS GRIEVING MANNER, more than his words—made Catherine Willows want to believe his story. Of course, Catherine had also believed her ex-husband, Eddie, and she knew how well *that* had turned out.

However much her heart wanted Lipton not to have done it, the evidence told another story: the videotape (beard or no beard), the history of fighting, the weapon . . . everything pointed toward Ray. Odds were, he'd done the murder—and these were a hell of a lot better odds than you could get at any casino in town.

Greg Sanders poked his spiky-haired head into her office. "No prints on that electrical tie."

Catherine looked up from the pile of papers on her desk with a frustrated frown. "Not even a partial?"

"Of the killer, I mean." Sanders stepped inside the office, hands on hips. "Couple of smudges and a couple on the sides—all the vic's." He shook his head. "Poor baby only had a few seconds before the strap would've cut off the blood flow to her brain, y'know."

Catherine nodded gravely.

The often jokey Sanders was dead serious. "She gave it her best—tried to get a hold of it and failed. So she was an exotic dancer, huh?"

"That's right."

"Yeah, okay . . . well, I'll just get back to it, then."

Sitting back and closing her eyes and sighing, Catherine let her weight rock the chair. She sat there for a long moment, just thinking, processing the new information, sorting out her emotional reactions and putting them in one mental pile (marked "Catherine"), placing the facts in another (marked "Grissom"). Something tiny gnawed at the back of her brain . . . small but tenacious.

"Hey."

With a start, Catherine sat forward to see Sara standing in front of her.

"Hey," Catherine said.

"You ready to go?"

". . . Sure."

Sara frowned as she studied Catherine. "Sorry, I didn't mean to startle you . . . I just thought we'd go check out Lipton's truck."

Catherine rubbed her eyes. "Good idea. I could stand getting out of here."

Sara gestured toward the PD wing. "Conroy has to book Lipton, and then she wants to meet us at Jenna's apartment, to search it? And to tell her roommate the bad news." A little what-the-hell shrug—"I thought we could do Lipton's truck on the way. We probably oughta log the overtime while the case is still fresh."

Catherine nodded and rose. "Okay."

Lipton Construction had a corner building in an industrial park east of the airport. A one-story stucco affair with smoked-glass windows, dating back decades—ancient history in this town—it crouched like an ungainly beast near the entrance to the park, far away from the heavier industry. A couple of pickups and a Honda Accord sat in the otherwise empty parking lot out front. To the left, behind a gate and an eight-foot cyclone fence, lurked a few heavy-construction machines. Down the side of the building, two garage doors opened onto the fenced-in lot.

Sara pulled the Tahoe into the parking lot and eased into the spot next to the green Accord. Catherine wondered if any of these people knew what had happened to their boss—and their boss's fiancée—last night. They parked and climbed out of the SUV, Sara lugging a field kit.

Sara, as if reading Catherine's mind, asked, "You think they know?"

"Probably not."

"Just the same, walking in there, cold. . . . Any ideas?"

Holding up a finger in a "wait" manner, Catherine said, "Just one." She plucked her cell phone from her purse, punched in a number, pushed SEND, and waited.

Finally, a voice on the other end picked up. "Conroy."

"Willows. Lipton still being cooperative?"

"Yeah. Still claims he was home alone, too."

"Innocent people don't always have alibis, you know."

"Is that what you think he is?" the detective asked. "Innocent?"

"I think he's a suspect. And if he still wants to impress us with his cooperative attitude, why don't you have him call his construction company and pave the way for us?"

"You really think that's necessary?"

"Detective Conroy, if Lipton makes the call, his people just might be more anxious to help, than if we just barge in and tell them that we've arrested their boss on suspicion of murder."

"Good point. Where are you?"

"At Lipton Construction—in the parking lot."

"Sit tight," Conroy said. "I'll call you back in five minutes."

Conroy more than kept her promise, Catherine's cell ringing in just under five.

"Lipton made the call for us," Conroy said. "He told them to play ball. They're expecting you."

"Good. Thanks."

"Catherine, I'll be questioning Lipton's people later today; but if you hear anything interesting, during the course of your evidentiary search, write it down, and let me know when we meet up at Jenna's apartment—so I have the info, going in."

"I hear you," Catherine said with a smile, and clicked off.

"We got the go-ahead?" Sara asked.

"Yeah. Lipton's staff is waiting for us . . . and Conroy gave us her roundabout blessing for a little off-the-cuff interrogation."

They walked into a roomy, undistinguished office with cream-colored walls, a handful of desks and a few file cabinets. Just inside the door they were addressed by a young woman sitting behind a metal desk, immediately to their left.

"You the cops, already?" she asked, her voice cold.

"LV Metro PD," Catherine said, displaying her I.D. "Crime scene investigators."

At a cluttered desk farther to the left, behind the woman's tidier one, sat a heavy-set thirty-something guy in an open flannel shirt and a Bulls T-shirt, eyeing the two female callers suspiciously over a mountain of papers. To his left, in the back corner, was a closed door; nearer them in the back, off to the right, a third desk sat empty.

"Ray said you were coming," the ash blonde said sullenly. "What, were you out in the parking lot all the time?"

Sara stepped forward, to the edge of the woman's desk. "Do you have a problem?"

Catherine quickly moved beside Sara, touching her arm, and said to the woman, pleasantly, "Who runs the office, please?"

"Mr. Lipton does." The ash blonde's voice was trembling and it seemed like she might cry. "And he's innocent. Ray Lipton has his faults, but he's not a killer."

"We don't decide that," Catherine said, rather disingenuously. "We just gather evidence."

The heavy-set man used the desk to help him rise. "Crime scene investigators, huh?" He had a deep, boomy voice that rattled up out of his chest like he was speaking from inside a trash can.

Catherine moved away from the secretary/receptionist's desk, to make eye contact with the hulking figure. "That's right. We'd like to see Mr. Lipton's office and his company truck."

Stepping out from behind the desk, which looked like a a playhouse toy next to him, the mountainous man lumbered forward, talking as he went: "Was that girl killed here or something? You saying this is a crime scene? Are you kiddin'?"

Sara, who did not suffer fools gladly, looked about to burst, and Catherine could just see the citizen's complaint forms come flying into the office, after the Sidle social skills went into full force.

Holding Sara back gently, Catherine said, "We need to investigate all aspects, all avenues, of a crime . . . not just the scene of the crime itself."

The big man deposited himself before them. "Ray's a stand-up guy," he said, his eyes burning into Catherine's. "He's not the killer type."

Chin up, Sara asked mock-innocently, "Is he the restraining-order type?"

The big man turned his gaze on the younger woman, sucking in air—the buttons on his flannel shirt threatening to pop and reveal the Bulls T-shirt in toto. Then the air rushed out: "That was *bull*-shit. He never did *nothin'* like that!"

"Like what?" Sara pressed

Catherine stepped between them. "Sir, we're not

going to debate the issue. This is police business. As I said, we're only here to have a look at Mr. Lipton's office and truck."

Still staring at Sara, the big man seemed to buckle a bit; then he said, "Well, all right—but we're only cooperatin' 'cause Ray told us to."

"So that's what this is," Sara said. "Cooperation."

Wincing, Catherine raised a hand. "Thank you, sir. We understand. And you should understand that we are here as much to look for evidence to exonerate Mr. Lipton as anything else."

He considered that, doubtfully, then said, "This way, ladies."

Catherine fell in alongside him, and Sara brought up the rear.

"I'm Catherine Willows, and this is Sara Sidle. And you are?"

"Mike. Howtlen."

He opened the door at the rear of the office, leading them into a corridor with another door on the left and one at the far end. "Ray's office is here." He gestured toward the closest of the doors. "And the truck, it's in the bay, in back."

The big man opened the office door and they all stepped inside. This was a colorless oversized cubicle with a messy desk, two filing cabinets, a couch against one wall, and—for the man who thought it unacceptable for his girl friend to be a stripper—a Hooters calendar.

"What's your job here, Mr. Howtlen?" Catherine asked.

"One of the job foremen."

"I see. And how long have you worked for Mr. Lipton?"

"Ever since Ray went into business for himself. . . . Six years."

"Do you have a Lipton Construction jacket?"

He looked at her funny. "Why do you ask that?"

"I'd appreciate it if you'd just answer, sir."

He shrugged, nodded. "Yeah, sure. I got a jacket. We all do."

"Define 'all.' "

Another shrug. "Twenty employees, here at Lipton Construction. We all got one. Ray's generous, and we're cheap advertising."

Well, Catherine thought, Howtlen would make a hell of a billboard, at that.

Sara had slipped on latex gloves and now moved around to the rear of the desk. She opened the top righthand drawer and fingered Scotch tape, a ruler, pencils, rubber bands. Slowly, she worked her way toward the back.

Howtlen's eyes were riveted on Sara—whether in suspicion or interest or just because Sara Sidle was cute, Catherine couldn't say.

What she could say, to Howtlen, was, "Can you put together a list for us, of everyone who has one of those Lipton Construction jackets?"

The foreman said nothing as he watched Sara shut the top drawer and move down to the next one. His face turned pink and he seemed to be gritting his teeth. So it wasn't Sara's good looks that had his attention: Howtlen was bridling at the indignity of their CSI invasion of Lipton territory.

Catherine took a step and gently laid a hand on his arm. "Mr. Howtlen?"

He shook his head and looked down at Catherine. "I'm sorry, what?"

"Sir, remember—what we find may clear Mr. Lipton."

"Should I believe you?"

"Off the record, sir—I have a hunch Mr. Lipton's innocent myself."

Sara flinched, but pretended not to hear it.

Howtlen said, "You're not just sayin' that."

"No. But it's my job to find out, either way—if Ray did kill his girlfriend, you wouldn't want him to have a pass, would you?"

"I . . . no. Of course not."

"Good. Now about that list, Mr. Howtlen? Of jackets?"

"Yeah, sure—puttin' that together shouldn't be a problem."

"Mr. Lipton told us he gave them to preferred customers, too."

"Oh, shit, come to think of it, yeah . . . but I have no idea who that'd be. But Jodi, that's the gal out front, she'd probably know. . . . Yeah, no problem. We'll get you that list."

The now truly cooperative Howtlen left then to fill Catherine's request, and the CSIs got down to work. Ninety minutes later they had pretty much dissected everything in the office and found nothing of value. The business records in the file cabinet, Catherine decided, could be left behind, for now; and there was no computer in here.

Gathering up their gear, they moved down the hallway into the bay.

Two roll-up garage doors dominated the left wall of the high-ceilinged concrete chamber. Men's and women's bathrooms took up the rest of the side they'd entered through. A workbench ate up a large chunk of the righthand wall; some green metal garden furniture and, at the rear of the room, a couple of wood-and-metal picnic tables comprised the break area. The center of the room held two blue pickups with Lipton Construction stenciled in white-outlined red on their sides. The one parked nearest to them had "Ray" in white script letters over the driver's side door. The back of the pickup was filled with tools and various piles of gear, as well as a steel toolbox mounted on the front end of the bed.

"I'll take the box," Sara volunteered, "if you want the cab."

Catherine shrugged her okay. "Dealer's choice."

They took photos of the truck from every angle, fingerprinted the doors and tailgate, and then each went to investigate their own part of the truck. In the cab, Catherine found very little beyond an empty soda cup and a McDonald's sack with a Big Mac wrapper and an empty french fry container.

"Got it," Sara said from the back.

Catherine came out of the cab. "Got what?" She moved down the driver's side of the truck to find Sara pointing the camera at something in the bottom of the truck bed. Following the line of the lens,

Catherine saw what "it" was: a nest of black man-made snakes in a plastic bag. . . .

Black electrical ties identical to the one that had squeezed the life from lovely Jenna Patrick.

The floor shook as Howtlen strode in, a piece of paper dangling from his massive paw. "Got your list, for ya!"

But Catherine was on to other things. "Mr. Howtlen, do you recognize this?" She pointed toward the bag.

Joining her alongside the truck, Howtlen looked down into the box, shrugged. "Sure—'lectrical ties. We use 'em all the time. I got a bag of them in back of my truck, too." He gestured at the other pickup. "Why? Is that important?"

"An electrical tie like these," Sara said, studying the man, "was the murder weapon."

"No shit! Really?"

Catherine gave him a hard look. "Really—tied around Miss Patrick's neck."

"Hell of a way to go." He was cringing at the thought, the tiny features almost disappearing into his fleshy face. "Don't ever think, just 'cause she was a stripper, Jenna wasn't a sweet kid . . . 'cause she was."

"Ray is said to have a temper," Sara said. "And yet you don't think he was capable of that? In the heat of anger?"

Howtlen shook his head quickly. "I've worked for Ray for six years—known him a hell of a lot longer than that . . . and, yeah, he can lose his top. But this is a sweet guy . . . and no killer."

Everybody was "sweet" to Howtlen, it seemed.

Sara didn't let up: "You do know the Dream Dolls club's manager was able to get a restraining order against him?"

The big head wagged, side to side, sorrowfully. "Yeah, yeah, I know . . . Ray caused scenes in there more than once. Sometimes when a guy dates a stripper, at first it's really great, and then it makes 'em crazy, other guys lookin' at their lady, naked."

"How crazy?" Catherine asked.

"Not *that* crazy, not Ray! He never hurt nobody in his life. Even that time when one of the bouncers hit him . . . with those brass knuckles? Ray yells, but he's not violent. Not really."

"Well if you're right," Catherine said, "our work will help clear him."

Howtlen held up the paper to Catherine. "Then take that list you said you wanted. I never had no idea just how many jackets Ray passed out . . . I admit I'm a little surprised, 'cause they're pretty expensive. But, anyway, Jodi found the receipts. Thirty-five."

Catherine accepted the list. "And how many of the jackets are accounted for on this list?"

"Twenty-seven we're sure of, who he gave 'em to, and a few maybes. The others . . . who knows? Maybe Ray can help. He'll probably remember."

"May we have copies of the receipts too?"

Howtlen nodded. "I'll get Jodi to do that for you right away."

"Thank you. And we'll need to take the ties from your truck too. Just to be sure."

"All right." He turned and lumbered to the door, then stopped and turned, sheepish—the big man was a big kid. "Hey, uh . . . sorry about before. You girls seem nice. You gotta understand—Ray's my friend, and he's a good guy."

"It's all right, Mr. Howtlen," Catherine said. "And we do understand—one of our coworkers was accused of murder, last year."

"How did that come out?"

Sara said, "He was innocent."

Catherine gave Howtlen a genuinely friendly smile. "Happy endings are still possible, you know."

"Yeah," Howtlen said, shaking his pumpkin head, "but not for that sweet kid, Jenna."

Ten minutes later they left Lipton Construction with the list, the photocopies of receipts, and two bags of electrical ties from both trucks. Catherine phoned Conroy again and the detective said she was on her way to Jenna Patrick's apartment. Did they still want to meet her there?

Catherine said yes, then clicked off, and said to Sara, "You don't mind? You are up for that?"

"We put in this much overtime," Sara said, at the wheel, with half a smirk, "why not?"

Catherine laughed silently. "Would you rather do your job than sleep?"

"Sure. So would you, Catherine."

Catherine said nothing; it was true. She loved her job, she loved solving puzzles. She just feared that she might become Grissom or, for that matter, Sara.

Jenna Patrick's apartment was off Escondido

near the UNLV campus. Conroy's Taurus already sat in front of the building when Sara pulled up and parked across the street. From the outside, the three-story building looked like an early sixties motel, all rust-color brick and crank-open windows. Concrete stairs ran up the right side of the building, and there seemed to be a small parking lot out back.

The three women—one detective and two criminalists—met up at the curb, where Catherine and Sara filled Conroy in on what they'd learned at Lipton Construction. Then the trio paraded single-file up the stairs (Conroy, then Catherine, then Sara) to the third floor, around the back and up the far side of the building to 312. A picture window faced them, curtains drawn over it keeping out any sunlight that might try to sneak through.

Strippers worked the night shift, too.

Conroy knocked on the white wooden door. Nothing. They waited, then Conroy knocked again and said, loudly, firmly, *"Police."*

Slowly, the door cracked open, chain latch still in place, and a tired woman peered out. "What? . . . Awful early . . ."

Conroy flashed her badge. "Are you Tera Jameson?"

The one visible eye widened enough to take in the badge. "That's me."

"Ms. Jameson, could you open the door, please?"

"Yeah. Sure." A sigh, and the door closed; they heard the chain scratch across the latch, then the door opened again. The voice of their hostess was more alert, now: "What's this all about?"

The three stepped in, Tera Jameson closing the door behind them. She was a buxom woman, her curly brunette hair flowing down her back but also framing her heart-shaped face. Tallish, maybe five nine, she wore only a 49ers football jersey about five sizes too large for her and a pair of baggy gray cotton shorts.

The living room was tidy if crammed with rent-to-own-type furniture. A low-slung dark coffee table with a glass top and piles of magazines crouched in front of a couch, and an overstuffed brown chair sat against the right wall with a hassock in front of it. In the opposite corner a twenty-five-inch color TV occupied a maple wall unit with a stereo, VCR, DVD and the attendant software.

"Thank you, Ms. Jameson," Conroy said, and she gestured to the couch, adding, "Maybe you should sit down. I'm afraid I have some bad news."

"What kind of bad news?" The woman's dark eyes flared, but she took Conroy's advice, sliding over to the couch and taking a seat. Sara sat down on her far side, not crowding the woman, and Catherine took the overstuffed chair, while Conroy got down on her haunches in front of Tera Jameson, parent to child.

"It's about your roommate," Conroy said. "I know you were friends."

"Best friends," Tera said. Then the eyes widened again, and she said, ". . . *were?*"

Conroy sighed and nodded. "I'm sorry to report that Jenna Patrick died last night."

Tera's hand shot to her mouth, her teeth closing on a knuckle as tears took the path over her high cheekbones down her face. "Oh, my God. But . . . she was in perfect health!"

"I'm afraid she was killed, at work, last night."

"What do you mean, 'killed'? An accident of some—"

"Murdered."

Tera covered her face with her fingers and began to sob.

Conroy eased forward, a hand rising to settle soothingly on the dancer's shoulder. "Ms. Jameson, I'm very sorry."

Now a certain anger seemed stirred into the sorrow. "What . . . what in hell *happened* to her?"

"Jenna was in one of the private rooms . . . and she was strangled."

"I *told* Ty those lap-dance rooms were dangerous. Goddamnit! I wouldn't work them . . . I refused. Goddamnit."

Catherine asked, "You did work at Dream Dolls, at one time, Ms. Jameson?"

"Yes . . . I've been at Showgirl World for, I don't know . . . three months?" Tera pulled a tissue out of a box on the coffee table and dabbed at her eyes. "Did you get him?"

Conroy, still on her haunches, blinked. "Excuse me?"

"That asshole Ray Lipton. It was him, wasn't it? It must have been."

Sitting forward, Catherine asked, "Why would you think that? He was her fiancé; he loved her."

She sneered, her lip damp with tears. "He's a fucking nutcase. He *hated* that she danced . . . *and* he hated that she lived with me, another dancer . . . I was a 'bad influence'! He fucking *met* her at the club! Jesus."

Catherine tilted her head. "Mr. Lipton said they were going to be married, soon. Was he lying?"

"Yes. No . . . I mean, yeah, that was the plan—they were getting married. Jenna was barely even my roommate anymore. To keep Ray happy, she moved out of here about a month ago."

Sara asked, "Was she quitting dancing for him?"

"Eventually, she planned to. I mean, most of us plan to get out, sooner or later. I have a nursing degree, you know. But she wanted to keep dancing for a couple of years, *after* they got married, to help build a nest egg. I mean, do you have any idea what those tits of hers cost?"

"Around ten thousand," Catherine said.

Conroy asked, "Well, was she living here, or not?"

"Her name's still on the lease, but she'd pretty much moved in with Ray. She still had a few things here, but it was mostly just stuff she hadn't picked up yet."

Conroy—squatting must have been getting to her—moved to sit down on the other side of Tera. She asked, "And why do you think Ray would kill her?"

"Probably over the dancing. That she hadn't

quit, that she wanted to keep going with it. . . . He hated that she danced even more than he hated her living with me. I mean, she liked it here—our hours were similar, it was close to work—but she moved in with him, to . . . what's the word? Placate the prick."

Conroy asked, "You think Ray hates you?"

Tera looked uncomfortable. "I *know* he does. You know about the restraining order Ty had against him, and what caused it?"

"We know that he tried to choke a customer," Catherine said.

"Well, that was just one particularly juicy time. It was me pulled his ass off that poor nerdy guy he jumped. More than once, when I was still at the club, he started trouble over our friendship, Jenna and me. He'd see us sitting together, or standing at the bar, laughing, and get all paranoid we were laughing at him. He'd start screaming at me. He probably yelled at me as much as he did Jenna."

"Why was that?" Conroy asked.

"You know how guys can be—jealous over their girlfriend's best friend. It's stupid, such a guy thing. He thought I had some . . . I don't know, kinda power over her. That I was this wicked witch trying to keep them apart."

"Why would he think that?"

Tera pulled her knees up under her, sat that way. Her chin was up. "Because I told her not to take any crap off him. If they were gonna be married, she still had to be her own person, and stand up for her rights, like dancing if she wanted to. I just generally encouraged her to do what she wanted to do."

"And Ray didn't like that."

"Oh, hell no. Ray's a typical control freak. He thought getting her away from me would make her fall in line with his plans. Get her to live with him, stop dancing, do whatever he said."

"Ray ever try to get physical with you?"

"No." She sat up straighter. "He's a coward, too—he knows I trained in tae kwan do. He figured, lay a hand on me and I'da sent his balls up to live in his throat . . . and he figured right."

"Okay," Conroy said, an uncomfortable tone creeping into her voice. "You mind if we look around?"

"Not at all. Anything that'll help." Tera shook her head, the dark locks shimmering. "Her bedroom's the one on the left, opposite the bathroom. Or it used to be."

Suddenly Tera's tough talk dissolved into another round of tears, and that quickly built into racking sobs.

Conroy stayed and held the dancer, tried to comfort her as Catherine and Sara moved to the bedroom. They slipped on latex gloves and entered.

Tera hadn't been kidding—Jenna had moved out, all right: no bed, no dresser, no furniture of any kind, just a few stray clothes hanging in the closet and a small pile of CDs sitting inside the door, the final artifacts remaining of Jenna Patrick's life in this tiny apartment.

The two criminalists went back to the living room where Conroy still sat on the couch next to Tera Jameson, holding the woman's hand—something she doubted Jim Brass would have done, and which would have mystified Grissom. Catherine caught Conroy's gaze and shook her head—they hadn't found anything.

Conroy rose, looking down at the young woman with a somber smile. "Ms. Jameson, we're sorry for your loss."

Tera, who was drying her eyes with a handkerchief, nodded bravely.

Conroy joined the CSIs at the door. "If we have more questions," she said to Tera, "we'll get back to you. . . . You have my card, if you think of something you consider important."

"I do, yes—I will . . . and thank you."

"Have you ever been back to Dream Dolls," Catherine asked suddenly, "since you quit?"

Tera shook her head, her long dark hair swinging. "No way. Good riddance to that hellhole."

Catherine knew the feeling.

"Thanks," Catherine said, and exchanged polite smiles with the woman.

Soon the trio from LVMPD were standing next to Conroy's car.

Catherine asked, "You didn't search Lipton's place yet?"

"No," Conroy said, "just picked him up and brought him in. We should get to that."

"Since he's in custody," Sara said, "maybe it could wait till tonight—we're way past the end of shift, and I'd hate to get the dayshift's sticky fingers in this."

Conroy said, "That should work out fine. Meantime, I'll ask Lipton if he'll give us the go-ahead, and see if we have to get a search warrant or not."

"You think he'll stop cooperating?" Catherine asked.

Conroy arched an eyebrow. "Wouldn't you, if you were about to go down for murder?"

"Yeah, I suppose I would . . . unless I was innocent."

"Which you think he is?"

"Well, he's cooperated with us so far—hasn't hidden a thing."

Sara asked, "Tera didn't paint a very pretty picture of him."

"She also didn't paint that violent a picture of him," Catherine pointed out. "Lipton and Tera hated each other, but it never went past shouting matches, didn't come to blows."

The three traded expressions that were made up of equal parts exhaustion and perplexity.

Catherine gave Conroy a wave, and she and Sara headed back to the Tahoe. They had plenty of work to do, though some of it could wait till tonight and, she hoped, the evidence would provide the right answers.

Concentrate on what cannot lie, Grissom liked to say: *the evidence.*

Hearing footsteps, Catherine turned to find Conroy right behind her. "I'm thinking of stopping at Circus Circus on the way back . . . you girls interested in some more overtime?"

Catherine looked toward Sara, and they both sighed and shrugged—at this point, what was the difference?

Twenty minutes later they pulled into the parking garage next to Circus Circus; then they were walking through the maze of halls to the second-floor casino where the familiar casino sounds—spinning slots, dealers calling out cards, rolling roulette balls—belied the breakfast hour. This large area was filled with slots, about half of which were in action; the cashier's cage stood immediately to the right, an Hispanic security guard making small talk with a cute redhead on the other side of the bars.

Conroy approached him and displayed her I.D. and a professional smile. "Who could I talk to about one of your employees?"

The stocky, wispily mustached guard had a radio mike clipped to the epaulet of his left shoulder. He used the mike to check with a Mr. Waller, who would receive the Las Vegas Metropolitan Police contingent in his office, which proved to be on the first floor, past the front desk, and down a deserted corridor behind a door labelled SECURITY.

A tall, thin man in a well-tailored gray suit and black and gray tie extended his hand to Conroy even as the guard showed them in. With a smile just a little too wide and teeth just a little too white, the casino man introduced himself as Jim Waller, and I.D.'s were proffered, hands were shaken,

Catherine finding the man's grip limp and his palm slightly moist.

Waller moved behind the desk and sat in a massive maroon leather chair, a computer whirring behind him, the screensaver showing fish swimming around. He motioned toward the three leather-covered chairs in front of his large darkwood desk.

Waller was a typical casino security man: unfailingly polite and helpful to the police, but wary as hell. "What can I do to help you, officers? Something about an employee, I understand? Is it a criminal matter?"

"Yes, Mr. Waller, it's criminal," Conroy said, and the security man's smile vanished, all those big shiny teeth tucked away in his face. "But the crime doesn't involve your employee."

Conroy explained the situation and soon Waller was using a walkie-talkie to summon Marty Fleming.

"Should only be three or four minutes," Waller said.

It was five, a security guard showing up, escorting a slump-shouldered, medium-sized man in his late forties with sandy hair, a bad complexion and gold-rimmed bifocals. A walking cast peeked out from the man's left pant leg; Catherine found him a rather pitiful-looking character. Waller rose, came around the desk and approached the man.

"Marty," he said, speaking to the dealer (though in a facility this size, the odds were scant Waller actually knew the employee), "these police officers need to talk to you."

The dealer's face turned anxiously inquisitive as his attention turned from Waller to the women.

"Detective Conroy," Waller continued, "I'll be at the front desk, when you've finished using my office."

"Very kind of you," Conroy said.

Then the security guard and Waller and the latter's shit-eating grin left them alone.

"Wh-what is this about?" Fleming asked.

Sara got up and vacated the chair next to Conroy, gesturing to Fleming to take it, saying, "Why don't you have a seat, Mr. Fleming, that cast doesn't look very comfortable."

He sat down, Conroy made the introductions, and explained the purpose of their visit, including the tragic death of Jenna Patrick.

"Damn it, anyway," Fleming said, shaking his head. He had a perpetual "why me?" demeanor. "I told Ty it was no big deal. Now he goes around telling the police."

Catherine said, "Mr. Fleming, it is a big thing—Mr. Kapelos did the right thing informing us. If Ray Lipton did attempt to strangle you, it might represent a pattern—a pattern of violence that culminated with him killing that young woman."

Fleming shook his head. "That's so sad . . . she was just the nicest girl. So beautiful. Nice and beautiful."

Catherine pressed: "Is Ty Kapelos telling us the truth? Did Ray Lipton choke you at Dream Dolls three months ago?"

Slowly, Fleming nodded; he seemed embarrassed. "About that—maybe a little longer ago. He saw me coming out of one of the backrooms with his girlfriend—I had, uh . . . you know, a private dance with her. Listen, you're not gonna talk to my wife, are you?"

Conroy said, "No, Mr. Fleming."

"I mean, she'll kill me, and then you'll be investigating *that.*"

"Tell us about that night, Mr. Fleming—the night Ray Lipton attacked you."

He sighed, thought back, pushing his glasses up on his nose—they didn't stay there long. "Jenna, she gave me a hug, you know, as we were comin' out of the booth—that's not something they usually do, I mean, when the dance is over, it's over. But she was a nice girl, and I used to have a dance from her, I don't know, a couple times a week."

Catherine nodded just to keep him going.

"Anyway, she hugged me and I gave her a peck on the cheek and the next thing I know, this guy is all over me, like ugly on a bulldog. Knocks me down, pins me to the floor in that, you know, that narrow hallway? On the floor there, digging his fingers into my throat. His face was all red . . . mine probably was, too. The girl was screaming and all, and I started to black out. I tell you, I thought I was dead."

Conroy asked, "Then what?"

He swallowed, pushed his glasses up again. "This brunette, another of the dancers, grabbed him by the hair and pulled him off. Saved me, sort of. She wasn't a very nice person . . . kinda cold, the other one, dark-haired. I had a private dance from her, once, too . . . brrrrr! But she did save me, I guess, from that Lipton guy. Anyway, she doesn't work there anymore."

"Tera Jameson, you mean?" Sara asked.

Fleming shrugged. "I didn't pay any attention to her name—I didn't like her. Anyway, the girls danced under different names, different nights. . . . So, then he and her started screaming at each other. He looked like he wanted to punch her, but he kept his distance. I just got up and a couple of the girls helped me back into the dressing room . . . only time I was ever back there."

He stopped and smiled as he thought back to that experience.

Conroy prompted him: "Mr. Fleming?"

"Yeah, anyway—I stayed back with the dancers, in their dressing room, till Ty and that Worm DJ guy hustled this Ray out of the club."

"Did you get the cast from that attack?"

Looking a little sheepish, Fleming said, "No. Got that about a month ago—accident at home. You know. Most accidents happen there."

Maybe his wife *would* kill him, Catherine thought.

Conroy asked, "That night at the club, that the last time you had contact with Ray Lipton?"

"Yeah."

"You're sure?"

"I'd remember."

"Guess you would." Conroy gave him a smile. "Thank you, Mr. Fleming."

He sighed, nodded. "You won't talk to my wife?"

"We won't talk to your wife."

Fleming rose and went out, and the trio lingered in Waller's office briefly, then did the same.

They stopped at the front desk and Conroy thanked Waller, and they made their way out of the gaudy casino, that pioneer in making Sin City family friendly.

Then they drove back to HQ, where they finally ended the night that had long since turned to day.

7

Lake Mead was born of Hoover Dam stemming the Colorado River's flow; downstream Davis Dam had given birth to Lake Mohave, and together the pair of man-made bodies of water—and the surrounding desert—comprised Lake Mead National Recreation Area, a million and a half acres set aside in '64 by the federal government for the enjoyment of the American tourist. Lake Mead's cool waters were ideal for swimming, boating, skiing, and fishing.

But some people had a peculiar idea of fun, which meant the CSIs were no strangers to the recreation area. They were at the end of another long shift, the day after the Toyota Avalon had been found at McCarran, when a phone call had come in, just as Nick Stokes and Warrick Brown were about to head home. Grissom had headed them off, announcing another discovery, this time a grisly one.

And now, once again, three nightshift CSIs, including their supervisor, were dragging their weary bones into the sunshine. Or at least Warrick and

Nick were weary: Grissom never seemed tired, exactly, nor for that matter did he ever seem particularly energetic—except when evidence was stirring his adrenaline flow.

Soon Warrick was steering one of the team's black Tahoes out Lake Mead Boulevard, Route 147, past Frenchman's Mountain and on toward the recreation area as he followed the twisty road west of Gypsum Wash and then down the Lake Shore Scenic Drive. The landscape was as untamed and restless as the Old West itself, rugged, chaotic, God working as an abstract artist, sculpting rocks in countless shapes in a raw rainbow of colors—snowy whites, cloudy grays, gentle mauves and fiery reds.

When Warrick swung into the parking lot for Lake Mead Tours, Brass's Taurus pulled up and parked next to them.

The autumn morning was cool enough for their windbreakers. None of them bothered with field kits yet—they would get the lay of the land, first—or maybe the lake, the endless expanse of which glistened nearby. Grissom and Nick climbed down and followed Warrick a few steps to where a man in a tan uniform stood next to a U.S. Fish and Wildlife pickup. Brass caught up quickly.

"Warrick Brown," the criminalist said, pointing to his necklace I.D. "Las Vegas CSI."

"Jim Tilson, U.S. Fish and Wildlife."

The two exchanged polite smiles and handshakes—the latex gloves weren't on, yet.

"This is Nick Stokes, CSI," Warrick went on as the rest of the group caught up with him, "and our supervisor, Gil Grissom, and Captain Jim Brass from Homicide."

Tilson nodded to them—more polite smiles, more handshakes.

Warrick was studying the guy, brow knitted. "I feel like I know you, Mr. Tilson."

A real smile creased Tilson's face now, revealing a row of uneven but very white teeth. "I played a little ball—Nevada Reno, then the CBA, couple years . . . till I blew my ankle out."

Snapping his fingers, Warrick said, "Yeah, yeah, I remember you! Jumpin' Jimmy Tilson. You spent some time with the Nuggets, too."

Tilson nodded. "That was a while ago."

"Mr. Tilson," Grissom said, "why did you call us?"

Tilson led them around his truck. "Over here . . . Not pretty."

Grissom smiled thinly. "They so seldom are."

They walked across the parking lot and down to the edge of the lake, where the water lapped at the sloping cement, and Tilson's USFW flat bottom boat was tied to the cruise boat's dock. If they looked hard, they could see the tour boat down at the far end of the basin; but that wasn't what they'd come to see. Warrick gazed into the flat bottom's bottom, where a canvas tarp covered something in the middle of the boat.

"I was on the lake this morning taking samples," Tilson said, a grimness in his tone.

"Samples?" asked Brass.

Tilson shrugged. "Testing chemical pollution in the lake, at various depths. It's an ongoing USFW concern. Anyway, I bring up my container, then start hauling up the anchor to move to another spot. Well, the damn anchor snags on something." Another shrug. "Happens once in a while. Lotta shit's ended up in this lake over the years."

"I can imagine," Brass said, just moving it along.

"So," the wildlife man said, "I start pullin' the anchor chain back in, and damn, it's heavy as hell." Tilson moved close to the boat, then glanced up toward the parking lot—to make sure they were undisturbed—and pulled back the tarp. "And this is what I found."

Even Grissom winced.

"That's one nasty catch of the day," Nick said, softly.

The lake had bleached the slab of flesh the gray-white of old newspaper. Someone had severed the body just above the navel and near the top of the femurs, leaving only the buttocks and vagina and the tops of the thighs. The unctuous odor of rot floated up and Warrick forced himself to breathe through his mouth.

"This is all you found?" Nick asked, frowning down at the thing.

"That's it."

Grissom was gazing out at the lake now. "Mr. Tilson, can you tell us where exactly you found this body?"

Now Tilson looked out across the water, gesturing. "Straight out—half a mile or more."

"You have GPS?"

Global positioning system.

Nodding, Tilson said, "I took a reading, but the damned thing flamed out on me. Bad batteries, I guess."

"We can send divers down," Nick suggested.

Grissom and Tilson both shook their heads at the same time, but it was Brass who said, "Too deep."

"Nearly six hundred feet in places," Tilson added.

"Besides which," Grissom said, "there's no telling how many different places parts were dumped into the lake."

"Whatever happened to dragging the lake?" Nick asked.

Tilson said, "You don't drag a lake that covers two hundred forty-seven square miles . . . and, man, that's just the water, never mind the seven-hundred miles of shoreline. And you take in the whole area, you've got twice the size of Rhode Island to deal with."

"And you have over ten million visitors a year, right, Mr. Tilson?" Grissom asked.

"That's right, sir."

"Lotta suspects," Warrick said.

And yet all of them knew, if this torso belonged to a certain missing woman, that one particular suspect would head their list. Warrick also knew that Grissom—whose mind had to be buzzing with the possibility of this being what was left of Lynn Pierce—would never countenance such a leap.

"I get the picture," Nick was saying. "So . . . what can we do?"

Warrick twitched half a humorless smirk, and

said, "We can do a DNA test on what we have, and hopefully identify the body."

Again, neither the criminalists nor the police detective said what they all were thinking.

"Mr. Tilson," Brass said, a mini-tape recorder at the ready, "can you tell us exactly what happened this morning? In detail?"

Though this version of the tale took longer, it added very little to the original, more succinct story Tilson had told earlier.

"Did you see anything unusual on the lake this morning?" Brass asked.

Tilson looked at Brass with wide eyes, and gestured down into the boat.

"Besides that," the detective said quickly. "Other boats, suspicious activity, anything at all noteworthy?"

The USFW man considered that carefully. Finally he said, "There were some boats . . . but, I mean, there's always boats. Didn't see anything odd, not like somebody dumpin' stuff into the water or anything. And we keep an eye out for that kinda thing."

For several minutes, Brass continued to question Tilson, without learning anything new. Tilson requested permission to confer with some of the recreation area personnel, who were nervously hovering at the periphery. Brass—after glancing at Grissom, for a nod—okayed that.

Finally, Brass said to Grissom, "We can't exactly go door to door with a picture of this, and ask if anybody recognizes her."

They were near the flat-bottom boat. Grissom

was staring at the torso, as if waiting for it to speak up. Then he said to Brass, "There's a body of evidence, here."

"Are you kidding?"

Grissom tore himself away from staring down at the torso to give Brass a withering look. Then he returned his eyes to the evidence and said, "Look at the edges."

The criminalist pointed first to the waistline, then the jagged cuts to the thighs. Warrick and Nick were looking on with interest.

Grissom was saying, "We'll figure out what made the cuts—that will help. She'll talk to us. . . . She already is."

Nick took pictures while Warrick carefully searched the boat for any other trace evidence. Once he had photos of the torso, where it lay in the boat, the two CSIs removed it from the snarled anchor chain and gently turned the body over.

Nick winced. "That left a mark . . ."

"Gris!" Warrick called. "You're gonna wanna see this!"

Striding over from where he'd been conferring with Brass, Grissom called, "What?"

Warrick raised an eyebrow and gestured in *ta-dah* fashion at the torso.

Glancing down, Grissom saw intestinal tissue sticking out of a slice in the back, like Kleenex popping out of a box.

Brass joined the group. "Something?"

"Whoever cut her up made a mistake," Grissom said. "He tried to cut through the pelvic bone.

Whatever he used got jammed up, and when he pulled it out, the blade snagged on the intestines."

Warrick didn't know which was grislier: the torso, or the glee with which Grissom had reported the butcher's "mistake." But Warrick also noted Grissom reflexively referred to the unknown killer as "he."

In the hour it took the CSI team to finish, the paramedics showed up, as did news vans from the four network affiliates. Uniformed officers held the reporters and cameramen at a distance, but there was no way Brass would get out of here without talking to them.

Gil Grissom did not envy Brass this part of his job. The CSI supervisor watched as the detective moved over to the gaggle of reporters. It was a calculated move on Brass's part: if the cameras were focused on him, they'd be unable to shoot the body being loaded into an ambulance.

Grissom watched as the four reporters and their cameramen vied for position, each sticking his or her microphones out toward Brass's unopened mouth. Grissom recognized Jill Ganine. She had interviewed him more than once, and he liked her well enough, for media. Next to her, Stan Cooper tried to look like he wasn't shoving Ganine out of the way. Kathleen Treiner bounced back and forth around the other two like a yappy terrier until her brutish cameraman managed to elbow in next to Cooper and give her some space.

Ganine got out the first question. "Captain Brass, is that the body of Lynn Pierce, the missing Vegas socialite?"

Leave it to the press to ask the question none of them had spoken. And just when had Born-Again suburban mom Lynn Pierce become a "socialite," anyway?

Grissom wished the TV jackals hadn't jumped so quickly to the conclusion that it was Lynn Pierce; more than that, he wished he could keep himself from making that jump. The torso could, after all, be any of hundreds of missing women. *Evidence,* he told himself, *just wait for the evidence and all will come clear.*

"We have no new information on Lynn Pierce," Brass said.

Cooper jumped in. "But you did find a body?"

Brass seemed unsure how to answer that. "Not entirely true," he finally said.

That was a nice evasion, Grissom thought; but as he listened to the reporters and the detective play twenty questions, Grissom kept his eyes on Ned Petty. Working carefully, the innocent-looking reporter was nearly around the tape line set up by the uniformed officers, as he and his cameraman moved toward the ambulance. The reporter was to Grissom's right, and slouching as he moved, no one—other than Grissom—seeming to notice Petty closing in.

Slipping behind the ambulance, to block the media's view of him, Grissom moved around until he was hidden by the ambulance's open back door, waiting.

With the body bag riding atop it—the rather odd shape of its contents plainly visible through the black plastic—the gurney was rolled by the EMS guys to the back door of the ambulance. Petty stepped forward, his microphone held up as he said, "Clark County paramedics load the body . . ."

"May I help you?" Grissom interrupted pleasantly, stepping out from behind the door and directly into the path of the cameraman's lens.

Petty didn't miss a beat.

The reporter swiveled, said, "On the scene is one of Las Vegas's top crime scene investigators, sometimes the subject of controversy himself—Gil Grissom. Mr. Grissom, what can you tell us about the victim?"

And Petty thrust the microphone toward Grissom, like a weapon.

Maintaining his cool, Grissom gave the camera as little as possible—a blank face, and a few words: "At this point, nothing."

Petty fed himself the mike, saying melodramatically, "That didn't *look* like a human body on that stretcher."

The mike swung back toward him, but Grissom said only, "That isn't a question."

"Do *you* believe you've found Lynn Pierce?"

Another shrug, this one punctuated by a terse, "No comment."

Finally the ambulance doors closed behind him, the paramedics all loaded up now, and the ambulance left—no siren; what was the rush? But the newspaper contingent made a race out of it anyway, peeling from the lot in pursuit of the emergency vehicle.

Having the scene to themselves again, Nick, Warrick, and Grissom gathered their gear, and left, finally letting Lake Mead start the process of getting back to normal—tourists would soon enjoy the sunshine shimmering off the lake, unaware of the gruesome events of the morning.

That night, a few hours before the official start of his shift, Grissom—blue scrubs over his street clothes—slipped into the morgue where Dr. Robbins still had the torso laid out on a table.

A whole body, a female body, Lynn Pierce's body. She is already dead. In a sparse bathroom, the body sprawls in a tub, unfeminine, undignified. A chainsaw coughs and sputters and spits to life, then growls like a rabid beast.

First it gnaws through the arms at the shoulders, then the legs below the hip sockets. The gnawing blade eats through the neck, severing spinal cord, nerves, and muscle. The body is limbless, headless.

The animal feeds on, but its keeper aims too low and the saw grinds to a halt in the middle of the pelvic bone and that blade is pulled out savagely, bringing with it a rope of intestine. With a snarl the blade shivers back to life, and this time the keeper aims higher, severing the body, just above the navel.

Pieces are packed into garbage bags with something to weigh them down, and hefted into the trunk of a car, driven to Lake Mead, loaded onto a boat beneath cover of night, dumped into the dark waters, here, there, scattered to the sandy bottom to never be found—save for one piece somehow freed, escaping the depths, floating, armless, legless, finding its way into the boat of the Fish and Wildlife man.

As Grissom approached, Robbins looked up. The

pathologist had been at Grissom's side for so many autopsies they had both long ago lost count. Robbins, too, wore a blue smock.

"You know," the coroner said, gently presenting the obvious, "the DNA test is going to take time . . . no getting around that."

Grissom shrugged. "I came to find out what you know *now.*"

Using his single metal crutch, Robbins navigated around the table. "I could share my preliminary findings."

Just the hint of a smile appeared at the corner of Grissom's mouth. "Why don't you?"

"There's this." Robbins pointed toward the victim's episiotomy scar. "She's had at least one child."

Grissom nodded curtly, and moved on: "Dismembered before or after her death?"

"After death." Robbins gestured. "No bruising around where the cuts were made. If she'd been alive . . ."

"There'd be bruises at the edges of the cuts. If the dismemberment didn't kill her, what did?"

Robbins shook his head, lifted his eyebrows. "No other wounds. Tox screen won't be back for a couple of days, at least. . . . Truthfully, Gil, I haven't got the slightest idea how she died."

"She is dead."

"Yes. We agree on that. But if the tox screen doesn't reveal something—and I doubt if it will—we may never know cause of death."

"Any other good news?"

"One very good finding—birthmark on her left

hip." Pulling the light down closer to the torso, Robbins highlighted the spot, which Grissom himself had glimpsed, earlier, at the lake.

Grissom rubbed his forehead. "Be nice to have a little more."

"Well, really we're just getting started," Robbins said, touching the corner of the table as if that might connect him to the victim in front of him.

"What's next?"

"We'll deflesh the torso."

"Good. Maybe the bones will talk to us."

"Yes. Let's hope they have something interesting to say."

"They often do," Grissom said. "Thanks, Doc. I'll be back."

"I'm sure you will."

Grissom made his way back to the break room where Warrick and Nick each sat with a cup of coffee cradled in hand. The coffee smelled scorched and the refrigerator in the corner had picked up a nasty hum. Although he liked working graveyard—because it helped him avoid dealing with much of the political nonsense, and obtrusive building maintenance, which happened nine to five, as well—Gil Grissom wondered why his dayshift counterpart, Conrad Ecklie, never seemed to get around to getting that fridge fixed . . . much less teach his people not to leave the coffee in the pot so long that it became home to new life-forms. That was one scientific experiment Grissom was against.

Filling Nick and Warrick in on what Robbins had

told him, Grissom concluded, "I want to know who she is."

Warrick shook his head. "Well, that could take a while."

Grissom's voice turned chill. "I want to know now. Not in a month or even a week, when the DNA results roll in—*now.* Find a way, guys," Grissom said, heading for the door, "find a way."

Still shaking his head, Warrick called out, "Gris! Two hundred people a month disappear in this town, you know that . . . a lot of them women. How are we going to track down one of them without DNA?"

From the doorway, Grissom said, "Eliminate the missing women who haven't had children."

Warrick, thinking it through, said, "And any that aren't white."

Nick was nodding. "And then we'll track one down who had a birthmark like that on her left hip."

"See," Grissom said, with that angelic smile that drove his people crazy. "We have a lot."

Moments later, Grissom was back in his office, seated behind his desk, jarred specimens staring accusingly at him from their shelves. A voice analysis report of the audiotape provided by the Blairs was waiting on his desk, and he read it eagerly.

He never would have admitted it to the reporters, and certainly not to his team, but Grissom was battling a small yet insistent voice in the back of his mind that kept telling him that they had just found Lynn Pierce.

And since one of his chief tenets was that the evidence didn't come to you, you went to it, Grissom picked up the phone and got Brass on the line.

"Jim, did you get a detailed description of Lynn Pierce beyond the photo her husband gave us?"

"I didn't, but the officer that spoke to Owen Pierce on the phone . . . he did. Why, what do you want to know?"

"Distinguishing marks?"

He could hear Brass riffling through some papers.

"A small scar on her left hand," Brass read, "an episiotomy scar, a bluish birthmark on her right shoulder . . ."

The torso didn't have a left hand or a right shoulder.

". . . and another birthmark, uh, on her left hip."

Grissom let out a long, slow breath.

"Jim, that was her in Lake Mead."

"Damn," Brass said, the disappointment evident in his tone. "I was hoping . . ."

"Me too."

"But if she's been killed, at least we have something to go on. We need to get over to Pierce's before the media . . ." The phone line went silent.

"Jim, what is it?"

"I just turned on a TV, to check . . . we're too late. It's already on channel eight."

"I'll call you right back." Grissom hung up and strode briskly toward the break room, pulling his cell phone and jabbing in Brass's number, on the move. In the break room (Warrick and Nick long gone), he turned on the portable television on the counter and punched channel eight. He heard the phone chirp once, and Brass answered.

"I've got it on," Grissom said.

They watched as Jill Ganine stood next to Owen Pierce, the physical therapist, in dark sweats, towering over the petite reporter, on the front stoop of his home.

"Mr. Pierce," Ganine said, her voice professional, her smile spotwelded in place, "as you know, the severed remains of a woman were pulled from Lake Mead this morning. Do you believe this to be your wife?"

Pierce shook his head. "As I've told the police, Lynn left us . . . both my daughter and myself. Lynn and I'd had some problems, and she wanted time by herself. . . . We *will* hear from her."

"But, Mr. Pierce—"

"I *have* to believe that the poor woman found today is someone else . . ." He touched his eyes, drying tears—or pretending to. "I don't wish anyone a tragedy, but . . . I . . . I'm sorry. Could I . . . say something to my wife?"

The camera zoomed past a painfully earnest Ganine in on Pierce. The big man steadied himself, rubbed a hand over his face, then looked into the lens.

"I'd just like to say to Lynn, if you're listening or watching—please, just call home, call Lori . . . that's the important thing. We so need to hear your voice."

Giving a little nod of understanding, Ganine turned to the camera, as Pierce disappeared behind his front door. "That's the story from the Pierce house, where the little family still holds out hope that Mrs. Pierce is alive and well . . . and will soon get in touch with them. . . . Jill Ganine for KLAS News."

Grissom clicked off the television.

"You believe that shit?" Brass asked in Grissom's ear.

"What I believe doesn't matter. Melodramatic TV news is irrelevant. What matters is the evidence."

"Like the birthmark?"

Grissom said, "And the audiotape."

"Shit! Damn near forgot about that tape."

Grissom said, "I just got the voice analysis back—and it's definitely Pierce talking. He threatens to cut his wife up in little pieces and now we have a piece of a woman . . ."

"Not a 'little' piece, though."

"No . . . but one with a birthmark identical to a marking his wife's known to have. Can I assume, Captain Brass, you'll be on your way to call on Owen Pierce, soon?"

"Meet me at my car."

8

At the same time Gil Grissom was meeting up with Jim Brass in the parking lot, Catherine Willows sat before a monitor at a work station in her office. The TV remote in hand seemed grafted there, as grainy images slipped by on the screen, rewinding, then playing again, rewinding. . . .

Despite her glazed expression—Catherine had been at this three hours—she was alert, and the unmistakable aroma of popcorn penetrated Catherine's concentration. Keenly tuned investigator that she was, she turned toward the doorway. There stood Sara Sidle, typically casual in jeans, blue vest and cotton blouse, holding out an open bag of break-room microwave popcorn like an offering to a cranky god.

"If that smelled any better," Catherine said to her colleague, "I'd fall to the floor, and die happy."

Sara placed the steaming bag on the counter, away from the stack of tapes they'd been plowing through, and wheeled her own chair up beside Catherine's. "Careful—don't get burned."

"In this job? When *don't* you get burned . . . ?" Taking a few kernels, Catherine blew on them, then popped the popcorn into her mouth. "You know, normally I have a rule against eating while I work—I don't have your youthful metabolism."

"Yeah, right. . . . Anyway, when was the last time you had a meal? Christmas?"

"Well . . . maybe New Year's. . . ."

Sara smirked triumphantly. "My point exactly. We've got to eat something sometime, don't we?"

"We'll *take* a break when we *come* to a break. . . . I just feel . . . I don't know, guilty somehow, taking off before anything's been accomplished."

"Feeling guilty is one thing," Sara said, shoving the bag at her again. "Feeling faint is another."

Catherine glanced at Sara—when an obsessively dedicated coworker tells you to slow down, maybe you ought to listen. And yet Catherine kept at it, the grainy video images crawling across the screen. Right now she was viewing the angle behind the bar. In the frame, the guy in the hat, dark glasses, and Lipton Construction jacket, strolled through then disappeared. Rewind. Again.

"That might be Lipton," Sara said, leaning in, eyes narrowed. "Then again, with this picture, it might be Siegfried or Roy."

"Or their damn tiger." Catherine sighed, shook her head. "We've *got* to get a better look. Where's Warrick, anyway?"

Audio-visual analysis was Warrick Brown's forensic specialty.

Sara shrugged. "Off with Grissom and Nick.

They're neck-deep in the Pierce woman's murder."

Catherine looked sharply at Sara. "That torso's been identified positively?"

"Close enough for Grissom to call it science and not a hunch. And I think our likelihood of borrowing Warrick for this, in the foreseeable future, is—"

"Hey! You remember that one guy?"

Sara's eyebrows went up. "I'm good, but I need a little more than that to go on."

Then Catherine traded the remote for her cell phone and punched in Grissom's number.

"Grissom," the supervisor's voice said, above the muted rumbling of motor engine and traffic sounds that told her he was on the road; he was, in fact, on his way with Brass to Owen Pierce's residence.

"Gil, I've got a problem."

"Jenna Patrick?"

"Yeah," Catherine said. "The videotapes are so grainy, not even Lipton's mother could ID our suspect. I'm assuming you can't spare Warrick—"

"Normally when you assume you make an ass of u and me. This is one of the rare other occasions."

Catherine rolled her eyes at Sara; a simple "That's right" would have been sufficient. Into the phone, she asked, "Gil, who *was* that guy?"

Again Sara raised her eyebrows. Grissom, however, had no problem deciphering who Catherine meant, answering without hesitation: "Daniel Helpingstine."

"Helpingstine," Catherine echoed, nodding. "That's right, that's right."

"Anything else?"

"Can I borrow Warrick?"

"No."

"Then I have to spend a little money."

"That's what we have—a little money. But do it."

At that, they both clicked off, no good-byes necessary. She rose and moved behind her desk. Sitting down, she quickly found the leather business-card folder in a drawer and riffled the plastic pages.

"Helpingstine?" Sara asked, still perplexed; she hated not knowing what was up.

"Yes." Catherine was flipping pages. "I guess you must've been out in the field, when he stopped by—manufacturer's rep from LA, who was here, oh . . . maybe six months ago. . . . Here you are! . . . He was pushing this new video enhancement device called Tektive—not computer software, a stand-alone unit."

"What's it do?"

Catherine started punching buttons on the cell phone again. "Just about everything short of showing the killer on the Zapruder film, if Helpingstine's to be believed. He might be able to out-do even Warrick, where this security tape's concerned."

On the other end of the line, the phone rang once, twice, three times, then a recorded message in Helpingstine's reedy tenor came on, identifying the West Coast office of Tektive Interactive.

Catherine waited for the tone, and said, "I don't know if you'll remember me, Mr. Helpingstine, this is Catherine Willows, Las Vegas Criminalistics. If you could call me, ASAP, at—"

She heard the phone pick up, and the same reedy tenor, in person, said, "Ms. Willows! Of course I remember you, pleasure to hear from you."

"Well, you're really burning the midnight oils, Mr. Helpingstine."

"My office is in my home, Ms. Willows, and I just happened to hear your message coming in—you're nightshift, if I recall."

This guy was good. But she could practically hear him salivate at the prospect of a sale.

"That's right," Catherine said, "nightshift. Never dreamed I'd get a hold of you tonight—"

"It's been what, Ms. Willows—six months? How may I help you? Are those budget concerns behind you, I hope?"

Maybe she could pull this off without spending even "a little money." "Mr. Helpingstine, are you still willing to give us an on-the-job demonstration of the Tektive?"

He was breathing hard, now. "Happy to! As I told you when we met, as good as our prepared demonstration is, it's far better for us to help *you* with something, and, uh . . ." She could hear pages turning quickly. ". . . how is Thursday?"

"I know it's terribly short notice, but . . . could you possibly fly in here tomorrow?"

Silence indicated he was considering that. "This isn't just . . . *any* demo, is it?"

"No," Catherine confessed. "It's a murder."

"Let me check on flights and I'll get back to you."

"You have my number?"

"Oh yes. In my little book."

She could almost hear his smile.

Catherine hung up, and with a wry smirk said to Sara, "He thinks he's got my number."

"That's only fair, isn't it?" Sara batted her eyes. "I mean, you've got his."

They returned to the tapes and the popcorn, and less than a half hour later the desk phone rang.

She answered, and Helpingstine asked, "Can you have someone pick me up at McCarran?"

Catherine smiled; now this was service. "Tell me what gate and what time, Mr. Helpingstine. Someone will be there, possibly my associate Sara Sidle or myself."

She could hear his pen scribbling Sara's name, then he gave the information, finishing with, "And would you please call me Dan?"

"Happy to, Dan. And it's Catherine. See you soon."

Catherine hung up and Sara asked, "How soon?"

"Six-thirty."

"Tomorrow evening?"

Catherine grinned. "No—this morning."

Sara grinned, too. "He have a thing for you, or what?"

"I think he has a thing for money—this little item sells in mid five figures." She sighed. "That means we can stop looking at these grainy videotapes until he gets here and concentrate on other things."

"For instance?"

"We could grab some food, if you like."

Sara half-smirked, lifted a shoulder. "Actually, I'm kinda stuffed."

"Demon popcorn. There's always searching Lipton's house."

Sara's eyes brightened. "About time!"

Reaching for her desk phone, Catherine said, "I'll call Conroy."

An hour later they met Detective Erin Conroy—crisply professional in a gray pants suit—in the driveway of Ray Lipton's house on Tinsley Court, not far off Hills Center Drive. A baby-blue split level built in the 'eighties, the house perched on a sloping lawn, looking well-taken care of in a neighborhood of other well-maintained homes, always a quiet area, particularly so at this hour of the night. The driveway ran alongside the house, a two-car garage around back.

The detective stood next to her Taurus, warrant in her hand, at her side, almost casually. "I've got it—let's go in."

"How are we getting inside?" Sara asked.

"Look what our buddy Ray gave me . . ." Conroy flashed a key. "The warrant's just to dot the i's. Lipton's still cooperative—insists he's innocent."

Innocent men always do, Catherine thought; *but then so do most guilty ones. . . .*

The three of them pulled on latex gloves, then the detective unlocked the door and they stepped inside.

"You want upstairs or downstairs?" Catherine asked her coworker.

"Cool stuff's always in the basement," Sara said, with a smile of gleeful anticipation. "I'll take that."

"Let's clear it first," Conroy said.

So the three of them walked through the basement, then Conroy and Catherine went up.

Stairs from the entryway opened onto the living room. Catherine noted the good-quality brown-and-tan carpet, and heavy brown brocade drapes hanging from ornamental rods, shut tight, the sunlight managing only a hairline or two of surreptitious entry. With everything shrouded in darkness like this, the house gave the impression it'd been closed up much longer than twenty-four hours. Only yesterday's *Las Vegas Sun,* on the coffee table and open to the crossword puzzle, indicated ongoing life. Beyond the coffee table, the cream-color plaster wall was occupied by an oversized brown couch accented by a couple of tan throw pillows; a starving-artist's-sale desert landscape hung straight above the couch. However neat the living room might be, one aspect seemed to indicate a male presence: the room had been turned into a formidable home entertainment center.

A thirty-six-inch Toshiba color TV ruled the room from a wheeled stand in a corner of the room, while a tan highback armchair sat to Catherine's left, where she stood at the top of the entry stairs, the chair's twin across the room next to the sofa. Both were placed at angles to the couch so they faced the TV. Speakers were mounted to the walls around the room and she noticed a black subwoofer on the floor next to the TV stand. A DVD player and VCR were stacked on the lower shelf of the stand and through a smoked-glass door below that, she could make out a row of DVDs.

"Why go out to the movies?" Conroy asked.

"It does beg the issue," Catherine said.

"So maybe he *was* home watching football."

"We'll see. . . ."

Using her Maglite, Catherine took a quick look at the DVDs, then at the other shelves of the TV stand, one of which had a few prerecorded tapes and a lot of T-120 cassettes, some with notations: "Friends season closer"; "Sat Nite Live w/ John Goodman"; and so on.

She checked the VCR: no tape. Question was, had Lipton recorded the Colts/Chiefs game, watched it after committing Jenna's murder, then hidden (or thrown away) the incriminating tape, just so he could have his TV ball game alibi?

Stranger things had happened, of course, but Catherine had a hard time buying that Lipton had strangled his girlfriend, come home, maybe had a beer while he watched the taped game, while at the same time getting his story ready for when the police came around. That seemed a reach to her.

Nonetheless, she gathered all the videotapes, including the prerecords, stacking them in front of the TV; she told Conroy to collect any video cassettes she might run across, and called the same instructions down to Sara. They would box them all up as evidence.

Catherine and Conroy checked the cushions of the furniture and behind the framed landscape over the sofa, finding nothing, not even loose change. They moved through the dining room, Conroy pausing briefly to riffle through the pile of mail on the table. She found nothing worth bagging.

The kitchen, a small galley-type affair, had a U-shaped counter at the far end, home to a double-basin sink with a couple of dirty plates and a glass in one side. The stove and refrigerator were a matching off-white, and Catherine found healthier food in the fridge than she would expect from a single guy. In the freezer and cupboards, she found nothing noteworthy.

The refrigerator had a piece of note paper held to the door by a Wallace and Gromit magnet: a list of names and phone numbers. Conroy put the list into an evidence bag and replaced the magnet on the refrigerator.

"Not much so far," the detective said.

"Well, we know Jenna was living here," Catherine said. "Or do you know a man who could keep a house this tidy?"

"Not many," Conroy admitted.

They moved down the hallway to where two doors stood opposite each other. The one to the right was a spare bedroom, the one to the left the bathroom. Conroy took the bathroom, Catherine the bedroom. Sparsely furnished with only a tiny dark dresser and a single bed covered with a tan quilt, the room with its bare cream-color plaster walls looked like a nun's cell.

A closet hid behind wooden, sliding double doors. Catherine opened one side and saw shoe- and other boxes stacked from the floor to the shelf, with more boxes occupying that space.

She heard Conroy pad in from the bathroom.

"Nothing in there," the detective said. "I'm going to check out the master bedroom."

"All right. I'll be going through these boxes."

The fourth box down in the back row, a flowered Mootsie's Tootsies shoebox, presented Catherine with the prize. Opening the box—the only woman's shoebox in the stack—she found a false beard, mustache, and a small brown bottle of spirit gum.

She felt her hopes that Lipton might be telling the truth start to fade, as this discovery seemed to confirm what she'd seen in the videotape . . . that he had, indeed, worn a fake beard and mustache to throw people off the track, and yet still had the bad sense to wear a coat with his company's name on the back.

Lipton didn't seem that thick, but plenty of other criminals had done dumber things in the commission of their crimes. She recalled one Don Dawson, who had worked at Castaways Bowling Center. Dawson had been smart enough to know the boss had a camera in the office, so when he'd gone in to crack the safe he'd worn a mask-style stocking cap. The cap had gone nicely with the satin jacket with Castaways Bowling Center embroidered on the back, and his name, "Don," on the breast. Dawson had lasted through almost thirty seconds of interrogation before he'd copped to the robbery.

Such stories abounded in national CSI circles. Like the two star athletes who robbed a local Burger King where their pictures hung in honor on the wall; or the numerous bank robbers around the country who would write their robbery notes on their own deposit slips.

Over the years, Catherine had seen enough reasonably bright criminals do enough dim things to know that anything was possible. She carefully dropped the beard and mustache into an evidence bag, the spirit gum into another, and the shoebox itself into a third.

Sara appeared in the doorway. "Any luck?"

Holding up the bag with the fake beard, Catherine said, "Jackpot."

Sara came over with "wow" in her eyes and had a look at the treasures Catherine had dug up.

Catherine asked, "How about you?"

"Well, I found a box in the basement with two Lipton Construction jackets in it. They look new, or anyway they've never been worn."

"Anything else?"

Sara shrugged, a little frustrated. "There's some stuff down there that doesn't fit Ray. Most of it looks like Jenna's—diet books, *Men Are From Mars, Cosmo*'s, and some other fashion magazines, buncha *Vogue*'s."

Conroy came back in from the master bedroom. "Nothing in there. Clothes from both of them. Obviously, Jenna was living here. You want to take a quick look around?"

This was addressed to Catherine, but Sara said, "I'll go, while you finish in here, 'kay?"

Catherine nodded. " 'kay."

She spent another hour going through boxes, but found nothing. When Sara and Conroy came back from the bedroom with a bag containing Ray Lipton's work boots, Catherine looked at the evidence curiously.

Sara said, "You lifted boot prints, didn't you, from the lap dance room?"

"Right," Catherine said, smiling, "and Lipton was wearing *tennies* when Conroy hauled him in . . . Good catch, Sara!"

"Thanks."

"That the only pair of boots in the house?"

"Didn't see any others."

"Well, Warrick says it always comes down to shoe prints . . . we'll see."

Back at HQ, the two CSIs and the detective logged in evidence for several hours. Catherine instructed Sara to line up some interns to go over the box of video cassettes, to check for a tape of that Colts game.

Shift was almost over, and the sun freshly up, by the time Catherine was back in one of the Tahoes, taking the 515 to 15 South, so she could get to the airport without having to fight morning traffic on the Strip.

Helpingstine was coming in on Southwest 826, which meant Gate C of Terminal One. A long hike, but after a cooped-up night of sitting in front of a monitor, then crouching in a closet at Lipton's, and finally logging evidence at CSI, the walk would seem like an invigorating relief.

As she made her way through the concourse, Catherine struggled to put a face with the name of the man she was picking up. They had met only once, briefly, about six months ago. Her memory was finally jogged, when the tall, fortyish man—glasses riding a pug nose, straight dark hair parted on the left, graying at the temples, his light gray suit looking suitably slept in—recognized her instantly, and strode up to her with a wide smile and a hand outstretched.

"Ms. Willows," he said, in a nasal but not unpleasant twang that indicated Chicago somewhere in his background, "good to see you again."

"Mr. Helpingstine," she said, smiling and allowing him to pump her hand, "you're very kind to come at such short notice, and so quickly."

He raised a gently scolding finger. "It's Dan, remember?"

"And Catherine," she said, falling in alongside him as he walked.

"Afraid we'll have to go to baggage claim to pick up the Tektive. They're understandably fussy about carry-ons."

Helpingstine's luggage consisted of a nylon gear bag with a Lakers insignia on it, and a square silver flight case on wheels that Catherine assumed contained the Tektive.

She led the way back to the Tahoe, with the salesman's small talk running to how well the Tektive was going over with various major metro police departments. But when Catherine tried to turn the conversation to the Jenna Patrick case, the manufacturer's rep waved a meaty hand. "Let's wait till I've had a chance to look at the tape."

"Fair enough, Dan. We'll follow your lead."

"I do have one other request."

"Name it."

"They didn't feed us anything on the flight. Can we go through a drive-thru or something?"

Suddenly she remembered her popcorn snack with Sara, a hundred years ago; her stomach growled its opinion. "I think I can manage that request."

They got McDonald's breakfasts, went back to headquarters and ate in the break room.

Sara ducked her head in. "I smell something very nearly like real food . . . What'd you bring me?"

Catherine handed her a breakfast burrito—vegetarian, of course—and Sara pulled up a chair and soon was digging in like she hadn't seen food since the Reagan administration.

"Dan, the dainty flower to your left is Sara Sidle."

Sara nodded and kept chewing.

"Dan Helpingstine," he said. "Tektive Interactive."

"Heard all about you, Dan—can't wait for you to work your magic." Between burrito bites, Sara said to Catherine, "Lots of footprints in the lap-dance room, and in the hall."

"Yeah, dozens," Catherine said between bites of a bagel sandwich. "Lots and lots of high heels. I remember."

"But just the one pair of work boots."

"I remember that, too."

Sara shook her head, shrugged, started a second burrito. "I haven't compared them up close yet, nothing Grissom-scientific yet . . . but the eyeball test says the boots we brought in tonight, from

Lipton's, are larger than the prints we lifted at the strip club."

Catherine said, "We'll check that out more thoroughly, as soon as we're finished with the video."

Setting up in Catherine's office, they got Helpingstine settled at a work station and lined up with the Dream Doll security tapes.

"First we'll digitize them," he said, working in his shirtsleeves, "then we shall see what we shall see."

"How long's the digitizing take?" Catherine asked.

"How long are the tapes?"

Catherine explained what they had, what they wanted, and why, for now, they were going to concentrate on just small segments representing two cameras: the one from behind the bar and the one from the end of the hallway.

Leaving the Tektive rep to his work, they went back to the footprints. Working in the layout room, they took prints from Lipton's boots and compared them to the one they got from the strip club.

"This print," Sara said, meaning what they'd just created, "is definitely shorter than the lap-dance boot."

"Are we *sure* Lipton had the boots on that night?" Catherine asked. "Is it possible that it's somebody else's boot, and we missed Lipton's print? Maybe he's one of the running shoes we found."

Sara shook her head. "The tennie he was arrested in's been ruled out . . . and the boot print was the oddest we got at the strip club, as well as the freshest, I mean it was on top . . . so we assumed it had to be the killer's."

Catherine wasn't sure whether to feel good or bad about this indication of Lipton's innocence; Grissom would advise her not to "feel" anything.

So she calmly said, "We'll check the videotape first, then if we get nothing, we head back to Lipton's to bring in all his shoes."

"It's a plan."

They returned to Catherine's office to find Helpingstine hunkered over his black box with its keyboard and built-in monitor screen.

"You ready for us?" Catherine asked.

The tech nodded. "These tapes are for shit, of course. Not exactly broadcast quality."

Catherine leaned in and patted his shoulder. "Which is why you're here, Dan, right?"

He gave the two women a little sideways half-smile. "You came to the right man. . . . I've cleaned up the images some, already, and I can isolate your guy in a couple of them."

"Any shots of his shoes?"

He returned his attention to his machine. "Let's see."

Catherine and Sara sat down on either side of him, facing the Tektive monitor, Helpingstine stationed at the keyboard. He punched some keys and the screen came to life, the angle on the tape playing from high behind the bar.

"That looks just the same to me," Sara said. "No offense."

"None taken," Helpingstine said. "Just wait."

He tapped some more keys and the picture improved, sharpening, the video garbage clearing somewhat.

But it was still disappointing, and Catherine groaned, "Dan, I was hoping for better . . ."

"Hey hey hey," the tech said, sounding mildly offended. "A mini-miracle I can do on the spot. You want an act of God, it's gonna take some time."

"Okay, show us a mini-miracle."

With a few keystrokes, Helpingstine outlined Lipton in the frame. Then the screen went blackly blank, except for the figure of the killer center screen.

"Now that is interesting," Sara said.

The murderer had no legs below the level of where the bar would have been, but was intact from the waist up except for a spot on his shoulder where a customer's head had been between him and the lens. They could barely make out the Las Vegas Stars logo on the ball cap, and the large dark glasses gave him the appearance of an oversized insect.

"Can you give us better detail on his face?" Catherine asked.

More work on the keys and the picture became slightly less blurry. "Quick fix," Helpingstine said, "that's what you get."

Catherine leaned forward in her chair. "That *is* a fake beard, isn't it?"

"Yeah," Sara said. She jabbed at the monitor screen. "And a mustache too. . . . Could be what you found at Lipton's."

Catherine asked the rep, "Any other quick tricks for us?"

Using a mouse, Helpingstine moved the killer's image into a corner. Then, fingers flying over the keys, he brought up another still, this one showing the killer from behind as he towed Jenna Patrick down the hallway, toward the private dance room where she was killed. A few more clacks from the keyboard and everything in the bar disappeared except for Lipton and Jenna.

A few keystrokes later, the grainy image sharpened further, the Lipton Construction lettering on the back of the jacket springing into sharp relief. From this angle, just barely able to see one side of the killer's partially turned head, they could clearly discern the fake beard.

"Is that a shoe?" Catherine asked, pointing at a dark spot at the end of the killer's leg.

Helpingstine said, "It would appear to be the toe of some kind of boot."

Catherine and Sara traded looks.

The killer stood practically upright, bent only slightly as he extended his hands back to Jenna's. She seemed taller than he was, but then she was wearing those incredible spike heels.

"Did you monkey with the aspect ratio on this?" Sara asked. "Is the picture squeezed or stretched in any way?"

"Not at all," the rep said. "That's reality, as seen by a cheap VHS security camera."

"And cleaned up by an expensive electronic broom," Catherine pointed out.

Sara pressed: "What's wrong with this picture?"

They all studied the frozen image for a long time.

Finally, Helpingstine said, "His head seems too big. Is that what you mean?"

The question was posed to Sara, but it was Catherine who said, "That could be part of it . . . but there's something else."

"What?" Sara asked. "It's driving me crazy . . . it just looks . . . *wrong* to me."

Catherine pointed. "Look at the shoulders—doesn't Ray Lipton have broader shoulders than that?"

"You're saying that's not Ray Lipton," Sara said.

"Call it a hunch," Catherine said.

Sara gave her a wide-eyed look. "You know what Grissom would say. Leave the hunches to the detectives—we follow the evidence."

"Let's follow it, then," Catherine said. To Helpingstine, she said, "Can you stay at this a while?"

"Absolutely," he said.

"Sometime today, call a cab, check yourself in to a hotel . . . there are a few in town . . . and save your receipts."

"Hey, Catherine, I'm here to help—no charge."

"You're here to make a pitch for your product; but we're not going to take advantage. You may have to stay over a night. We'll cover it."

He shrugged. "Fine."

She explained that their shift started at eleven P.M., but gave him her phone and pager numbers, should he come up with something sooner.

"Are you clocking out now?" Helpingstine asked.

"No, Dan. I have a little more work to do, before I call it a night."

"Or day," Sara said, hands on hips. "What do you have in mind?"

"I'm going to check Ray Lipton's alibi."

Her eyes getting wider, Sara said, "But he doesn't *have* one."

Catherine shrugged, smiled. "Let's follow the evidence, and see if you're right."

9

Not as many lights were on in the Pierce castle, tonight—a few in the downstairs, one upstairs. Distant traffic sounds were louder than those of this quietly slumbering neighborhood, the only voices the muffled ones of Jay Leno and David Letterman.

Out on bond on his possession charge, Owen Pierce opened the door on Brass's first knock—as if he'd been expecting them—the physical therapist's handsome features darkly clouded, the blue eyes trading their sparkle for a dull vacancy. He slouched there in a black Polo sweatshirt, gray sweat pants and Reeboks, like a runner too tired even to pant. His eyes travelled past the homicide captain to Grissom.

"What you found . . ." Pierce began. "Is it . . . Lynn?"

But it was Brass who answered: "Could we come in, Mr. Pierce? Sit and talk?"

He nodded, numbly, gestured them in, and soon Brass and their host sat on the couch with its rifles-and-flags upholstery, while Grissom took the liberty of pulling a maple Colonial arm chair around, so that he and Brass could casually double-team the suspect.

"It's Lynn, isn't it?" Pierce said, slumped, arms draped against his thighs, interlaced fingers dangling.

"We think so, Mr. Pierce," Grissom said. "We won't have the DNA results for a while, but the evidence strongly suggests that what we found was . . . part of your wife's body."

Pierce stared at the carpet, shaking his head, slowly. *Was he trying not to cry?* Grissom wondered. *Or trying* to *cry . . .*

Grissom had a Polaroid in his hand; he held it out and up, for Pierce to see—a shot close enough to the torso to crop out everything but flesh. "Your wife had a birthmark on her left hip—is this it?"

Swallowing, he looked at the photo, then dropped his head, his nod barely discernible but there. "Is it . . . true?"

Brass asked, "Is what true, Mr. Pierce?"

He looked up, eyes red. "What . . . what they're saying on television . . ." Pierce's voice caught, and he gave a little hiccup of a sob; a tear sat on the rim of his left eye and threatened to fall. ". . . that Lynn was . . . cut up?"

Brass sat, angled toward the suspect. "Yes, it's true. . . . I'd like you to listen to something, Mr. Pierce." Pulling a small cassette player from his suitcoat pocket, already cued up, Brass pushed PLAY.

Pierce's angry voice came out of the tiny speaker: *"You do and I'll kill your holier-than-thou ass . . ."*

Another voice, Lynn Pierce's terrified voice, said, *"Owen! No! Don't say—"*

"And then I'll cut you up in little pieces."

Brass twitched half a humorless smile. "Gets a little ugly after that. . . . Wouldn't want to disturb you in your time of sorrow."

Pierce had a poleaxed expression. "Where did you get that?"

Brass ignored the question. "Maybe now would be a good time to advise you of your rights, Mr. Pierce."

The therapist's dull eyes suddenly flared bright, as he rose to loom over the detective and the criminalist, and the sorrow—possibly fabricated—turned to unmistakably real rage. "You're *arresting* me? What for? Having an argument with my wife?"

"You threatened to cut her into pieces," Brass said, "and shortly thereafter . . . she was in pieces. We don't view that as a coincidence."

"That tape probably isn't even admissible. Who gave it to you? What, the Blairs? Those religious fanatics? Probably doctored that tape . . . edited it. . . ."

"We've had the tape closely examined," Grissom said. "It's your voice, and the tape is undoctored."

A half-sigh, half-grunt emanated from the therapist's chest, and he sat back down, hard, shaking the couch, jostling Brass a little.

Pierce fixed his red-rimmed blue eyes onto Grissom. "Are you a married man?"

"No."

Then Pierce turned to Brass. "How about you detective? Married?"

Brass said, "My marital status isn't—"

"Ha!" Pierce pointed at homicide captain. "Divorced! . . . And I suppose you never threatened your wife? You never said, I could just *kill* you for that? One of these days, Alice, pow!, zoom!, straight to the moon?"

"Ralph Kramden," Grissom pointed out, "never threatened to dismember his wife."

Brass glanced at the criminalist, surprised by the cultural reference.

Backing down now, Pierce ran a hand over his forehead, removing sweat that wasn't there. "I see your point, guys, I really do . . . I have a nasty temper, but it's strictly . . . verbal. I'm telling you, those words were just me losing it."

"Your temper," Brass said.

"Yes. No question."

"Lost your temper, killed your wife, dismembered her. You're a physical therapist—you have some knowledge about anatomy."

"I *didn't* kill her. It was just an argument—we had them all the time, since her . . . conversion, that Born-Again crapola. But do you honestly think I would kill my wife over *religious* differences?"

Brass was about to respond when the front door opened and a teenage girl stepped into the foyer.

Grissom didn't recognize the girl—she had short, lank black hair, a pierced eyebrow, enough black mascara to offend Elvira, black form-fitting jeans, and a black Slipknot T-shirt. He wondered if this was a friend of Pierce's daughter, Lori, come to visit.

"Daddy, what is it?" the girl asked in a mousy voice that didn't go with her punky Goth look.

Pierce's eyes went from Brass to Grissom to the girl. "Lori," he said slowly. "These officers have some information about Mom."

Grissom looked harder—this was indeed Lori, formerly blonde and rather wholesome-looking, perhaps getting an early start on Halloween.

The girl froze, her eyes wide, the whites of them making a stark contrast with the heavy black mascara. "Is she . . . al . . . all . . . right? What they found . . . on TV . . . was it . . .?"

Pierce was on his feet, nodding gravely, motioning to her. "Come here, baby . . . come 'ere."

A short, sharp breath escaped her, then Lori ran to her father's arms and he held her tight, saying, "She's gone, honey . . . Mom's gone." They stayed that way for a long time. Finally, Pierce held his daughter at arm's length.

"What *happened?*" Lori asked, her pseudo-adult makeup at odds with eyes filled with a child's pain.

Pierce shook his head. "No, honey. It's not the time for that. . . . I have to deal with these . . . the authorities."

"Dad . . ."

"Lori, we'll talk about this later."

She pulled away from his grasp. "I want to know, *now.*"

Grissom had a shiver of recognition: he'd said almost exactly the same thing about Lynn Pierce to Warrick and Nick.

Brass was on his feet. He moved near the father, and said, almost whispering, "Why don't you let me talk to her, Mr. Pierce. I have a daughter, not much older than her. . . ."

Turning to face him, Pierce said, rather bitterly, "Your compassion is noted, detective. But I don't think that's such a good idea."

"I do need to ask your daughter some questions," Brass said. "I'm sure you want to cooperate . . . both of you?"

The girl's eyes were tight, her expression paralyzed, as if she couldn't decide whether to scream, cry, or run.

"Lori's had a great shock," Pierce said, reasonably. "Can't this wait until later?"

"Frankly, Mr. Pierce . . . no. This is a murder investigation. Delays are costly."

Exasperated, Pierce turned to Grissom. "Can't you stop this? You seem like a decent man."

With a tiny enigmatic smile, Grissom rose and said, "You seem like a decent man, too, sir. . . . Maybe you and I should leave Lori and Captain Brass alone, so they can talk . . . and you can show me the garage."

Pierce was looking at Grissom as if the criminalist were wearing clown shoes. "What?"

"Your garage," Grissom said, pleasantly, pointing. "It's this way, isn't it?" He started toward the kitchen.

Reluctantly, with a world-weary sigh and one last glance at his daughter, Pierce followed the CSI.

"Sit down, Lori, please," Brass said, gesturing toward the sofa. "You don't mind if I call you Lori?"

"Do what you want," Lori sniffled. Tears were trailing down her face, mascara painting black abstract patterns on her cheeks. She looked at him skeptically, then demanded, "Are you going to tell me what happened to my mother?"

"Lori . . . please. Sit."

She sat.

So did he.

"I'm Detective Brass. You can call me Jim, if you like."

Her response was tough, undermined by a teary warble in her Sniffles the Mouse voice: "I feel so close to you . . . *Jim.*"

Brass took in a deep breath, let it out slowly through his mouth. No sugarcoating this; the girl had seen the television news, after all. He said, "Your mother was murdered."

He watched her as she took that in. Her face auditioned various emotions, one at a time, but fleeting—surprise, fear, anger—as she struggled to process and accept what he'd just told her. Her internal struggle, barely letting any emotion out beyond the unstoppable tears, reminded Brass a great deal of his own daughter. He wondered if Ellie had cried when his wife told her that he had left them; he wondered where Ellie was now, and if she still hated him.

"Are you all right?" he asked the girl.

"No, I'm not all right! . . . Yeah, right, I'm fine, I'm cool! You got a *touch,* don't ya?"

Brass felt a fool—just as his own daughter had so often made him feel. Of course Lori wasn't "all right," and for that matter, probably never would be. Mothers were not supposed to get murdered.

Then the girl's toughness dropped away. "I . . . I can't believe it," she finally managed.

"It's hard to lose family," he said. "Especially a parent. Even if you had trouble with them. Sometimes that only makes it harder."

The streaky face looked at him differently now. "You . . . ?"

He glanced around, making sure they were alone. "Yeah, both of mine are gone. Not as rough as you, Lori."

"No?"

"Natural causes, and I was an adult."

"But . . . it was still hard?"

"It's always hard. Lori, I don't like this, but we all owe it to your mother to find out what happened to her, and clear this up as much as possible."

"What, like that'll bring her back?"

"Of course it won't bring her back. But it could mean . . . closure, for you. And your dad."

"Closure, huh? Everybody talks about closure. You know what I think, Detective? Closure's way fucking overrated."

". . . You may have a point, Lori. . . . Now, I've got to ask you some questions—you up to it?"

She took a deep breath and nodded, what the hell.

Brass hated this part of the job, and wondered where he should start. If he hit a raw nerve, the girl—who had warmed to him some—might come unglued; and then he'd have a hell of time getting her to answer any questions. If she truly broke down, he'd have to call in the Social Services people, to provide the girl counseling . . . and his investigation would take a backseat.

Best to tread carefully, he thought. "Did you get along with your mother?"

Shrug.

"You're what, Lori? Sixteen?"

Nod.

"So, how did you get along with your mother?"

"You already asked me that."

He'd gotten *some* words out of her, anyway. "Yes, Lori, but you didn't really answer me."

Another shrug. "Not good, really. She didn't want me to do, you know, anything."

"What do you mean . . . 'anything'?"

"You know—go out with guys, go to concerts, get a job. She wanted me to be the girl in the plastic bubble. She barely tolerated my boyfriend, Gary."

"Tell me about your boyfriend."

This time the nod carried some enthusiasm. "Gary Blair. He's cool."

"Cool? Aren't the Blairs a pretty straight-laced family?"

A tiny smile appeared. "Basically. I don't know about lace, but he's pretty straight. His parents are in a church group with Mom . . . otherwise, I don't think she'd even let me go out with him."

"How strict was your mom?"

She snorted. "She's way past strict into . . ." Her expression turned inward. ". . . I mean, she *was* way past strict. . . ."

Brass could have kicked himself for the past-tense slip. She'd just been opening up, when he made the faux pas, and now he had to find a way to save the interview, before the kid caved.

"What do you and Gary like to do together?" Brass asked. "Movies? Dancing?"

Lori, lost in thought, didn't seem to hear him. She was still on his previous question, mumbling, "Yeah, Mom made the 700 Club look like, you know, un-psycho."

"You and Gary?"

She seemed to kind of shake herself out of it. "We, uh . . . you know, go to the movies, we hang out at the mall. Sometimes we just stay here."

"Ever go to the Blairs?"

"Not much. His mom is really weird, kinda . . . you know, wired? Like a chihuahua on speed?"

Brass smiled at that, though the drug reference was disturbing. "So when you and Gary hang out here, what do you do?"

Yet another shrug. "Listen to CDs in my room, watch DVDs, stuff like that. Sometimes surf the 'net. Go in chat rooms and pretend to be people, you know, like pretend I'm a nympho or a dyke or somethin'—typical shit."

Brass was starting to wonder if the shrugging was a nervous tic, or simply generational—his sullen daughter had shrugged at him a lot the last time he'd seen her. Somewhere along the line, shrugging had become a substitute for speech. "Gary ever around, when your parents argued?"

She gave him an odd, sideways look. Her response turned one syllable into at least three: "No."

"But you did? See them argue?"

"I . . . I don't know if I should be talking about stuff like that. . . . That's personal. Family shit."

"It's all right, Lori. I'm a . . . public servant. I'm just trying to help you . . . help your family get through this."

She drew back. "*That's* bullshit."

He froze, then laughed. "Yeah . . . I guess it is, sort of. Lori, this is a crime. I have to find out what happened to your mom. If you don't talk to me, you'll have to talk to somebody, sometime. Why not get it out of the way?"

Lori considered that for a moment before answering. "Yeah, well. They fought sometimes. All parents do. All married people do, right?"

"Right."

"I don't think they fought any more than anybody else. I mean, I never saw Gary's parents fight, but they're such . . . pod people. My other friends' parents fight, at least the ones that are still together do."

Out in the large, tidy garage, Pierce stood on the periphery, arms folded, while a latex-gloved Grissom poked around.

One of the two parking places stood empty, the therapist's blue Lincoln Navigator occupying the other. A workbench made out of two-by-fours and plywood ran most of the length of the far wall, tools arrayed on the pegboard above it, larger power tools stored on the shelf below. Three bikes and two sets of golf clubs in expensive bags lined the nearest wall. A plywood ceiling held a pull-down door with stairs that gave access to the crawl-space up there.

"Do you own a chain saw?" Grissom asked affably.

"A chain saw!" Pierce's eyes and nostrils flared. "I resent this harassment! I'm trying to—"

Holding up a traffic-cop palm, Grissom interrupted. "I'm not harassing you, Mr. Pierce."

"That's how it looks to me."

"I'm sorry you see it that way. I'm doing my job, which is to find and eliminate suspects based upon the evidence."

"I'm automatically a suspect, I suppose, because I'm the husband."

"Based on that tape you heard Captain Brass play, it's fair to say you had argued with your wife, threatening her with violence . . . and when she turns up dead in just the manner you described, you tell me? Are you a reasonable candidate for the crime?"

The therapist looked dumbfounded. "Well . . ."

"Your cooperation helps me eliminate you as a suspect. Remember that."

Pierce turned conciliatory, sighing as he walked over to the criminalist. "I'm sorry, Mr. Grissom. I guess I lost my head, because I do know how it looks."

The question, the CSI thought, *is how did your* wife *lose her head?* But Grissom had enough sense and tact not to blurt as much.

Instead, Grissom said only, "Understandable, sir. Understandable."

"Lynn and I had some really good times, before she was . . . *born* again. I'm telling you, it's like she joined a cult. Do you know that she told me, once, that she felt it was so sad that good people like Gandhi and Mother Teresa had to go to hell, 'cause they hadn't been saved, like she had? I can't lie to you, Mr. Grissom—we were definitely in the divorce express lane."

"The chain saw?"

Pierce sighed, pointed. "Under the workbench. . . . Want me to . . . ?"

Grissom nodded, followed him over and watched as Pierce pulled out two chain saws and hauled them, one at a time, up on the bench. One, a brand new STIHL, was still in the box.

"This box is sealed," Grissom said, giving it a close, thorough look.

"Yeah, just bought it yesterday. Got the receipt."

The other, an old Poulan, was so rusty that Grissom could tell just by looking that the saw wouldn't even start, let alone cut through a human body.

"What do you generally use a chain saw for, Mr. Pierce?"

"Cutting firewood, mostly. Pile out back."

Grissom nodded at the door leading outside. "May I?"

"Be my guest."

Behind the house, in the moonlight, Pierce showed Grissom to the woodpile. Using a pocket flash, the CSI knelt and inspected several of the cords.

"These are freshly cut, Mr. Pierce." He stood. "You've got one saw that's inoperable, and another still in the box. How is it you have fresh cut firewood?"

Pierce didn't miss a beat. "Nextdoor neighbor. Mel Charles, he loaned me his chain saw."

"When?"

"Couple of days ago. I like to watch a fireplace fire . . . helps me think, relax. So, I cut some wood. That's relaxing, too—use some muscles I don't, in my work."

Grissom nodded; he'd have Brass check with the neighbor.

They went back into the garage, Pierce saying, "Is that all, Mr. Grissom?"

"Crawlspace?"

Pierce pulled the steps down, and Grissom and his Maglite went up for a look—nothing. He would send Warrick and Nick in for the fine-tooth comb tour, later.

The physical therapist ushered Grissom back into the house, where Brass and Lori were just wrapping up their interview. Brass glanced up as they came in, but continued the interview.

"Lori, you've gone through some pretty big changes," Brass said. "The dyed hair, the pierced eyebrow, weren't you worried about what your mom would say when she came home?"

Lori's eyes shot to her father's, but she said nothing.

Pierce, sitting next to his daughter, putting a hand on her shoulder, said, "Lori was so upset when we thought Lynn had abandoned us, well . . . I thought a few changes wouldn't hurt anything, and would help Lori's state of mind."

"But wouldn't her mother have been furious?" Brass asked.

Pierce waved that off. "Lori had every right to be angry. At least, she thought so at the time."

Brass's eyes moved to Grissom. The CSI supervisor shook his head: nothing in the garage. Rising, Brass said, "Thank you, Lori—I really appreciate your cooperation."

The girl shrugged—but a tiny one-sided smile indicated the slight but significant rapport Brass had established.

To Pierce, Brass said, "I'm sure we'll have more questions for Lori, as the investigation continues. But I promise you we'll keep her best interests in mind."

"I'm sure," Pierce said dryly.

"We'll also have more questions for you."

"Then you're not arresting me?"

"No," Brass said, a "not at this time" lilt in his voice, "but you may wish to consult with your attorney."

Pierce's reply was quietly sardonic: "Because you have my best interests in mind."

The investigators moved to the door and Pierce shut it wordlessly behind them.

Out in the yard, Grissom gestured to the sprawling stucco ranch-style house next door. "We need to stop by the neighbor's house."

"Kinda late."

Grissom explained what Pierce had told him about the chain saw. "I want that chain saw, now."

"Are you saying Owen Pierce borrowed his neighbor's chain saw to cut up his wife?"

"He could have. Any way you look at it, I want that chain saw."

They crossed the well-manicured yard, a dwarf fruit tree perched in the middle of a brick circle surrounded by a moat of mulch. Brass rang the bell.

"They're gonna love us," Brass said.

But it was only a moment before an auburn-haired woman of about thirty answered the door. She wore jeans, tennis shoes, and a T-shirt with the "Race for the Cure" logo splashed across the front. Green-eyed with milky skin, she had a small rabbit-twich nose and an inquisitive expression—but she didn't look annoyed.

The muffled sound of Conan O'Brien came from the living room. *Good,* Brass thought. *We didn't wake anyone.*

"I don't normally open the door at this time of night," she said, and her voice, though quiet, carried a backbone of authority. "But I've seen you before, stopping next door, and on TV, too—you're the police officers on the Lynn Pierce case, aren't you?

Brass already had his I.D. out to show her. "That's right, ma'am. I'm Captain Jim Brass and this is crime-scene investigator, Gil Grissom. Is Mel Charles here?"

"Mel is my husband—I'm Kristy Charles." Her smile disappeared. "The house is kind of a mess—you mind if I bring Mel to you?"

"Not at all," Brass said. "This shouldn't take long."

"Any help we can give, we're glad to—Lynn's a

great gal, but her husband . . . well, I'll get Mel for you."

Soon Mel Charles filled the doorway, his wife staying just behind him, taking it all in. She seemed to have a satisfied expression, as though relishing this call by the police.

"Mr. Charles," Grissom said, "did you loan a chain saw to your nextdoor neighbor, Mr. Pierce?"

"Couple days ago," Charles said.

"Have you loaned him the saw on other occasions?"

Charles considered that for a moment, then shook his head. "Never needed it before. He had his own. He's always out there cutting wood."

"Why'd he need yours?"

"Said his had rusted up on him, and he hadn't had a chance to get a new one."

"Are you and Owen Pierce close, Mr. Charles? Hang out, shoot the breeze, loan each other garden tools and so on, pretty casually?"

"No. We just nod at each other. . . . Kristy and Lynn are friendly, share a cup of coffee now and then . . . I wouldn't say 'close.' "

"Obviously, you've seen the news about the disappearance of Mrs. Pierce, and what was found out at Lake Mead, today . . ."

Mrs. Charles's face was etched with dread. "You don't mean . . . he used *our* chainsaw to . . . oh my God. . . . Excuse me."

And she was gone.

Brass said, "Your wife liked Mrs. Pierce."

Eyebrows rose above the Buddy Holly rims. "You make it sound like Lynn's dead, Captain Brass."

"The evidence leans that way, yes."

Charles shook his head, mouth tight. "Well, that's a damn shame, God, a pity. She was real nice—kind of straight-laced? But nice."

"Straight-laced?" Brass echoed, remembering using the term himself when questioning Lori.

"You know—Born-Again Christian, conservative as hell."

"How about Mr. Pierce?"

With a shrug, Charles said, "We don't know them that well, really. But I get the idea he wasn't the church-going type, himself."

"What makes you say that?"

Charles was clearly trying to decide how much it was fair to say. ". . . I've seen rough characters stop by the house."

"Any you might be able to identify?"

"There was this one guy . . . I don't want to sound prejudiced."

"Black? Hispanic? Asian?"

"Black guy—dreadlocks, jewelry, baseball cap backwards."

"Often?"

"No. Few times, when Pierce's wife was away. He had different women in the house, too, when Lynn was visiting relatives or even just off doing some church thing."

Brass frowned. "Different women? Not one woman?"

"Hookers, is my guess. Right in his own house."

"What about his daughter? Would she have witnessed it?"

"She wasn't home that much, especially when the mom wasn't around."

Mrs. Charles's voice chimed back in; she'd returned, drying her eyes with a tissue—maybe she'd been off throwing up. "That daughter's got a smart mouth . . . but I suppose people think the same thing about our kids."

Brass was not surprised the Charleses and the Pierces weren't close—typical for neighbors in a city growing as fast as Vegas. It was one of the things Brass hated about living in the fastest-growing city in the United States. In the last ten years, the population had expanded by the size of Minneapolis, and every single day the equivalent of Salt Lake City came to visit. He lived in a city of strangers, some good, some bad, and one of them had killed and dismembered Lynn Pierce.

Mel Charles did not object when Grissom collected the chain saw into evidence.

As they drove back, Brass turned to Grissom. "What do you think?"

"If Pierce used this chain saw, all the cleaning in the world didn't get the blood off. The luminol will tell."

But an hour later Grissom was in his office, on the phone to Brass. "This chain saw hasn't cut anything but cord wood."

"Jesus," Brass said into the phone. "This guy Pierce has an answer for everything."

"Too many answers, Jim—and too pat. Don't despair—this tells us a lot."

"What does it tell us? A chain saw with no blood on it? That doesn't tell us a damn thing!"

Patiently Grissom said, "It tells us there's a missing chain saw—probably at the bottom of Lake Mead."

"Where we'll never find it—but how do you figure . . . ?"

"I should have known," Grissom said, disgusted, "when Pierce all but walked me over to that nextdoor neighbor. He was sending us on a wild goose chase, Jim, while trying to build a sort of alibi. Doesn't wash, though."

"Because there's a third chain saw?" The skepticism in Brass's voice was thick.

"No, there are *four* chainsaws. Think it through, Jim—Pierce has an ancient, rusted-out chain saw. That thing hasn't been used for some time. Yet the neighbor has seen him, fairly recently, cutting cord wood."

"There's also a brand-new, in-the-box chain saw."

"Yes—to replace the chain saw used to dismember Lynn. The one now, presumably, at the bottom of the lake."

Brass was getting it. "And after he tossed that chain saw in the lake, he borrowed his neighbor's . . . to cut some firewood, and to throw us off the trail."

"Exactly. To make it appear that there had never been a chain saw in the Pierce household between the old rusted one and the new-in-the-box."

Brass grunted a humorless laugh. "Well, Gil—I'll

let *you* walk your new proof over to the D.A. That's about the most circumstantial circumstantial evidence I ever heard."

"I didn't say it would hold up in court. But it's a piece of the puzzle, and we need all the pieces we can get our hands on."

"Particularly since we only have one piece of Lynn Pierce. Can you make the picture out yet, Gil, of this puzzle you're working?"

"I can tell you Owen Pierce cut up his wife with the missing chain saw."

"After he murdered her?"

"That," Grissom said, "I can't say."

"Great. If we can prove he cut his wife up, but not that he murdered her first, we can book him on his other crime."

"What other crime?" Grissom asked.

"Littering."

And the phone clicked in Grissom's ear.

10

WELL PAST THE END OF HER SHIFT, THE LONG HOURS SUDdenly catching up to her, Catherine Willows sat at her desk, on the phone, talking to a lawyer—and the hell of it was, it had been her own idea.

She was speaking to Jennifer Woods, in "legal" at ESPN, and had introduced herself. The woman—whose voice was alto range, self-confident, professional—did not seem at all surprised, or for that matter impressed, to be hearing from a Las Vegas PD criminalist.

"How may I help you, Ms. Willows?"

"Ms. Woods, we have a suspect in a murder case who claims he was watching television at the time of the murder."

"Our network, I take it."

"That's right."

"What day, what time?"

Catherine read from her notes: "Thursday, October twenty-five, from five thirty Pacific time until, let's say midnight."

"And what are you after, Ms. Willows?"

"First, your program listing. Second, a VHS dub of your file tape, assuming you keep such a thing. As I said, we're checking a murder suspect's alibi."

A pause—ducks were being gathered into a row. "All right, Ms. Willows, here's how it works. We need a letter of request sent to us. If it's not in writing, it doesn't exist."

"May I fax it?"

The lawyer's silence indicated consideration. "You may fax it to get the process started, but I can't really divulge any information or share any videotape until we have the letter mailed to us."

"This is a murder investigation."

"Exactly, Ms. Willows. And we're the legal department of a major company."

"I would appreciate any help you can provide," Catherine said, holding her temper in check. As much as she wanted them to rush, the truth was she did understand their hesitancy—right now, Catherine Willows was just a voice on the phone. "I'll fax you a copy in ten minutes and overnight the letter. What's the fax number and the address?"

Woods told her, then added, "I'll begin looking into this now; I'll call you when I have something."

Catherine recited all her phone numbers and said, "Thanks—you getting started on this really means a lot."

"No promises."

And the lawyer hung up.

Five minutes later, Sara strolled in, less than

bright-eyed after another endless shift. "Find out anything?"

Shaking her head, Catherine said, "Only that even when a lawyer does me a favor, I don't like 'em much."

"Is the network going to help?"

"After their lawyers assure them that there's no way anybody can ever sue them for doing their civic duty, I think so."

"What do we do in the meantime?"

"Here's a thought—why don't we go home?"

Sara's eyebrows lifted and she nodded. "It's an idea."

"You up for coming in a hour or two early? Maybe by then the elves will have polished all our boots for us." Catherine was reaching for her purse.

"Elves like Greg Sanders," Sara said, as they walked down the hall toward the locker room, "and Dan Helpingstine?"

"Great big elves like that, yeah."

And the women went home, like Vegas headliners, to sleep away the day.

The city wore the blue patina of dusk, the sky streaked a faded orange along a horizon made irregular by the lumpy spine of the slumbering beast of the dark blue mountain range; dark gray clouds, like factory smoke, encouraged the night.

In her stylish black leather jacket, a turquoise top and new black jeans and black pointed-toe boots, Catherine Willows walked briskly across the parking lot, feeling fresh, well-rested, and ready to get back to solving Jenna Patrick's murder. She had not yet admitted to herself that this case was special, that her emotions had been touched by the thought of a young woman, about to leave that life, having hers ended prematurely.

She collected Sara in the break room, where the brunette criminalist was giving the dayshift's coffee a down-the-drain mercy killing.

"Hey," Sara said.

"Hey," Catherine said. "Let's see what the elves have come up with."

"Greg first?"

Catherine nodded. "Greg first."

Greg Sanders was hovering over one of his state-of-the-art machines. God, he was young, Catherine thought; with his spiky hair and mischievous smile, he looked more like a kid than a gifted scientist—still, there was no doubting his ability.

Catherine stood across from the slender blue-smocked figure, Sara leaning on the counter, not yet awake. This was morning to them, after all.

"What do you have for us?" Catherine asked.

Sanders shuffled some papers, and smiled—a smile that might mean disaster or triumph, one never knew. "Last things first, I guess. The fake beard and mustache you found in Lipton's house? Human hair."

"Human scalp hair," Catherine said.

Sara was frowning, not quite following.

Sanders picked up on Catherine's thought. "Human scalp hair's what they use to make really high-quality wigs." He brought out two plastic bags with the beard in one and the mustache in the other.

"Okay," Catherine said, with Sanders and yet not with him. "So what does that tell us?"

He turned his palms up. "Well, the hair in the beard and mustache, that you took from Lipton's closet, doesn't match any hairs you collected in Dream Dolls."

"No?"

He held up a tiny bag with a single straight brown hair in it. "No—for example, this is from the club, and I identified it as wig hair, but the cheap variety . . . *not* human hair: rayon."

"Okay," Sara said, not ready to process this information just yet, "what else?"

Sanders showed them two more evidence bags. "The spirit gum bottle, and the shoebox you got all this stuff from? The only fingerprints belong to the victim, Jenna Patrick."

Sara shrugged. "So Ray Lipton wore gloves, or wiped off the bottle and box."

Sanders was already shaking his head. "Not likely."

"Why?" Catherine asked.

"No wipe marks, but plenty of clear prints—the Patrick woman's prints would've been smeared, if the box'd been wiped. Near as I can tell, only Jenna Patrick ever touched this stuff."

"Okay," Catherine said, "so Ray Lipton didn't touch any of it. Maybe this is some other fake mustache and beard, hard as that might be to buy. . . . What about the back room at the strip club?"

"Yeah," Sara said, eager, "any sign of our man back there?"

Sanders sighed, took a swig of coffee, shook his head. "You brought in a ton of stuff; I'll still be going through this evidence when I reach retirement. Y'know, I never knew female pubic hair could be such a bore."

Sara made a face. "Thanks for sharing, Greg."

"Anyway, none of the fingerprints belong to Ray Lipton. His hair wasn't back there, either."

Sara suddenly seemed animated—finally awake. "Wait, Greg—what are you telling us . . . Lipton didn't do it?"

"I'm not saying that. Anyway, you've still got the videotape, don't you?"

Catherine said, "That's starting to look a little iffy, its own self."

After another sip of coffee, Sanders raised his eyebrows, shrugged and said, "It's not that Lipton *couldn't* have done the deed—it's just that there's no real evidence from the strip club that he did, other than the security videotape. And if you think that's not him on the video . . . well . . . where does that leave you?"

Sara turned to Catherine. "Where does that leave us?"

"Where else?" Catherine said. "Back to square one: find evidence that Lipton did it . . . or evidence that exonerates him."

"And, hopefully, points to someone else," Sara said. "Greg, you got anything else for us?"

"Fingerprints, lots of them. Hair, fibers, and

DNA. We just don't know who they go with. I need samples from the dancers and the customers."

Catherine shook her head. "We've got the customers who were there when the murder was discovered—O'Riley and Vega have been interviewing them, collecting fingerprints; maybe dayshift can help us out and gather those samples for you."

"That'll help," Sanders said.

"As for customers who might've been there earlier that day or night," she went on, "or more crucially, any who slipped out before Jenna's body was found . . . there's no way to track them down."

"Unless they were regulars," Sara said, "and that Kapa-what's-it guy'll give us their names."

"Kapelos," Catherine said. "He might help." She used her cell phone and caught Detective Erin Conroy, telling her, "We need another visit to Dream Dolls."

"Got a lead?"

"We may have, after you've done some questioning. . . . Meet Sara and me there, and I'll fill you in when I see you."

Fifteen minutes later, they met the detective in the mostly empty parking lot of the strip club, the fancy DREAM DOLLS sign doing its neon dance for no one in particular.

"Why so dead?" Sara wondered aloud.

Catherine surveyed the vacant spaces. "Early evening . . . weeknight."

Still, strip clubs in Vegas rarely had empty parking lots, no matter what hour it was.

"You mind telling me," Conroy said, her mouth a

tight line, "why we've returned to this delightful scene of the crime?"

"Ray Lipton," Catherine said quietly, "may not be our guy."

A convertible Mustang rolled by, a male passenger catcalling at the three women standing in the parking lot, possibly mistaking them for strippers on their way into the club. A low-rider BMW drove by, its bass speaker rattling windows in the surrounding older buildings.

"Lipton not our man?" Conroy asked, numbly.

Catherine shook her head.

Conroy was frowning. "What the hell? We have him cold, on videotape."

"That might not be him," Sara admitted. "If it was, he somehow managed not to leave any prints."

"You CSIs ever hear about gloves?" Conroy asked.

"It's not that easy," Catherine said.

She filled Conroy in on Greg's reading of the evidence, and Helpingstine's preliminary enhancement of the video, which seemed to bring out a figure that didn't entirely resemble Lipton's build.

Rather glumly, Conroy asked, "Suggestions?"

Catherine said, "Sara and I'll get hair and blood from the dancers, and I thought you might want to re-interview."

"Yeah," Conroy said, "probably a good idea. But maybe you should chat with the owner some more."

The two CSIs gathered their equipment from the Tahoe, Conroy giving them a hand, and headed into the club. While Sara and Conroy kept a respectful distance, Catherine approached Ty Kapelos, who ruled the roost from behind the bar, wearing what appeared to be the same white long-sleeved shirt as the other evening.

"Hey, Ty," she said.

"Hey, Cath . . . knew you couldn't stay away—missed me, didn't ya?"

"That's it, Ty," Catherine said. "You're irresistible."

The club was quiet, only a handful of college-age guys, hanging out near the stage, and a few white-collar types at tables, whether conventioneers or local businessman "working late," Catherine couldn't hazard a guess. The music was thankfully silent—Worm in his booth, going through CDs looking for tunes, reminding her of Greg Sanders examining clues—and no women were currently on the stage.

"Jeez, Ty," Catherine said. "I'd like to have the tumbleweed concession in this place, about now."

Kapelos shrugged. "Changeover time, Cath. You know how that is. Girls are in the back."

"That the *whole* story, Ty?"

His good humor evaporated, and he answered her, but in a hushed tone. "Nothing like a murdered dancer to chase business away."

"Sure—your patrons like things discreet. Murder happens, you never know when the cops are going to show back up."

"You said it, Cath, I didn't—at least, the sheriff had the decency to send around pretty cops."

"You're still a charmer, Ty," she said, and explained what they needed.

"Sure, go ahead," Kapelos said.

Catherine turned to Conroy, who gave her a

look. The CSI nodded just a little, getting it, and said, "You two go ahead. . . . I'll catch up."

Conroy smiled a little as she and Sara moved toward the hallway in back.

Returning her attention to Kapelos, Catherine asked, "Which of your dancers makes the most money?"

He shrugged as he polished a glass.

"Come on, Ty—I'm not the IRS. I don't want to bust anybody's chops, particularly not yours—I just want to know if Jenna was the object of jealousy."

Another, more cooperative shrug. "Yeah, some—she was really cute, y'know, had this girl-next-door kinda thing goin'. She did pretty well even before her boob job, which came out great, and made her even more popular. . . . Some of the girls didn't like that. You know how it goes."

Catherine was aware that Jenna's life at Dream Dolls wouldn't have been easy. Under the added pressure of her jealous boyfriend, Jenna couldn't have been very happy; no wonder she'd wanted out. "Had Jenna ever talked about quitting?"

Kapelos waved off the question. "Yeah, sure. They all do."

"So, you didn't take her talk of quitting seriously?"

"Question is, did *she* take it serious. I mean, hell, I knew this boyfriend, Lipton, wanted her to quit . . . even though he *met* her here . . . and she usually talked about it, right after they argued. 'Maybe Ray's right, maybe I am prostituting myself.' I learned a long time ago not to put too much stock in that kind of talk. These are messed-up kids—you know, Cath . . . low self-esteem, high drug abuse, and more incest victims than a week of Springer."

"Was Jenna a drug user?"

"I don't know about her private life. I don't have to tell you, I don't allow none of that shit in here, not in my business . . . but what they do on their own time, how they spend all this money they make, that's *their* business."

"Jenna ever mention anything about her and Lipton getting married?"

"Yeah, but I figured she was just talkin' about that to keep Lipton on the hook. Sure he's a hot-headed prick, but he's also a good-looking fella with a successful small business."

"So you figure she did want to marry him?"

"I think so, but my take is, she wanted to work a few years, and put a little money away, of her own, before she walked away from show biz to be a baby-making machine."

"Did she say that? Indicated Lipton wanted a big family?"

"Yeah. She'd be a normal housewife, those were the words she used. Look, I don't have to tell you Dream Dolls and even the glitzier clubs, like Showgirl World and Olympic Gardens, ain't exactly Broadway or Hollywood . . . but it's still show business, and Jenna was a star, in her little universe . . . and it's hard to walk away from that kind of attention."

"But Jenna did want to marry Ray," Catherine said, pressing Ty, "if not now, eventually?"

Kapelos turned up his palms. "Who can say? You ever know anybody talkin' about marriage didn't have their head up their ass?"

Suddenly her ex-husband Eddie's face popped up in her memory, like a jack-in-the-box, and she shook her head to dismiss the image.

"Damn straight," Kapelos said, misreading that as a gesture of agreement with him.

Catherine didn't bother to correct him. "Which of these dancers would you say disliked Jenna the most?"

Kapelos harumphed. "Hell, take your pick. It ain't like the old days when you girls watched out for each other. These days, these girls just as soon spit at each other as say hello. This is a more lucrative business than when you left, Cath. Some of these girls are makin' a good six figures."

Catherine squinted—had she heard right? "You serious?"

"As a heart attack . . . and Jenna was one of those girls. She did the circuit, made some serious green, but this was home for her. . . . Y'know, when she did L.A., she had the porn producers hounding her, all the time."

"She interested?"

A groove of thought settled between his thick eyebrows. "Frankly, I think she mighta been considering it. She told me that some of the top girls in the adult industry work a few years, and retire millionaires."

"Did Lipton know she was considering a porn career?"

"If he did, well . . ."

"Well what, Ty?"

"I was gonna say . . . he'd kill her."

Their gazes held for several long seconds, then Catherine twitched a smile and said, "Thanks, Ty. I'm going to the back, to help out. I know Detective Conroy's going to have some more questions, possibly about regulars. I'd appreciate if you'd be as open with her as you have been with me."

Kapelos grinned. "Not a chance, Cath . . . not a chance."

She chuckled, as Kapelos turned his attention to one of college kids, who'd ambled up to the bar.

Pushing through the curtains at the corridor's end, Catherine entered a different facet of the world of Dream Dolls.

The dressing room was much brighter than the dark bar and it took a moment for her eyes to adjust. Once the tiny stars dissipated, she found herself in a room deeper than she remembered, going back a good thirty feet and leaving space for nine tiny dressing tables along each side wall. Globe lights on four ceiling fans ran down the center of the ceiling. At least, Catherine thought, Ty had finally got rid of those fluorescents that painted the dancers a ghostly white. Walls a pastel green, the room felt soft and inviting compared to the overbearing blackness beyond the heavy curtains.

Conroy was in the far left-hand corner interviewing a lithe, chocolate-skinned dancer wearing a red sequined g-string and nothing else. About halfway back on the right side, Sara was taking a blood sample from a blonde woman in red bikini lingerie, a voluptuous girl of maybe twenty.

Seven or eight other women stood around in various stages of undress, none of them the least bit modest or seemingly even aware of the three fully clothed women in their midst. The unforgiving illumination revealed cellulite, stretch marks, scars and other imperfections that the low, blue-tinged lighting out front would conceal; a couple of them wore a shiny patina of perspiration that told Catherine they had been dancing recently.

A redhead with breasts as fraudulent as her hair color strode forward on spike heels that lifted her to a height of six feet. Probably pushing thirty or even thirty-five . . . ancient in this trade, Catherine knew . . . the busty dancer had the cold eyes of a veteran and a narrow severe face framing a small round mouth that looked perpetually angry. She used a large white beach towel to dry herself as she walked over, saying, "You with them?" The woman tilted her head toward the back of the room.

Nodding, Catherine introduced herself, adding, "Crime scene investigator—and you are?"

"Pissed off . . . Thanks for askin'." She saronged the towel around herself, plucked a package of cigarettes from the nearby dressing table and lit herself up. She blew smoke and said, "I was just wonderin' when you people are gonna be done with this place so we can go back to makin' money."

Ignoring the stripper's belligerent attitude, Catherine asked, "You have *my* name—yours is . . . ?"

Chin high, proud of herself, the dancer said, "Belinda Bountiful."

Catherine laughed out loud. "That wouldn't be a stage name, by any chance?"

The redhead glanced around, making sure no one was listening, and whispered, "Pat Hensley."

"Don't the other girls know your real name?"

"We're not that close. I like to keep my private life private, that's all. . . . I got a husband and two kids to feed."

Catherine sat on the edge of a dressing table. "So, the money's dried up around here?"

With a shake of her ersatz-auburn mane, the dancer said, "It was hard enough to make money here when Jenna was alive—this ain't exactly the Flamingo, you know. But now . . ."

"What about now?"

"Whose fantasy is it, to go into the club where there's been a murder, anyway? Jeffrey Dahmer's maybe? Ted Bundy's? And those two ain't been hittin' the club scene much, lately. Plus which, we've had cops in and out of here, almost nonstop since Jenna bought it."

That was touching. "You have a few customers out there. It's early, yet."

"Probably as big a crowd as we'll see all night."

Trying to catch the dancer with her guard down, Catherine asked, "Bother you at all, how much money Jenna was pulling down?"

The Hensley woman scoffed at that. "Hell, no. You're kidding, right?"

"You were making your fair share then?"

Moving a well-manicured hand to her cleavage, the dancer asked, "You know anything about this life, then you know that as long as I have these, I'm going to make my fair share."

"You happen to know if Jenna Patrick was using her real name?"

The belligerence was gone, now. "That was her real name—had the right sound, y'know? Lots of 'Jennas' around the strip circuit, right now. Hot porn star name."

"You knew that was Jenna's real name, but she didn't know yours?"

"Hey, just 'cause I'm belly-achin' about business, don't think I'm glad Jenna's gone. Truth is, we were friends. I get along with her roommate, too."

"Tera Jameson, you mean?"

"That's right—ever see that one dance? Now she is class; she was born with a great rack, and she studied ballet and shit. Yeah, before Tera left for Showgirl World, the three of us was pretty close."

Catherine cast an eye toward Conroy who was still talking to the African-American dancer. "Has Detective Conroy talked to you yet?"

The dancer shrugged. "Last time you guys was here."

"Not this time around?"

"No, why?"

"I had the impression," the CSI said, "that the girls around here weren't all that tight."

Pat nodded. "That's true enough, but I'm kinda the . . . den mother, I guess. And the three of us, Tera and Jenna and me, we hung out together quite a bit. Shopping, the occasional breakfast after we got off, stuff like that."

"How well do you know her boyfriend?"

"Hothead Ray? Not all that well." Pat smirked sourly. "I was a little surprised when Jenna hooked up with *his* ass."

"Surprised, why?"

Again the dancer looked around to make sure they weren't being overheard. "I never knew what was goin' on with Jenna and Tera, not exactly, not really . . ."

Catherine nodded, even though she didn't know what she was agreeing with.

". . . but I just assumed . . . well . . . you know."

The CSI's antennae were tingling as she said, "No—I don't know."

"Knowing that Tera was a lez, I just assumed that Jenna was too. Anyway, that's why I was so surprised when Jenna hooked up with Lipton. I mean, I didn't know Jenna was bi—but what the hell? Whatever gets you through the night . . . or workin' *these* hours, the day!"

Catherine's eyes bored into those of the dancer.

"Ooooh shit," Pat said, eyes as big as her bosoms. "You didn't know Tera leaned that way, did you?"

"Never came up before. All we knew was, she and Jenna lived together; but nobody mentioned a relationship between the two, other than that they were roommates."

"Didn't you talk to Tera yet?"

"Yes. She didn't say a word about it."

The dancer shrugged. "Well, even these days, people don't always advertise it."

However you figured it, Catherine knew, this little sexual tidbit would call for another trip to Tera Jameson's apartment.

The criminalist decided to push on; she had in Pat a close friend of the deceased, after all. "Any idea who would be jealous of Jenna, either here in the club, or, I don't know . . . maybe somebody out of Lipton's life? Coworker at the construction company, maybe?"

Pat looked slowly around the room. "Here at Dream Dolls? Any of these girls who haven't saved up for new ones were jealous of her. And she had really nice work done . . . I'm saving up to get mine overhauled."

Catherine's eyes travelled around the dressing room and she realized Pat's words might apply to all of these other dancers. That meant if Lipton really was innocent, they would have no shortage of suspects.

Sara strolled up and looked at Pat. "You ready to give at the office?"

Before Catherine's eyes, Pat Hensley disappeared and in her place stood Belinda Bountiful, returning in all her bitchy glory. "Is this trip really necessary? Ain't it enough you're keeping us from makin' a livin'?"

Sara shrugged with her mouth. "You can either do it voluntarily, or we can get a court order. Do it now and we're out of your hair—your choice."

Making a real production out of it, star stripper

Belinda Bountiful finally agreed to follow Sara back and have the blood drawn. Turning privately to Catherine, Pat peeked out from behind the Belinda mask to whisper, "Can't ever let 'em forget who the real diva is around this hellhole."

While Conroy and Sara finished up, Catherine moved back to the tiny room where a murder had occurred. Using her Swiss Army knife, the CSI sliced through the yellow-and-black crime-scene tape and eased the door open. Having been closed up for this long a time, the cubicle hit Catherine in the face with a hot, fetid aroma, as if not an atom of air conditioning had penetrated the police seal.

Pulling on latex gloves, she stepped in. They were missing something—something *important*, she thought; and maybe they had missed it in here. . . .

Standing there at the threshold of the murder, Catherine saw it happen.

Lipton—in a fake beard and mustache, dark glasses on, cap pulled down tight, the LIPTON CONSTRUCTION *lettering on his jacket standing out in bold red letters against the denim background—walks down the hall, leading Jenna Patrick down the familiar path to the lap-dance cubicles. Naked except for the flimsy lavender thong, Jenna trails behind a few steps, an apprehensive smile on her pretty face as she wonders why her boyfriend is tempting fate by coming in here. Still, it excites Jenna, knowing that he would disguise himself so they could be together here, at the forbidden place that Dream Dolls has become. . . .*

They enter the little room, he sits on the chair and Jenna closes the door. She goes to him; perhaps they even kiss. He is, after all, no ordinary customer. Jenna spins around, sits on his lap and begins to gyrate to the music filtered in through the speakers, even as behind her back, he pulls on gloves, takes the electrical tie out of his pocket, and at the critical moment, slips it down over her head, and around her slender throat.

He yanks it tight. Within seconds it cuts off the blood in her carotid arteries. She struggles to get a grip, her eyes wide with fear and pain and betrayal and sorrow; but it's too late. . . . Essentially unconscious, brain death only a few short minutes away, she stops fighting as the electrical tie does its terrible work. All Lipton has to do is sit quietly and watch her die.

When she is dead, dropped to the floor, he need only rise, and make his way through the bar, out the door, and into the cool night, where a new life awaits, where he will find some new woman who will not betray him with this sorry, sordid lifestyle.

"You all right?" Conroy asked.

Catherine shook herself to awareness. She hadn't even heard the detective come up behind her. "Yeah—fine. I was just thinking it through."

Sara strolled up in the hallway. "Four of the girls aren't here, but they're scheduled to work tomorrow. We can go to their apartments, or stop back, then."

"Tomorrow'll do fine," Conroy said, as the three women confabbed in the corridor. "We got plenty to work on."

"You get anything interesting?" Catherine asked them.

Conroy shrugged. "Hard to say. The dancer that

spoke to you . . ." She checked her notes. ". . . Belinda Bountiful, aka Pat Hensley?"

"Yeah?"

"She brought out some things that might be worth looking into. Especially if you're still unsure about Lipton."

"Namely that Tera Jameson is gay," Catherine said, "and Jenna bisexual."

"Well," Sara said, taking this new information in stride. "I think we need to drop around at the roommate's again."

"Yeah," Conroy said. "That's a swell idea." The detective let loose a long sigh. "So—should we kick Lipton, you think? Are you sure he's not the guy?"

"Not sure at all," Catherine said. "We've got Jenna potentially in a love relationship with her roommate, but Ty tells me Jenna was being courted by Los Angeles pornographers, offering the world to her on a blue movie platter. Other than his half-assed alibi and the security videotape, it's all pretty shaky where Lipton's concerned . . . and if this tech we've got working on the tape says that's *not* Lipton . . . well . . ."

"That doesn't really answer my question," Conroy said. "Do we kick him loose, or don't we?"

Catherine thought about it. Then she asked, "How long can you hold him?"

"Without pressing charges?" Now Conroy thought about it. "We may be pushing it already. He'd be on the streets by now, if he'd asked for a lawyer."

Sara asked, "Can't you hold him as a material witness?"

Conroy turned up her palms. "How? If Ray boy wasn't here, then he can't be a witness . . . and if he *was* here, that makes him our number-one suspect. Ladies, you better talk to your videotape expert, and find out where we really stand."

A little over half an hour later, with Detective Conroy's blessing, Catherine was back in an interview room with Ray Lipton. A lidded medium-sized evidence box was on the table before her.

The construction mini-magnate looked like hell. The last forty-eight hours had seemed to chew him up pretty bad, his eyes red and puffy and locked into a vacant, not-quite-there holding pattern. He hadn't shaved or bathed and he carried the heavy, sour scent of sweat that came from living in the same clothes in the same small cell for way too long. He sat alone at the table, his head hanging. Though physically much smaller, the CSI towered over him.

His voice was low, strained, as if he hadn't taken a drink of water since the last time they had seen him. "I need a lawyer, don't I?"

"If you want one, you have every right to make that phone call." In her one hand, Catherine held a fax from Jennifer Woods of the ESPN legal department. Along with a stern reminder to make sure the letter was in the mail, Woods had sent a log of all programming from noon until midnight, October 25, 2001; a videotape had been Fedexed.

"But before you make that call," Catherine said,

"I'd appreciate it if we could talk, just a little more, about your alibi."

"I don't have a damn alibi." He shook his head. "I told you, Ms. Willows—I was home alone, watching a football game."

"That's my point, Mr. Lipton. The football game can help give you an alibi."

He looked up. "You're shitting me, right?"

"No—not one iota, Mr. Lipton. It won't clear you, but it would be a good start. Now . . . what time did you say you started watching the game?"

Lipton shrugged. "Game started at five-thirty. Got home about seven, took a shower, nuked some dinner, probably sat down just about seven-thirty. Second half had started. Like I told you before, Peterson kicked a field goal; then this guy I never heard of ran the kickoff back for a touchdown."

Catherine checked the sheet in her hand. According to the ESPN log, Dominic Rhodes ran back a kickoff for a touchdown with 4:50 left in the third quarter. The action occurred at 7:34 P.M. Pacific Time. "Dominic Rhodes ring a bell?"

Lipton brightened. "Yeah! That's the guy."

"Then what?"

"Couple of minutes later, the Chiefs scored a touchdown. It was a hell of a half—I think there were four touchdowns in the fourth quarter alone."

"Do you recall how many were made by each team?"

"Two," he said, with confidence. But then his expression dimmed a bit. "Now . . . can you tell me something?"

"I'll try."

"How does this help me?"

"The game was broadcast live, right?"

"Yeah. Of course. I don't care about that tape-delay shit."

"Did *you* tape it?"

This had apparently not occurred to him. Lipton shook his head.

"I'm pretty sure of that myself," Catherine told him. "There was no tape in your machine, and we've checked every videotape in your residence, and the game hadn't been recorded on any of them. You would have had to tape it, watch it, and dispose of the tape before the police arrived. More importantly, you'd have had to anticipate we would ask you specifics about the game, and you'd have to be ready for our questions. Not impossible, but in real life, in the time frame we're talking about, highly unlikely."

His eyes had come alive. "Does that mean I'm finally free?"

Catherine gave him a "sorry" smile, and shook her head. "Not just yet. We're still working on the security videotape."

The contractor retained his hopeful expression, nonetheless. "I'm not worried—that's not me on the tape, 'cause I wasn't there. . . . And you don't think it's me on the tape yourself, do you, Ms. Willows?"

With a quick glance at the two-way mirror where she knew Conroy and Sara were watching, she said, "This isn't about my opinion, Mr. Lipton."

"Sure it is. You can't tell me you people don't look at this evidence from some kind of point of view. Everybody knows that instincts are just as important as facts."

Gil Grissom would disagree, Catherine knew; but she said, "Let's just say I'm not entirely convinced one way or the other."

That took some of the air out of him.

"Also, I need you to explain these." She took the lid off the box that contained the evidence bags from the house: the beard, mustache, spirit gum and shoebox.

Lipton looked in at them without touching anything. He shrugged. "That's Jenna's stuff."

"A beard and a mustache?"

"Yeah—it's from her act."

"Her act?"

Lipton nodded matter of factly. "She had this routine where she'd put this stuff on, dance around the bar dressed as an old man. She didn't make a stage entrance, you know? And another girl would still be dancing. Jenna'd just sort of show up out in the club, kinda sneak out there." He grinned, shaking his head, remembering. "She'd have 'em all fooled."

"Did she?"

"Oh, yeah, she was really good. She'd rub against these guys as she moved through the bar, drove 'em batty—they thought she was an old gay guy tryin' to get lucky or somethin'! Eventually, she'd work her way to the stage and got up there with the girl that was dancing at the time, and rub all over her."

"Uh huh."

"It's just about the only bit I ever liked about her dancing. See, the other dancer would pretend to be grossed out by the old man and'd leave the stage . . . then this 'old man' would start stripping. When the stiffs finally figured out they had pushed *her* away, they went ballistic. She had them all in the palm of her hand."

"That must have got under your skin," Catherine said.

"Naw," Lipton said, shaking his head. "Just the opposite. That act wasn't about cheap sex, her act was . . . social commentary. Jenna liked making that point; she was smart, you know, and sensitive. Don't turn someone away until you get to know 'em. It was subtle, but it was about a hell of a lot more than just Jenna taking off her clothes. Like I said, it was the only bit of hers I liked."

"Why hasn't anyone mentioned this act before?"

"Well, she hadn't done in quite a while. After she, you know . . . had her augmentation surgery, it wasn't so easy for her to pretend to be a man. . . . Does this clear me?"

"No."

His face fell.

She continued: "I need to confirm that this act really existed."

"That Kapelos character'll tell you."

"I'll call him right now and find out," she said. "You see, it's like I told you when this started, Mr. Lipton."

The suspect's eyes were poised between hope and despair, now.

"If you are innocent," she said, "we'll find that out, and we *will* catch the killer."

"Not for my sake," he said.

She wasn't following him; her expression said, *What?*

"For Jenna's," he said.

11

AT THE SAME TIME GREG SANDERS WAS GIVING CATHerine Willows and Sara Sidle the skinny on wig hair, Gil Grissom—in a loose long-sleeve dark gray shirt and black slacks—was striding down the hall, a file folder in one hand, his heels clicking softly on the tile floor. Finally arriving at his destination, he knocked on a door with raised white letters spelling: CAPTAIN JAMES BRASS.

"It's open," came the muffled voice from the other side.

Grissom walked in and granted Brass a boyish grin; the detective was sitting in a large gray chair behind a government-issue gray metal desk.

The office was a glorified cubicle, the wall to the left filled with file cabinets, a chalkboard all but obscuring the wall at right, with a table covered with stacks of papers camped beneath it. Brass's desk, however, was tidy, bearing only the open file before him, a telephone, and a photo of his daughter, Ellie.

"Chic," Grissom said.

"You came by for a reason, or just to brighten my evening?"

Standing opposite Brass, ignoring a waiting chair, Grissom deposited his own file on top of the one Brass had been perusing. "Results of the tox screen on our torso—no drugs, no alcohol."

"Sounds like a good Christian corpse," Brass said, cocking an eyebrow over the file. "But is it Lynn Pierce?"

"Still waiting on DNA confirmation. Replicating the DNA, heating it and cooling it, over and over, takes time."

Brass nodded, put down the file, locked eyes with the CSI. "Tell me we've got something to hold us over till then."

"Doc Robbins defleshed the torso, and used the bones to run some numbers, which reveals significant information, through wear."

Though Brass had once supervised CSI himself, he still considered much of Grissom's information to sound like gibberish. "Which in English means what?"

Nick Stokes—in a long-sleeve tan T-shirt and dark tan chinos—appeared in the open door, but didn't interrupt. Brass waved him in, and Nick moved to the side and leaned against the corner file cabinet.

"It means," Grissom said, "that the torso belonged to a white woman between the ages of thirty-five and forty-five, weight approximately one-ten, height about five-four . . . and she was definitely dismembered with a chain saw."

With an amazed shake of his head, Brass asked, "Robbins got all that from the pelvic bones?"

"Yeah, that and that she was in a heavy exercise program . . . did a lot of sit-ups."

"You can tell me all this, including her dismemberment by Black and Decker . . ."

"We don't know the brand name. Yet."

"But you can't confirm who she is or how she died."

"That's true to a point. But we have the husband's identification of the birthmark, and now, a lot more."

"Such as?"

"Female between thirty-five and forty-five, weighing one-ten and standing five-four . . . who does that remind you of?"

Brass shrugged one shoulder. "Sure, those figures fit Lynn Pierce . . . but how many other missing women?"

Slowly, Grissom said, "Factoring in the birthmark, and the episiotomy scar? . . . Not another in Nevada."

Silence stretched in the little office.

"Well . . ." Brass sighed. "We already knew it was Lynn Pierce, didn't we? . . . And yet we still don't have a thing to hang on that bastard husband of hers."

Grissom held Brass's eyes, and then slowly moved both of their gazes over to Nick, standing on the sidelines, leaning against that file cabinet.

Wearing a tiny enigmatic smile, Nick straightened. "We may have him. . . . You tell me."

"I will," Brass said. "Go on."

"I've been working on the Lynn Pierce computer and credit-card records."

"Any movement since her disappearance?" Brass asked.

"Nothing on the e-mail front. She's still getting them, a few friends, church announcements, spam; but she hasn't answered any of 'em, since the day before she went missing. And nothing new on the credit cards or ATM."

"What woman does not use her charge card?" Grissom asked.

"A dead one," Brass admitted.

Nick said, "Hey, I got more—something really interesting. Going through the old credit card receipts, I found this." He stepped forward holding out a slip of paper.

Brass took the slip and studied it. "A receipt for a box of forty-four caliber shells . . ." His head went sideways. "Didn't Pierce say . . ."

". . . that he never owned a gun?" Grissom finished. "Yes he did. . . . Gentlemen?"

Somehow, Brass managed to arrive in front of the Pierce home in less than ten minutes. The sun had long since dipped below the horizon, leaving the sky the purplish hue of a huge bruise. The evening was cool and only a few lights were on in the castle-like house. Grissom and Nick hurried to keep up with Brass who moved onto the porch, skipped the bell, and pounded on the front door with his fist.

Pierce, in an open-neck navy Polo shirt and dark blue jeans, opened the door displaying the same hangdog expression they'd seen on their last visit.

He had not shaved; perhaps, Grissom speculated, the physical therapist had stayed home from work again today.

Brass held out the photocopy of the receipt like a bill collector demanding a payment way overdue. He didn't even wait for their reluctant host to speak. "You lied, Pierce! You told us you never owned a gun—so how do you explain a receipt for bullets you bought?"

The detective kept walking as he spoke, backing Pierce inside the house with the force of his words and forward motion. Grissom and Nick followed them in, the former even shutting the door behind him, as the group gathered in the foyer by the winding stairway.

"And don't bother feeding us some bull about buying them for a friend," Brass ranted. "This time, I want the truth." Finally, when the detective stopped to take a breath, Pierce got a word in.

"All right!" the therapist said. "All right, I admit it. . . . I . . . I had a gun in the house . . . for a while."

Brass seemed ready to blow again, but that statement brought him up short. He looked hard at Pierce. "*Had* a gun?"

"*Had* a gun," Pierce repeated.

Brass's open hand shot to his right temple, as if he were either fighting off a vicious migraine or a sudden stroke. Neither option struck Grissom as positive.

The therapist held up his hands in a fashion that was equal parts surrender and calming gesture; then he led them into the living room, gesturing to the rifles-and-flags sofa. "Please, please . . . sit down. Let me explain."

In a stage whisper in Grissom's direction, Brass said, "This should be prime."

But Brass took a seat on the couch, while Grissom again sat at the edge of the maple chair opposite; Nick hovered in the background, while Pierce settled in chummily beside the skeptical detective.

"I know what you're thinking," Pierce said, reasonably, with a tone usually reserved for children. "Cocaine in the house, gun in the house, Born-Again wife . . . he had to have killed her."

"Now that you mention it," Brass said.

Running a hand over his unshaven face, the therapist sighed in resignation. "Okay. I had a gun. A .44 Magnum I bought from . . . an acquaintance."

"And of course it wasn't registered."

"Your negative attitude, Captain, doesn't keep that from being any less true."

"The name of the acquaintance?"

Pierce hesitated.

The sarcasm in Brass's tone had been replaced with matter-of-fact, almost cheerful professionalism. "One of you is going to jail this afternoon, Mr. Pierce—either you or the person who sold you an illegal weapon. You make the call."

"I can't tell you, Captain."

"Can't? *Won't,* you mean."

"I bought it from the man I was buying cocaine from. He doesn't even know my wife—he's no suspect in this."

Brass frowned in shock. "And you're *protecting* him?"

"I'm protecting myself and my daughter. Do I have to tell you that these kind of people are dangerous?"

Grissom said, "You were friendly enough with this person to purchase a weapon from him . . . what, to protect your family from the likes of the man you *bought* it from?"

"You might say . . . Guys, fellas . . . this is hard to admit."

Brass smiled an unfriendly smile. "Try."

Pierce sighed. "For a while, I was . . . when Lynn got involved with her church, gone all the time . . . well. She used to be . . . God!"

Grissom said, "Mr. Pierce, if you are innocent, you need to be frank us, so we don't waste our time going down your road. Do you understand?"

Pierce swallowed thickly, nodded. "My wife used to be a wildcat . . . in the bedroom? Do I really have to say more? . . . Anyway, when she . . . got religion, certain things suddenly seemed . . . perverted to her. We hardly . . . had relations at all, anymore. . . . I need something to drink. Just water."

"Nick," Grissom said, and gestured toward the kitchen.

Nick nodded and went away.

"I'm not proud of it," Pierce said, "but . . I started seeing prostitutes. They're not exactly tough to hook up with in this town. Sometimes I brought them to my office, sometimes to a motel, and sometimes . . . I brought them here."

The son of a bitch was confirming the nextdoor neighbor's story!

Nick delivered the glass of water, Pierce took it, saying, "Thanks . . . You know how some of these girls, these women can be. How they sometimes bring their pimps or whoever around . . . and my . . my coke connection said I should be careful. Said I needed protection in the house. . . . So I bought the Magnum."

Brass said nothing; then glanced at Grissom, who shrugged. It was a good story.

"Okay, Mr. Pierce," Brass said softly, "then where's the gun now?"

Pierce looked at the floor, then at Brass, and back at the floor. "I had second thoughts about having it around the house, and, anyway, I stopped seeing those kind of girls."

"You haven't answered my question."

"I threw it away."

Grissom, wincing, said, "You threw the gun away?"

"Yes."

"Where?"

"Lake Mead."

Grissom felt as tnough he'd been slapped; he glanced at Brass, whose expression said he felt the same.

Brass asked, "You own a boat?"

"No. I went out on one of those excursions. Just

tossed the thing overboard when nobody was looking."

Grissom said, "Don't suppose you kept the receipt for that ride?"

"No. Why should I? Wasn't deductible."

Brass rose, reaching for his cuffs. Grissom, still seated on the edge of the chair, touched the detective's elbow, then—with his head—signaled for Brass to come with him.

Rising, Grissom said, "We'll be right back, Mr. Pierce. If you don't mind, we're going to borrow your kitchen for a moment."

Pierce sipped his water. "Be my guest."

The three of them adjourned to the kitchen.

"Lake Mead?" Brass said, eyes wide with fury, though he kept his voice low. "He's rubbing our goddamn faces in it!"

"No, that's good," Grissom said, with a hand gesture and a little smile. "He's cute. He thinks he's smarter than us."

"Maybe he *is* smarter," Brass said.

"Than some of us . . . maybe." And Grissom grinned sweetly, while Brass shook his head in utter irritation—only some of it at Pierce.

"You *are* going to arrest him for the pistol?" Nick asked Brass, also keeping his voice low.

"Damn right," Brass said. "That much we *do* have on the son of a bitch."

Now it was Grissom shaking his head. "It'll never hold up, Jim—you know that. There's no gun. All we really have is a receipt for bullets dated six months ago."

"He confessed to having a gun!"

"Remind me—which one of us read him his rights?"

Brass's face was red; he was breathing hard. "I can't believe this! It's crazy. Insane . . . That evil bastard killed his wife, cut her up and dumped the pieces of her in the lake. There's gotta be something here! Where's the justice?"

"No justice yet," Grissom said, gently, touching the detective's sleeve. "But there will be. Now, let's get out of here before we screw something up."

They took their leave quietly, and let Pierce have the last word.

At the doorway, he said, "I hope I've been of some small help."

Nick Stokes parted company with Grissom and Brass at HQ, and headed into the lab where Warrick had been working. He found Warrick practically spotwelded to the monitor of a computer.

"What's up?" Nick asked.

"I'm trying to track down that red triangle we found on the bag of dope at Pierce's."

"Timely," Nick said. "Pierce just copped to getting not just coke from a dealer, but a gun as well."

Nick filled Warrick in on the latest visit to the king of the Pierce castle, including the therapist's refusal to I.D. his connection.

Nick asked Warrick, "Getting anywhere?"

"Not yet . . . but I just know I've seen that signature somewhere, it's ringin' a bell . . . a distant one, anyway. I'm gonna keep diggin'."

"All right." Nick yawned. "I'm fried—Grissom had me in early today, to keep at those computer records . . . I gotta go home and catch some z's."

"It's a plan. . . . Later."

"You may want to try getting some sleep one of these days yourself," Nick said, at the doorway. "Latest thing—they say it's really catching on."

Warrick expended half a smirk. "Not around here."

Warrick Brown stayed with it, going through file after file looking at drug dealers the LVMPD had busted in the last few years. An hour later, he was still rolling through files looking for the odd little red triangle.

A knock at the doorframe took him away from his work, and he turned to see one of the interns, a young, dark-curly-haired guy named Jeremy Smith, slight of build, in a black UNLV sweatshirt and blue jeans. A criminal justice major at the university, Smith had been working part-time for the last few months, sometimes days, occasionally nights.

"Hey, Jeremy," Warrick said, mildly annoyed to be interrupted. "What's up?"

Smith stepped gingerly into the lab, as if not sure he had permission. "I talked to every glass company in the metro area—remember, to see if they replaced the driver's side window of a '95 Avalon?"

"Right. And?"

The young man shook his head. "Zip zally zero."

Warrick muttered a "damn," but the kid was stepping forward, more sure of himself now.

"Then I thought I better check the car dealerships too."

"That was good initiative, Jeremy—any luck?"

"Not really."

"Yeah. Well. Good thought, though. Thanks."

"All right, then . . . Warrick?"

Warrick sighed to himself, suddenly sorry he'd told the kid to call him by his first name.

Smith was beside the computer, now, bright-eyed as a chipmunk. "Anything else I can do for?"

Why not tap into all this energy? Warrick considered the offer for a long moment, then said, "Junkyards, Jeremy—try the junkyards."

Smith nodded, grinned. "I'm on it."

The kid was halfway out the door when Warrick called out, "One more thing, Jeremy! You ever see this before?"

The intern came back over and Warrick passed him the evidence bag with the baggie of coke inside.

Turning it over and over, Smith studied it, then handed it back. "Yeah, I've seen this mark."

Warrick knew the intern had been working a lot of days, and gave him the benefit of the doubt. "Bust you were in on?"

The intern shook his head, saying, "No, this is something I've seen on campus. . . . Small-time dealer, sells mostly grass. I don't know if he's been in the system or not."

"He wouldn't have a name, would he?"

"Well, I don't know his real name—his street

name is Lil Moe. Supposed to be once you've tried his stuff, you always want . . . a little mo'."

Warrick just looked at Smith.

Jeremy gave him a quick nervous smile and patted the air with his hands, like an untalented mime. "Hey, that's just what I heard."

"Uh huh."

"Honest, Warrick!"

Smith used some of his nervous energy to haul his ass out of there, and Warrick immediately tried "Lil Moe" in the database, coming up blank. He checked pending files and struck out again. Finally, he went in search of Jeremy the intern and found him in the break room with a phone book in one hand and a phone in the other, a notepad and pencil before him.

The kid looked up, saw Warrick, and said, "Starting on the junkyards. Some of 'em work at night, y'know. Anybody I can't talk to, at least I can have a list of numbers ready for tomorrow."

"Table that. Would you know Lil Moe if you saw him?"

"Sure."

"Help *me* know him."

"Five-nine, -ten maybe, a hundred twenty-five or thirty. Real skinny. He's got dreadlocks to his shoulders and always wears this big Dodgers stocking cap."

"Stocking cap in Vegas?"

Smith shrugged. "Makes him easy to find."

"Find where?"

"He kind of bounces around the edges of the campus . . . but he'll probably be somewhere around the Thomas & Mack Center."

Easy for students to find him, Warrick thought, and nodded. "Thanks."

"What now?"

"Junkyards."

"Junkyards," Jeremy said, and got back to it.

Warrick found Brass in his office and shared his new information.

"Lil Moe, huh?" Brass said.

"A little is better than nothing at all." Warrick stood with his hands on his hips, his eyebrows high. "You wanna go for a ride, and see if we can score?"

Brass was already on his feet. "Let's do that—even a drug dealer'll feel like a step up from Owen Pierce."

The home of the Runnin' Rebels basketball teams squatted on the far southwest corner of the UNLV campus, but the Taurus came at the Thomas & Mack Center from the campus side. The detective made the trip just below the speed limit, but not too slow. The Taurus stuck out enough without them crawling along in an obvious search. It wasn't midnight yet, and the campus hadn't quite yet gone to sleep.

People (kids mostly) dotted the sidewalks here and there, quiet students heading to their dorms, louder ones off to the next kegger, the occasional professor walking with briefcase and sometimes a young teaching aide, a few joggers working off the stress of the day in the cool of the night . . .

. . . and another strata more in the shadows, harder to see, unpredictable, even dangerous, some searching for drugs, and—more important to Brass and Warrick—some selling. On their first lap, as their eyes probed the shadows and recesses of doorways, they didn't see anyone fitting Lil Moe's description . . . and not on the second lap, either, or even the third.

By lap four, midnight had come and gone, the sidewalks had thinned, and they hadn't gotten even a whiff of Lil Moe.

"Maybe he's not out tonight," Brass offered.

"Or maybe he's making the car. Just 'cause it's unmarked, that doesn't mean Moe doesn't know a police car when he eyeballs it."

"We could disguise ourselves," Brass commented dryly from the wheel, "as cheerleaders."

"I got a better idea. . . . Let me out."

Brass just looked at him. "You have your weapon, Brown?"

"No—I don't wear it around the lab."

"We're not in the lab. You're asking to do some kind of half-assed, impromptu undercover dance, and that's not—"

"C'mon, Brass! I'm not saying leave me alone. Just back me up from a distance. Let me see if I can smoke this guy out."

"You're a criminalist, Brown—not a cop."

"And you're a middle-aged white guy. Which of us stands to score easier?"

Brass considered that. "Well, it's plain this plan isn't working."

"All right then—Plan B."

Hopping out at the corner of Harmon and Tarkanian Way, Warrick ambled down the street named after the legendary UNLV basketball coach. Taking his time, not wanting to appear anxious or in a hurry, Warrick strolled toward the arena, enjoying the cool evening. In the dusky light he could barely make out the sign for the Facilities Management Administration Building (whatever that was) across the street. Passing the single-story building, he continued inexorably toward the Thomas & Mack Center.

Warrick turned left, keeping the basketball arena on his right as he circled the building. The streetlights spaced their pools of light about every ten yards, giving a sense of security to a gaggle of passing coeds, but only made Warrick feel more like a moving target. The shadows deepened and became fathomless in contrast to the spheres of white.

He glanced up to see Brass's Taurus turning off Gym Road into the Thomas & Mack parking lot near Tropicana Avenue. Then he shifted his gaze around, as if aimlessly looking at this and that, so that anyone watching him wouldn't realize he'd been keeping tabs on the unmarked car.

The CSI had almost made it to the Jean Nidetch Women's Center when a male voice called out to him from the shadows. "Bro!"

Warrick swiveled that way but stayed on the sidewalk. He said nothing.

The voice from the darkness said, "You lookin' for somethin'? Or you jus' lost?"

"That depends. What kinda map you sellin'?"

A figure took a step closer, remaining in the shadows, but now visible as a slight, sketchy presence. "Roadmap to bliss, bro—happiness highway."

Warrick settled into place on the sidewalk. "Who couldn't use a little happiness?"

The guy took another step toward the light. Warrick got a better look at him now: a tall, gangly man in a silk running suit, a Dodgers stocking cap perched atop a tangle of dreadlocks. Just a kid, Warrick thought, maybe twenty-one tops.

"You lookin' for happiness, I got it. Just not out there, man—light hurts my eyes. Ease on down the road."

After a glance around, Warrick stepped out of the pale circle of streetlamp light, and into the shadows in front of the guy . . .

. . . who fit the intern's description of Lil Moe like a latex glove. *Long time since I hit a jackpot in this town,* Warrick thought.

The dealer was saying, "What kind of happiness you in the market for?"

"You might be surprised what makes me happy."

"Hey, bro—I'm strictly pharmaceutical . . . strange sex stuff, try the yellow pages."

"Not sex, Moe . . ."

Eyes and nostrils flared. "How you know my name? I never done bidness with you."

"Information, Moe—that's all I want."

"You want infor*mation* from me? Do I look like a fuckin' search engine? What am I, some Yahoo Google shit?"

Lil Moe snapped his fingers, and before Warrick could move, a third party grabbed his left arm, wrenched it behind him, and pain streaked up his arm, spiking in his shoulder. He heard a sharp metallic *snick,* and suddenly felt the point of a blade dimple his throat, next to his Adam's apple. He froze—and hoped to hell that somewhere Brass was watching this, somewhere *close,* calling in some backup.

"I'm gonna ask you again, homey," Lil Moe said, moving in on Warrick, the dealer's face contorted, waving his hand like a pissed-off rapper. "Why you want information from *me?*"

The knife pressed deeper, and Warrick felt the sting before something warm began trickling down his neck. Behind him, whoever held his arm was strong, and kept Warrick's hand high between his shoulder blades, the muscles stretching and ready to explode, if the assailant snapped the bone.

In front of Warrick, the young man in the Dodger stocking cap hopped from foot to foot, as if the sidewalk were a bed of coals under his expensive sneakers. "Who *sent* you, man? What's this about?"

Forcing himself to slow his breathing and to remain calm despite the situation, Warrick's mind raced over possible outcomes—most of them grim.

"I'll pay for what I want," Warrick managed.

"Oh, you gonna pay, all right! Who you workin' for? You with Danny G?"

His unseen assailant's breathing came in sharp, rapid gulps, breath hot on Warrick's neck and reeking of liquor and garlic. The assailant sucked his teeth as if trying to control his salivating over the urge to plunge the blade into Warrick's throat.

And the dealer was singsonging, "You better fuckin' talk, boy, while you got your vocal cords."

Rasping, his voice little more than a hoarse whisper, Warrick asked, "You don't wanna cut me."

Looking older suddenly, Lil Moe eyeballed the CSI, the anger shining through even in the darkness. "Aw fuck this, Tony—fuckin' *cut* him, man!"

Even as Warrick tensed for the cold invasion of steel, he felt the pressure go slack on his arm and the blade drew away from his neck. Then he heard steel clatter to sidewalk, followed by Brass's quiet voice saying, "Smart move—and I didn't even have to tell you to drop it."

Lil Moe's eyes went wild, his mouth dropped open; no words exited, but he did: spinning on his heel, he ran like a starting gun had sounded. Turning, Warrick saw his assailant, a wiry black kid, this one in baggy UNLV jersey and baggier jeans and no more than sixteen, the nose of Brass's automatic kissing the boy's right temple.

"You just gonna stand there bleeding?" Brass asked Warrick. "Or are you gonna go catch him?"

Warrick took this gentle hint, and spun and sprinted after the drug dealer.

Moe had a good twenty-yard head start. But he was also stoned and pumping his arms wildly, his knees pistoning up and down, his stride lengths varying as the drugs kept him from running smoothly. And instead of heading toward the mass of buildings to the east, where he would have had options for escape and possibly obstacles to benefit his youth, he had taken off across the vast expanse of the parking lot.

Before he'd got halfway to Tropicana Avenue,

Moe started to slow, and—by the far side of the lot—Warrick caught up and grabbed his jacket, slowing him as they both ran. "Stop! . . . It's over!"

Lil Moe fought frantically with the zipper, trying to escape the jacket and still keep running at the same time. The drugs prevented him from doing either very effectively. Suddenly lurching to the right, Moe snatched the jacket from Warrick's grasp, but tumbled, elbows and feet flying at odd angles, and he whumped onto the cement and rolled and came to a skidding stop at the parking-lot curb, in a fetal position, one hand going to his face, the other arm wrapping around ribs that were at least cracked if not broken.

Barely breathing hard, Warrick bent down over him. "That's it—there ain't no Moe."

Sweat beading on his face and looking like he couldn't decide whether to bawl or vomit, the young man stared up, all the fight gone from his face. "Okay, man, okay—so I'm Lil Moe. You five-oh?"

Warrick grinned. "Criminalist."

"What-the-fuck 'ist'?"

"Don't sweat the details—you're still in a world of trouble."

Brass strolled up, towing the other one by his elbow, the kid's hands cuffed behind him. "Brown—you caught him," the detective said, looking very pleased. "Nice job."

Touching the small wound on his neck, Warrick returned his attention to Lil Moe. "You got a customer named Owen Pierce?"

The young man was shaking his head before

Warrick finished the question. "Never heard of the dude and I ain't sayin' shit till I see my lawyer."

Looking down at the dealer, Brass asked, "You got a name?"

"Told you! Talk to my lawyer."

"He admits he's Lil Moe," Warrick said.

"What's your real name?" Brass asked.

"Lawyer me up, or kick me, Barney Fife!"

Brass sighed. "Who's your lawyer?"

Lil Moe shrugged. "P.D. my ass."

Brass rolled his eyes and Warrick felt himself growing very weary. Public defender—this was going to be a long night.

"I got Band-Aids in the glove compartment," Brass said.

Warrick said, "I've been cut worse shaving."

"Probably." Brass managed one of his rumpled smiles. "But that you can't brag about."

And they hauled the drug dealer and his scrawny "muscle" back to the Taurus.

12

AT JUST BEFORE TWO A.M., WAITING IN THE PARKING LOT for Catherine Willows and Sara Sidle, Detective Erin Conroy for the umpteenth time questioned the wisdom of her decision to apply for a police position in Las Vegas. How glamorous it had sounded, how inviting the travel books had made the desert mecca seem, how foolishly she had booked Rat Pack-era images into the theater of her mind.

Only recently had Erin admitted to herself that she missed her family—her folks, her sister and husband; and almost immediately she'd longed for the changing of the seasons. There were no beautiful autumn colors in Nevada, no leaves putting on their last mighty show before exiting to make way for the white blanket of winter—no sledding, no sleigh rides . . . and you could get hot chocolate, sure, but what was the point?

In the desert, they had . . . the sun. Winter sun, spring sun, summer sun (with the bonus of unbearable heat), and now, in the fall, just for a change of pace, more sun . . . with these cool desert nights the only respite.

Erin Conroy fought to shake off her melancholy and tried to dismiss the thought of another Christmas with no snow, no family, and not even the prospect of a New Year's Eve date.

"You all right?" Willows asked.

The homicide detective hadn't even seen Willows and Sidle exit CSI. "Uh, yes, sure, fine."

"We signed out a Tahoe—we'll follow you over."

The trio planned to call on the late Jenna Patrick's roommate, Tera Jameson.

"Oh?" Erin said.

"Yeah," Willows said, "we have to meet our video wizard, Helpingstine, back here at four A.M."

"Has an early flight out," Sidle said.

"Does he have anything good for you?" Erin asked.

"Guess we'll see."

The CSIs in their Tahoe followed Detective Erin Conroy in her Taurus through typically bustling Vegas wee-hours traffic to the three-story motel-like apartment house where Tera Jameson (and Jenna Patrick had once) lived.

Again Erin led the way up the stairs to the third floor and around the building, stopping in front of Tera Jameson's door; no light filtered through the window curtains. The detective knocked and got no answer, knocked twice more and again got no response. The three of them looked at each other for a long moment.

"She does work nights," Sidle said.

Willows raised her eyebrows. "Should we try Showgirl World, you think?"

"She isn't scheduled there tonight," Erin said. "I already checked."

"Maybe she's asleep," Sidle offered.

Erin used her cell phone, dialed the police department switchboard and got Jameson's number. She dialed again and they could hear the phone ringing, inside. Finally, the machine picked up: "It's Tera. You know the drill: no message, no call back . . . 'bye."

"We could use a warrant about now," Sidle said.

Erin left a message for Tera to contact her, then punched END and turned to start the long walk back around the building and down the stairs. "You two go on back and keep your date with that video techie."

"Gonna stake the place out?" Sidle asked.

"Maybe . . . but first, I'll think I will drop around Showgirl World and see if maybe I can't get a line on her, there. Maybe she traded shifts with somebody, last minute."

"Call us if you need us," Willows said, in step with the detective. "And sooner is better than later—Mobley's on our case about all the overtime."

Erin nodded and kept walking. She'd gotten the same memo; problem was, some nightshift work simply had to be done during the day, and there was a rivalry between them and dayshifts that discouraged helping each other out.

Soon the Tahoe was peeling off in one direction, and the Taurus in the other, as Erin Conroy drove across town, to Showgirl World . . .

. . . which was everything Dream Dolls and so many other strip clubs in the greater Vegas area wanted to be when they grew up. The exterior was black glass and blue steel, the sign a green-and-blue rotating neon globe with SHOWGIRL WORLD emblazoned across it in red neon letters that chased each other to a finish. Erin parked in the massive lot, which was almost full—though it was approaching three in the morning, that was prime time in Party Town.

She opened the door, took a step inside a foyer whose gray-carpeted walls were arrayed with framed black-and-white photos of the featured dancers and had to pause until her eyes adjusted from the brighter parking lot. With the spots before her eyes dissipating to a hard white glow, Conroy approached the doorman—a big, bald, olive-skinned, Tony Orlando-mustached ex-linebacker in a white shirt, black bow tie and tuxedo pants.

"Fifteen bucks," he said, voice naturally gruff but tone noncommittal, his eyes on hers nonjudgmentally. Erin plucked her I.D. wallet from her purse and showed the doorman her badge and a smile.

"Or not," he said, and—completely unimpressed—waved her on through.

Stepping through the inside door, Erin had to again stop and allow her vision to adjust, as the club itself was much darker than the foyer. The ventilation was better in here than Dream Dolls, but a mingled bouquet of tobacco, beer, and perfume nonetheless permeated. Techno throbbed through the sound system at a decibel level just a notch below ear bleed, and Erin could feel the beat pounding in her chest, like a competing heartbeat.

Where Dream Dolls had cheap industrial-strength furniture, Showgirl World had heavy black lacquered wooden tables surrounded by low-slung black faux-leather chairs. Each table accommodated five chairs and those along the mirrored walls squatted within partitioned-off nooks that largely screened patrons from view while allowing a full view of the stage. Even the chairs lining the stage were comfortable swivel affairs, albeit bolted to the floor.

Right now, the main, kidney-shaped stage—around and over which red and blue lights flickered in sequence—held two statuesque if bored-looking women, gyrating more or less in time to the music, occasionally draping themselves on one of two brass poles to swing their forms around, sometimes upside down. To the left, a bar extended toward the back, behind which a four-foot-high mirror ran its length. Three bartenders in tuxedo shirts and black ties worked briskly, mixing drinks and raking in money as fast as possible.

Erin approached the nearest one, a guy older than she would have expected to find working in a place like this; he was in his mid-fifties, easy, with short, neatly trimmed gunmetal-gray hair, darker-gray-rimmed glasses and the burly bearing of a cop or, anyway, security man.

Pulling out the badge-in-wallet again, Conroy asked, "The boss around?"

"We're clean, detective," the bartender said, reflexively defensive. "Everything here's aboveboard."

"That's a good answer—I just don't remember asking a question that goes with it."

He made a face. "All right, all right, don't get your panties in a bunch—I'll get him." The burly, bespectacled bartender moved to a phone on the back counter, punched a button, spoke a few words, listened a second, then hung up. He returned with his expression softened, seeming even a little embarrassed. "Boss'll be right out. . . . Look, detective, I didn't mean to give you attitude."

"I'll live."

"No, really. It's just that I used to be on the job, myself, and I know these guys run a clean joint. I just don't like to see 'em hassled."

"No problem. Vegas PD?"

The guy shook his head. "Little town in Ohio. Moved out here when I retired. Looking to get away from the midwest winters."

Conroy nodded, smiled. "Only now, you miss them. How long were you on the job?"

"Twenty-eight years."

Erin frowned, curiously. "Why didn't you stay for a full thirty?"

"They put me behind a desk and I couldn't take it. . . . *Now* look what I'm behind."

She chuckled, and a door she hadn't realized was even there, down at the far end of the bar, opened like an oven to blast a wide shaft of light into the darkness of the club, only to be sucked away as the door swung shut. A brown-haired, thirtyish, stocky man in a dark business suit approached her warily.

He glanced at the bartender, who nodded her way, then seemed to get very busy farther down the bar.

The new arrival stuck out a hand. "Rich McGraw," he said, his voice deep.

She introduced herself, practically shouting to be heard over the blare of music. She showed McGraw her I.D wallet, but the fine print was lost in this pitiful light, though the glint of her badge made its point.

"What can I do for you, Detective Conrad?"

"Conroy," she said, almost yelling, and explained the situation. A new song came on but the intensity of the volume had lowered just enough to make conversation possible, if not easy. Now and then she had to repeat herself.

"She's not here," McGraw said.

"I know—I called earlier. I don't think it was you I talked to, Mr. McGraw."

"Must not've been."

"I'm hoping to get in touch with her tonight, or tomorrow at the latest. When does she work next?"

"You tried her place? You got that address?"

"Yes, sir." Then she repeated: "When does Tera work next?"

But he shook his head. "She won't be back till day after tomorrow, earliest. Said she wanted a few days off."

A sinking feeling dropped into the detective's gut. *Where the hell was Tera Jameson? And why had she picked now to disappear?* "Say where she was going?"

Again, McGraw shook his head.

Erin wondered how he managed that so well

without the benefit of a neck. "And you don't know when she'll be back?"

"Nope. Maybe day after tomorrow." Shrug. "She's gonna call in."

In the mirror, Erin noticed that the two girls dancing to Samantha Fox were not the ones who'd been on when she arrived—a bosomy brunette and a leggy black girl were reigning over their male court.

"You seem to give Tera a lot of leeway, Mr. McGraw."

"She's popular. Exotic. She was in *Penthouse*, you know."

"No, I didn't. Could I see her dressing room?"

"She's okay, no prima donna, like some of them. So I give her leeway, yeah."

"Her dressing room?"

The oddly handsome features beamed at her. "You got a warrant?"

Erin shook her head.

He half-smiled, his expression almost regretful. "I don't mean to be a prick about it, lady, but I do have to protect the privacy of my employees—and we are talkin' about one of my star dancers, here."

"You know I'll just be back, once I've got a warrant."

He nodded. "And at that time I will personally escort you to her dressing room."

Detective Erin Conroy left the club wondering if the management had just covered for Tera; maybe the dancer was even camped out there, in a back room or dressing area. One thing the detective knew: she needed search warrants for both

Jameson's apartment and dressing room and she needed them now.

She would check with Captain Brass for his advice on which judge to wake up.

Catherine Willows was at a table having coffee in the break room, killing a few minutes while Helpingstine—who had arrived after checking out of his hotel to make a presentation of his evidence to them—got his fifty-thousand-dollar toy up and running again.

Sara ambled in, with the latest from Greg Sanders. Getting herself an apple juice from a fridge that thankfully held no Grissom experiments at the moment, Sara said, "None of the shoes from Ray Lipton's house match the prints from Dream Dolls."

Catherine couldn't find it in her to be surprised. "Did our boy Ray ditch them, y'suppose?"

Sara shrugged, sat, sipped. "Don't know . . . but what I do know is, the top print is the killer's, and Ray Lipton's shoe size is *way* bigger than the print. I'm starting to agree with you."

"About what?"

"That he's innocent."

"I didn't say he was. We don't have any evidence that proves he *didn't* do it either."

"Jeez, Cath—do you want him to be guilty, or innocent?"

"Yes," she said.

On that note, they finished their drinks and made their way down the hallway until they reached Catherine's office, where the door was open, Dan Helpingstine pushing his glasses up on his nose and waving for them to join him.

The tall, pug-nosed manufacturer's rep had his Tektive video machine all fired up, and he motioned for them to sit on either side of him. Catherine eased down on Helpingstine's left, Sara to his right, while on the monitor screen they could see the security tape from the front door at Dream Dolls.

"I spent a very long day getting to know these tapes," he said.

"Find anything?" Sara asked.

"I think so—you'll have to be the judge."

Catherine felt a spark of hope.

"This," Helpingstine said, "is your killer coming in."

They watched as their suspect moved through the door, face turned away from the camera, trying to slide through the frame quickly. The tech did his thing with the keyboard and the picture cleared somewhat. Again he separated their suspect from the surroundings and improved the picture even more.

"Freeze that for a moment," Catherine said.

Helpingstine obeyed.

"Look at the shoulders," she said. "Remember we said they didn't look broad enough to be Lipton's?"

"Yeah," Sara said slowly.

"Now look at the hips."

Helpingstine was smiling. "I was hoping you'd notice that. Men's shoulders are wider than their hips—women are the opposite."

Catherine and Sara traded significant looks, while Helpingstine unfroze the image and allowed it to move in slow motion, even as he worked on it some more.

From this high angle, they now were looking down on the figure from the side. All they could see of the head was the ball cap, an ear, the glasses, the beard and the corded muscles of the neck.

"Freeze that again!" Catherine said.

Helpingstine did.

"Can you zoom in?" Sara asked.

Catherine and Sara again traded glances—they were on the same page.

Helpingstine zoomed in on the head. Though they got significantly closer, the resolution grew worse accordingly, and it wasn't a big help.

Sara pressed closer, her nose practically against the screen, pointing. "What's that dark spot on the ear?"

The others leaned in closer too.

"I can't make anything out except a discoloration," Catherine said.

Helpingstine punched the keyboard and the ear blossomed to fill most of the screen.

"Is that just . . . pixelation?" Sara asked.

"No way," the tech said. "It's *something*—I just can't squeeze out enough res to tell *what*. Earring, maybe. Probably, in fact."

Eyebrow raised, Sara said, "Lipton doesn't have a pierced ear, does he?"

"No," Catherine said.

They sat back and looked at each other.

"Ray Lipton *is* innocent," Sara said.

Catherine nodded. "And Tera Jameson hated him."

"Well," Helpingstine said, "based upon unequivocal standards of anatomy, your killer is a female—in fake facial hair."

Catherine stood, pacing; Sara stood also, but planted herself. The wheels were turning now, for both of them.

"One of the strippers at Dream Dolls," Sara said, "told you Tera was a lesbian, and indicated Jenna was bisexual, right?"

"Right," Catherine said. "She also suggested that maybe Jenna Patrick and Tera Jameson weren't just roommates."

"But we don't have any evidence that they were having an affair," Sara said.

"Yet," Catherine said.

Sara rose. "Better call Conroy."

Catherine already had her phone out and was punching in numbers. By the time Catherine and Conroy had compared information, they came to the mutual conclusion that they needed to meet back at Tera Jameson's apartment.

"Let's roll," Catherine said to Sara.

"Conroy meeting us there?"

"Oh, yeah—with a warrant and the landlord."

But before they exited the office, Catherine went to thank Helpingstine. "Your next trip to Vegas," she said, "will be entirely on us—we may need you to testify."

"My pleasure," Helpingstine said, grinning. "Anything to get the word out about my baby. . . . Will you recommend to your superiors that they buy a Tektive?"

"Dan," Catherine said, pausing halfway out the door, "I'll recommend we invest in the company."

In the hallway, coming around a corner, Catherine and Sara almost collided with the burly, crew-cut Sergeant O'Riley.

"Just the lady I was lookin' to see," O'Riley said to Catherine, pleasantly. "Those jackets you had me tracking down—the Lipton Construction jackets?"

"Yes?"

He dug a notepad out of his breast shirt pocket, referred to a page as he said, "Twenty-six positive I.D.'s out of the twenty-seven . . . and all three that the Lipton Construction office girl had marked 'maybe' were correct. No idea about the other five . . . or the one we're short, outa the positive list."

"Nice work, Sergeant. Thanks."

He gave Catherine a little grin. "Getting along out there all right, without me?"

Catherine smiled at the big man. "Yeah—but don't think you're not missed."

"Holler if you need me," he said, and headed back toward the PD wing.

Thirteen minutes later, Catherine and Sara pulled up in their Tahoe to find Conroy standing on the sidewalk out in front of the brick apartment house, speaking with a silver-haired senior citizen in a gray sweater, white slacks, black socks and sandals.

"This is the landlord, Bill Palmer," Conroy said. "I've already apologized for bothering him, this time of night."

"Morning," the older man corrected, trembling

slightly as he shook their hands. He had wireframe trifocals, and one gigantic overgrown white eyebrow that looked like a caterpillar had died on his forehead.

"I've served Mr. Palmer with the warrant," Conroy said, "and he's about to let us in."

"Let's get on with it," Palmer said.

The three women followed him up the stairs and around behind the building. They'd made this trip enough that Catherine was considering adding it to her normal exercise routine. Palmer worked his way through half a dozen different keys—apparently there was no single master—before he finally managed to unlock the door of the apartment. Once they were inside, Conroy escorted the landlord back outside, to clear the scene, while Catherine and Sara snugged on their latex gloves and went to work.

As was so often the case in their job, they didn't know what they were looking for, exactly; so they started right there in the living room. Moving slowly, the two CSIs went over the single-armed couch, the chair, the hassock, and the rest of the living room, finding nothing of any apparent significance.

"If you take the bathroom," Sara said, "I'll take the kitchen."

"What a deal."

"I'll buy breakfast later, if you do."

"That is a deal."

In the bathroom, a gold-metal basket sat empty on the back of the toilet lid and Catherine knew at once that Tera Jameson had taken all of her cosmetics and such with her. Nonetheless, Catherine opened the medicine cabinet, but found nothing of use in there.

Whether the killer was Lipton or Tera or someone else, they would need DNA evidence on each of their suspects. Using a forceps like a spoon, Catherine dug around in the sink drain and came up with a wad of hair. Actually, she noticed two different colors of hair—Tera's and Jenna's, most likely. She stuffed it all into an evidence bags and slid over and did the same thing with the tub drain.

Sara came in from the kitchen and stuck her head in the door. "Nothing."

"Not much here either. Hair for DNA samples."

"Care for a double-team in the bedroom?"

"Sounds like more fun than it will be."

A king-sized bed with an ornate bookshelf headboard dominated the far wall of Tera's bedroom. A good-sized matching dresser stood against the left wall, a small television perched on top of it. The right wall was all closets and the wall with the door was home to a small dressing table, with a framed *Penthouse* magazine cover on the wall nearby . . . and Tera—wearing a golden chainmail outfit that most of her flesh showed through—was the cover girl.

Sara went directly to the dressing table, while Catherine started with the headboard. Dark oak and sturdy, the headboard contained two shelves and a drawer on either side. The top shelf was lined with paperbacks, mostly Grisham, King, Koontz and various other thrillers. The bottom shelf held magazines and a small electric alarm clock radio. Opening the nearest drawer, Catherine looked inside and found a tie-on seven-inch sex toy.

"Well hello, big fella," Catherine said.

"What?" Sara said.

"Have a look at this."

Sara came over and peered into the drawer. "DNA on a stick!"

Catherine snapped several photos of the device then she carefully slipped it into an evidence bag. "I'll let *you* drop this one off with Greg," she said.

Sara gave her a "gee thanks" expression, then said, "Found a couple of wigs, but nothing like the short-hair one in the security video. And no mustache, beard or spirit gum."

"Let's keep looking. There's a surprise in every drawer. . . ."

"Be nice to find a Lipton Construction jacket."

Sara went from the dressing table to the closet. The second drawer of the headboard was empty and Catherine moved to the bed. The RUVIS showed a few spots of bodily fluids on the spread and Catherine bagged the spread, too. Recently washed, the sheets were clean under the ultraviolet. Stripping off the sheets, Catherine immediately saw small dark stains in numerous places on the mattress.

Sara was pulling several pairs of jeans from the closet; these and a couple of baseball caps, she bagged, saying, "No boots."

"None?"

"Cowboy or otherwise—nothing."

After taking pictures, Catherine took scrapings from the dark spots on the mattress. It appeared to be menstrual blood, but she bagged each scraping separately.

They spent hours combing the apartment, but never found any boots or Lipton Construction jackets or any other evidence that seemed to point toward Tera Jameson's guilt.

Finally finished, they packed up their silver field kits and met Conroy and the landlord outside.

"Anything?" the detective asked.

Catherine shrugged. "Some material to send through the lab . . . then maybe we'll know more."

Conroy frowned. "No jacket? No beard?"

"No jacket. No beard."

The elderly landlord was looking at them like they were speaking in Sanskrit.

At the bottom of the stairs, a sporty black Toyota eased by them, and Catherine recognized the woman behind the wheel: Tera Jameson.

The car parked, the engine shut off, and the woman unfolded herself out of the car and started in on a brisk walk. Carrying a purse on a shoulder strap, she wore tight denim shorts, a black cropped T-shirt exposing her pierced navel, and high-heeled sandals. Her bushy brown hair was tied back in a severe ponytail.

Then she saw the little group at the bottom of the stairs and froze in mid-stride.

"Is that my stuff?" she asked, her voice shrill, angry. "What the hell are you doing with my stuff?"

Conroy stepped forward and held out the folded

paper. "Tera Jameson, we're serving you with a search warrant."

The exotic eyes were wide, nostrils of the pretty face flared like a rearing horse; she did not accept the warrant. "What the hell *is* this? I got rights like anybody else, you know!"

Conroy's voice was coldly professional. "Ms. Jameson, this warrant allows us to search your residence for evidence, which we have done in your absence."

"Evidence of fucking what?"

Catherine stepped forward and said, "Ms. Jameson, we're gathering evidence in the case of Jenna Patrick's homicide."

Tera shook her head angrily, the ponytail swinging. "You've *got* that abusive son of a bitch in custody, don't you? Why aren't you searching *Lipton's* house?"

"We have," Catherine said, calmly.

"Well . . . isn't *he* the *killer?"*

With a noncommittal shrug, Conroy said, "We have several suspects."

"Oh, and I'm one of them now? I was *working* the night Jenna was killed. Jesus! He's a crazy jealous asshole! He did it, you *know* he did it."

"Well we do know one thing for sure," Conroy said. "Lipton never lied to us."

"Right!" she laughed, bitterly. "Lie is all Ray Lipton does." Then she stopped as she realized what Conroy meant. "Wait . . . you think *I* lied to *you?"*

"I don't remember you telling us you were a lesbian."

Tera Jameson backed up a step, horrified and offended. Words flew out of her: "Why the hell does that matter? What business is it of yours? What could it possibly have to do with Jenna's death?"

Catherine asked, coolly, "Ms. Jameson—were you and Jenna involved?"

"No! We were just friends."

"We've been told Jenna was bisexual."

"Who by? That cow Belinda? That's crazy! That's nonsense! Jenna was straight—you think gays don't have straight friends? Odds are one of *you* three is a lesbian!"

"Jenna was straight?" Conroy repeated, arching an eyebrow.

"Yes, she was straight! So why should I have mentioned my sexual preference? It has nothing to do with this."

Sara asked, "So you two just lived together?"

"I told you—Jenna wasn't like that. What, you think we were a couple of teenage girls playing doctor? Get real."

"Well," Catherine said, edging past the dancer, the bagged bedspread piled under one arm, "we'll know soon enough."

"Is that my bedspread? Are you taking my bedspread?"

Catherine said nothing.

Now Tera was following them as they headed for the Tahoe. "What *else* of mine are you taking?"

"Some jeans," Sara said, casually, "some other stuff."

"Shit! You lousy bitches!"

Conroy swung around and faced the dancer. "Maybe we should take you in, too."

Tera's face screwed up in rage. "For what?"

Catherine knew Conroy wanted to say murder . . . but right now? They had no proof.

So the CSI stepped forward and said, in a friendly manner, "Ms. Jameson—you liked Jenna. She was your friend. Let us do our job. We're just trying to eliminate you as suspect . . . that's all."

Tera thought about that, and said, "Yeah, right," not seeming to believe Catherine, but not as worked up, either.

Then the dancer was heading quickly up the stairs, ponytail bouncing.

When Tera was out of sight, Catherine said, "Greg had better come through for us, or we might find ourselves on the crappy end of the lawsuit stick."

Conroy sighed. "Thanks for playing diplomat, Catherine—I was kind of stepping over the line, there. And with the mood Mobley's been in lately, I don't want any part of pissing off the sheriff."

"I hear that," Sara said.

But Catherine knew it was worse than just department politics. Detective Erin Conroy had taken in one bum suspect, and doing that a second time could make the case practically impossible to prosecute . . . if they ever got that far. Any decent defense attorney would make mincemeat of them for arresting two wrong suspects—talk about reasonable doubt—and Jenna Patrick's killer, whoever he or she might be, would walk smiling into the sunset.

"Well, if I can't come up with something solid,"

Conroy said to the CSIs as she helped them load up the SUV, "you ladies better find it for me, somewhere in all this evidence we've been gathering . . . and soon."

Then the detective went to her Taurus, and Catherine and Sara to their Tahoe, to head back. The sun was coming up, and another shift was over.

13

THE NEXT NIGHT'S SHIFT HAD BARELY BEGUN WHEN Warrick Brown stuck his head into Grissom's office, waving a file folder. "Lil Moe's real name is Kevin Sadler."

Grissom looked up from files of his own. "The pusher you busted? What was that about? Bring me up to speed."

Warrick remained in the doorway. "Sadler's a two-bit dealer, done some county time, never handled enough weight to go the distance."

"And this has to do with our case how?"

Warrick offered up a sly smile. "Sadler stamps his bags with a little red triangle."

"Like the bag of coke we found at Pierce's?"

"Exactly like."

Grissom rocked back. "So—does this mean we have a new suspect?"

Warrick leaned against the jamb. "You mean, did Owen Pierce hire this scumbag to off his wife? Or maybe did Owen and his connection have a falling out, and Lynn Pierce caught the bad end of it?"

Impatiently, Grissom said, "Yes."

"No," Warrick said. "Sadler was in lockup for three months—grass bust. Just got out."

"Just?"

"Two days after Lynn Pierce went missing."

Grissom made a disgusted face. "Didn't take him long to jump back into business. Well, at least you got him off the street. . . . What's next?"

"Gris, Little Moe's *not* a dead-end."

"There's mo'?"

Warrick actually laughed. "That wasn't bad, Gris. Anyway, just two short years ago, Sadler was a baseball player at UNLV. Guess who his physical therapist was?"

Grissom's eyes glittered. "Does he live in a castle?"

"How's this for a scenario? Kevin Sadler, aka Lil Moe, enters his new, lucrative line of chemical sales. And maybe his physical therapist is not just a member of the Hair Club for men . . ."

Grissom frowned thoughtfully. "He's the president?"

Warrick shrugged a shoulder. "People who come to massage therapy are hurting—and massage isn't cheap. Pierce pulls down seventy-five an hour for a session . . . so he's obviously attracting a clientele who could afford recreational drugs to help ease their pain."

Still frowning, Grissom—already on his feet—asked, "You run this by Brass?"

"Oh yeah—more important, he's about to run it

past our friend Kevin . . . which is to say Moe." Warrick checked his watch. "They should be heading into the interrogation room about . . . now."

Through the two-way glass they could see the slender, dreadlocked Sadler, in one of the county's orange jumpsuits, sitting sullenly at the table, a bandage on his forehead. Seated beside him was Jerry Shannon, the kind of attorney who was glad for whatever scraps the Public Defender's office could toss his way. Short and malnourished-looking, the attorney looked superficially spiffy in a brown sportcoat, green tie and yellow shirt, which on closer inspection indicated his tailor shop of choice might be Goodwill.

Brass was on his feet, kind of drifting between Sadler and his attorney, whose arms were folded as he monotoned, "My client has nothing to say."

Warrick and Grissom exchanged glances: they'd encountered Shannon before; low-rent, yes, threadbare, sure . . . but no fool.

Brass directed his gaze at Sadler, and with no sympathy, asked, "How's the ribs?"

"They hurt like a motherfucker!" Sadler said, and grimaced, his discomfort apparently no pose. "I'm gonna sue your damn asses, police brutality shit. . . ."

The skinny attorney leaned toward his client and touched an orange sleeve. "You don't have to answer any of the captain's questions, Kevin—including the supposedly 'friendly' ones."

"You prefer Kevin, then?" Brass asked. "Not Moe?"

The dealer looked toward his lawyer, then back

at Brass, blankly. Shannon leaned back in his chair, folded his arms again, smiled to himself.

Brass was saying, "Found a lot of grass on you last night, Kevin—not to mention the coke and the meth, and the pills. County just won't cover it. This time you're gonna get a little mo' yourself . . . in Carson City."

Trading glances with his attorney, Sadler tried to look defiant and unconcerned; but the fear in his eyes was evident.

"You positive you don't want to answer a few questions for us? Help us out?"

"Hell no! You—"

But Sadler's attorney had leaned forward and touched that orange sleeve again, silencing his client.

Pleasantly, Shannon inquired, "And what would be in it for my client? If he 'helped you out.' "

"That would depend on the answers he gives," Brass said.

Shannon shook his head. "You want Kevin to answer your questions, and *then* you'll offer us a deal? That's a little backwards, Captain Brass, isn't it?"

Brass shrugged. "Fine—we can let the judge sort it out. What do you think, Kevin? You're young enough to do ten years standing on your head—you won't even be all that old when you get out."

"Captain Brass," Shannon began.

But Sadler shook the attorney's hand off his sleeve and said, surly, "Ask your damn questions."

Brass took the seat next to Sadler. He even smiled a little as he asked, "Kevin—last night you told us you didn't know Owen Pierce . . . was that true?"

Sadler's forehead tightened in thought.

"I guess ten years isn't such a long time," Brass said, reflectively. "You might even be out in five. They even have a baseball team at Carson City—how is the knee, anyway?"

Sadler got the message, and shook his head, disgustedly. "I only know him *that* way . . . Pierce worked on my knee, some. That's it. End of story."

Brass rose, and looked toward the two-way window.

"That's my cue," Warrick said to Grissom.

Moments later Warrick entered the interrogation room waving a clear evidence bag; carrying it over to Sadler, Warrick let him see the bag within the bag, the red triangle winking at him. "How did this end up in Owen Pierce's house, if he was just your physical therapist?"

The attorney said, "Pierce could've got that from anybody. There are countless sources in this town."

Warrick showed the bag to the attorney, now. "But those sources don't use this particular signature. . . ." And now the CSI turned toward the dealer. "Do they, Kevin?"

Sadler turned away from Warrick's gaze.

"Were you paying Pierce in coke, Kevin?" Warrick pressed. "Is that how it worked? Him tradin' you physical therapy for his chemical recreation?"

The dealer settled deeper into sullen silence.

"The hell with this!" Brass said, roaring in off the

sidelines. "Kevin can rot in jail for the next decade or so—that's a given." The detective leaned in and grinned terribly at the sulky face. "But I will promise you this, Mr. Sadler—when we put Pierce away for murder, I'll find a way to latch onto you as an accessory."

Brass motioned with his head to Warrick and they headed toward the door.

"Accessory?" Sadler blurted, his eyes wide, batting away his lawyer's hand. "Hey, man I ain't accessory to shit!"

Brass stopped, his hand on the knob. "Did you know Lynn Pierce?"

"I never even met the wife. I was never over there when she around—mostly we did business at his office."

Brass strolled back over. "What kind of business, Kevin?"

Sadler looked at his attorney a beat too long. They had him.

"I seen the papers and TV," Sadler said, tentatively. "Is she . . . missing or, she dead?"

"Mrs. Pierce?" Brass said, conversationally. "Dead. Cut up with a chain saw."

That stopped Sadler, who blew out some air. "Man, that is cold. . . . I had nothing to do with that. You sound sure he did it . . ."

Warrick said, "If he didn't, we want to prove that, too."

Sadler snorted a laugh. "Yeah, right—I forgot all about where the police was into justice and shit."

Tersely, the attorney said, "Kevin, if you *must*

speak . . . think first. And check with me if you have doubts about—"

"I'm on top of this," Sadler said sharply to Shannon. Looking from Brass to Warrick and back, he said, "That stuff last night . . . the blade and all—that was goin' no place. You dig? That's just, you know—theater."

Warrick, who still had a small Band-Aid on his neck, said, "Theater."

"Yeah—people got to take this shit serious."

"Dealing, you mean."

Sadler shrugged. "Anyway, I never killed nobody. I scare people if I have to—to buy me, you understand, *street* cred."

Brass said, "Kevin—when your knee went south, and you dropped out of school, and entered your new line of work . . . did Owen Pierce help you line up clients by introducing you to certain of his patients?"

". . . If I answer that, it'll help clear up this murder? Won't be used to nail my sorry ass to the wall?"

Brass said, "All we want is Lynn Pierce's killer. I'm a homicide captain—I don't do drugs."

"That's a good policy," Sadler admitted. Then, smiling broadly, the dealer said, "It is a sweet deal—his clients, my clients, got a lot in common, y'know: money and pain."

"Are you and Pierce still in business together?"

"Oh yeah, we tight—ain't shit could come between us. I even let him borrow my boat."

Brass's eyes widened. "*You've* got a boat?"

"Yeah," Sadler said, misreading the detective's reaction. "What, a brother can't own a boat?"

Warrick asked, "What kind of boat is it?"

"Three hundred eighty Supersport. That is one fast motherfucker, man."

Brass again: "And you let Pierce borrow it?"

"Sure . . . We might come from different places, but, hey—we understand each other, 's all 'bout the benjamins, baby. Hell, he even kept an eye on my crib while I was in the lockup—brought my mail in, let the housekeeper in and shit."

"This was during your recent vacation with the county?"

"Yeah—I only jus' got out. Don't you got that in your computer?"

Leaning in alongside the dealer, Brass said, "Kevin, you seem to have heard about Lynn Pierce's disappearance."

"Yeah. I don't live in a fuckin' cave."

Warrick, seeing where Brass was going, dropped in at the young man's other shoulder. "Then you heard about the body part that was found at Lake Mead?"

"Yeah, sure, I . . ." Once more, Sadler looked from Warrick to Brass and back again, this time with huge eyes. "Oh, shit . . . are you sayin' he used *my* boat to . . ."

The attorney said, "Kevin, be quiet."

"Your good friend Owen Pierce," Warrick said, "made an accessory-after-the-fact out of you."

"But I was in jail!"

"An accessory doesn't have to be present, just help out—lend a boat, for example."

The attorney said, "Gentlemen, I think my client should confer with me before this goes anywhere else."

But Brass said, "How would you like a pass on the drugs?"

Sadler said, "Hell, yes!"

And his attorney settled back in his chair, silently withdrawing his demand.

"Then," Brass continued, "give us the address and key to your house, and the location of your boat."

Sadler frowned. "Just let you go through all of my shit?"

"That's right—and we don't need a search warrant, do we? After all, you're going to be a witness for the prosecution."

Shannon was way ahead of his client, leaning forward to say to Brass, "And anything you might find, beyond the purview of your murder investigation, goes unseen?"

Brass thought about that, then glanced at the two-way glass.

Moments later, Grissom entered the interrogation room, conferred briefly with Brass, who then said, "We can live with that."

Sadler looked at his attorney, who was smiling. Shannon said, "So can we, gentleman," with a smugness not at all commensurate with how little the lawyer had had to do with the deal.

* * *

Gil Grissom, Jim Brass, Nick Stokes and Warrick Brown—the latter behind the wheel—rode together in one of the black SUV's, their first stop the Quonset hut–style storage building where Sadler kept his speedboat. One of half a dozen adjacent cubicles, the oversized shed was at the far end of a U-Rent-It complex not far from where Sadler lived.

Warrick dusted the metal door handle for prints, but the CSI found nothing; no surprise, as the desert air caused fingerprints to disappear sooner than in more humid climes.

With that pointless task completed, they swung the overhead door up and moved inside to have a look at the drug dealer's very expensive boat. With no electricity in the garage, they compensated with flashlights. Forty-feet long, the sleek white craft was crammed into the shabby space with barely enough room to shut the door, a beautiful woman in a burlap sack. Triple 250 horsepower Mercury motors lined the tail and, as Brass played his beam of light over the engines, he let out a long low appreciative whistle.

"Fast boat," he said.

"If you say so," Grissom said, eyes on the hunt for something pertinent.

Nick and Warrick climbed up into the craft while Brass and Grissom remained on the cement floor. Warrick started at the stern, Nick in the bow, and they worked toward the center. To the naked eye, the boat appeared pristine, and the lingering scent of solvent and ammonia suggested a fresh cleaning.

"When was the last time Sadler had the boat out?" Nick called down.

Shining his flashlight on his notebook, Brass said, "If our charming cooperative witness can be trusted, right after the Fourth of July. He was in lockup most of the time after that."

Nick glanced back at Warrick. "Then where's the dust?"

"Boat's way too clean," Warrick said, shaking his head. "Ask me, somebody used it, and cleaned it."

From below, Grissom said, "Don't ask yourself—ask the evidence."

Nick and Warrick dusted the controls and the wheel for prints. Everything had been wiped. Opening the fish box, Nick shone his beam inside and saw that it too had been hosed clean.

"There's nothing here," Warrick said finally. "There'd be more dust and dirt if it had come straight off the showroom floor."

"Keep at it," Grissom said, working the cubicle itself.

Up in the boat, the indoor/outdoor carpet covering the cockpit floor was a mix of navy, light blue, and white swirls. Even on his hands and knees, with the beam of his light barely six inches off the deck, Warrick doubted he would see anything even if it was there. Fifteen minutes of crawling around later, he had proved himself correct.

Nick jumped down onto the cement, nimble for the big guy he was. "I don't know what to say, Grissom."

Grissom's smile was barely there. "Remember the old movies when the Indians were out there, about to attack? 'It's quiet . . .' "

" 'Too quiet,' " Nick finished, with a nod. "And this is too clean, way too clean for sitting as long as it's supposed to . . . but we can't find anything."

Grissom's head tilted and an eyebrow hiked. "If a dismembered body was disposed of from the deck of that boat, Nick—what should we expect to find?"

Nick smiled, nodded, went to Warrick's field kit, picked out a bottle and tossed it up to him.

"Luminol, Gris?" Warrick called down. "You don't really think he cut her up on the boat, do you?"

"I don't know," the supervisor said. "I wasn't here when it happened . . . see if anything's *still* here that can tell us."

Nick walked forward to where Brass stood with his arms crossed.

"I thought we had the bastard," said the detective.

Shrugging, Nick said, "Grissom's right—the cuter they think they are, the smarter they think they are, the surer a bet that they slipped somewhere." He looked down, his gaze falling on the end of the trailer. "Anybody dust the hitch?"

Brass looked at him, a tiny smile beginning at the corners of his mouth. "Not yet."

With the luminol sprayed over the cockpit, Warrick turned on the UV light source. He moved from bow to stern on the port side: nothing; going the opposite way on the starboard side, Warrick made it as far as the console before he saw the first glow . . .

. . . a fluorescent dot.

His breath caught and he froze, willing the tiny green spot to not be a figment of his imagination.

Two more drops to the side, one more on the gunnel, and Warrick knew he was seeing the real thing. Retracing his steps to the center of the boat, he opened the fishbox. Though it had appeared clean at first glance, it now had a tiny fluorescent stripe on the bottom, against the back wall. One bag of body parts had leaked, he thought.

"Got blood," he called down, coolly. "Not much, but it'll give us DNA."

Grissom smiled at Brass. "If Lynn Pierce's dismembered body took a trip on that boat, we're going to know."

Removing the tape from the trailer hitch, Nick shone his light on the tape to reveal a nice clean thumb print. "Got a print off the trailer hitch!" he called.

The quartet locked up the garage feeling pretty good about themselves—they knew to a man that they were finally making progress in this frustrating case.

"Next stop," Grissom said, "the home of Kevin Sadler."

"And more puzzle pieces?" Nick asked.

"Maybe," Grissom admitted. And then he went further: "Maybe enough pieces to tell us what picture we're putting together."

The house, a rambling ranch in need of repair and paint, squatted on one of those side streets that never made it into the "Visit Vegas!" videos, much less the travel brochures.

Brass unlocked the door and the CSIs moved in, carrying their silver field kits in latex-gloved hands, their jobs already assigned by their supervisor, the detective ready and willing to pitch in on the search. Nick took the kitchen, Grissom the bedroom and bathroom, Brass the living room, and Warrick the basement.

Arrayed with contemporary, apartment-style furnishings, many of them black and white (the walls were pale plaster), the place was tidy, perhaps—like the boat—too tidy. On the other hand, Sadler had been away for some months, and only recently returned; so it was not surprising that the place had been cleaned while he was away (while watching the place, Pierce had let the housekeeper in, the dealer had said), nor was it startling that Sadler hadn't had time yet to get it very dirty, since.

The television in the living room was smaller than a Yugo—barely; next to it, stacks of electronic equipment thumbed their noses at Brass, who knew what little of it was. A large comfy-looking white leather couch dominated the center of the room with chairs set at angles facing the television on either side. Thick white pile carpeting squished beneath the detective's feet, the type that particles of evidence could hide themselves away in; still, Brass knew there was little hope of finding any evidence in here, which (he also knew) was why he'd drawn this room in the first place.

In the bedroom, on the nightstand, Grissom found an ashtray full of smoked joints and, in a drawer of the nightstand, a large resealable plastic bag full of grass. As he went through the closet, Grissom began to realize he wasn't going to find anything to help him in here. He had hopes for the bathroom, but found nothing there, either. To his surprise, luminol showed no blood in the tub . . . or the sink. . . .

In the kitchen, Nick found some blood in the drain, as if someone had washed it off their hands. And luminol showed a few spots of blood in the sink. He took samples of all of it, but found nothing else.

"You're gonna wanna see this!" Warrick called from the basement.

They trooped downstairs, an eager Grissom in the lead. The windowless room was illuminated by a single bulb dangling from the ceiling, *Psycho*-style. In the far corner, a shower head was attached to the wall, feeding a drain in the floor a few feet away. Though a curtain rod made a square enclosure, the shower curtain was long gone, bits of it still entangled in the metal rings of the rod.

The latter detail struck Grissom as possibly significant.

Next to the shower, a large sink was mounted on the wall, with a toilet along the same wall beyond that, no walls around any of the fixtures.

With the others looking on, a calm but focused Warrick said, "I sprayed the shower, the floor, the sink and the toilet with luminol."

No one said anything as the lanky CSI turned on the UV light. Nor did they speak when the entire room seemed to supernaturally fluoresce before them, freezing even these seasoned investigators into shock.

Shaking his head, Brass finally said, "Oh, my God . . ."

His expression grim, Grissom hung his head, the vision of it playing before his closed eyes.

Pierce has a key to the house. He comes down here, into this cement dungeon, with the body of his wife. He places her in the shower like the lump of flesh she's become, and goes back upstairs for his chain saw. Soon, he returns, and fires it up. . . .

Trying to keep the mess to a minimum, he begins a one-man assembly line, cutting off a piece of his dead wife, then cutting off part of the shower curtain—with scissors?—and wraps it up like a piece of meat from the grocery store. Then he puts the pieces in garbage bags, taking care to weight down each bag—rocks? sink weights?—before he ties it off.

All the time he's doing this, Pierce has no emotional response to the fact that he's chopping up his wife. It's a job—nothing more. He has had so many bodies stretched out before him on his massage tables that the human body has no surprises for him—bones, muscles, fat, his fingers know them all so well.

If anything, he takes a grim satisfaction that he's obliterating Lynn's identity, this new identity, this born-again prude who replaced the woman he married. It somehow isn't enough to just kill her—she had been so concerned with spiritual matters, so obsessed with the heavenly world beyond this one, well, he would just relieve her of that cumbersome suit of flesh, removing it from existence: no body, no Lynn.

He also relishes outsmarting the police. If they somehow do come after him, and he is cornered, he will blame that squalid little dope dealer.

"Sadler did it," he will say. "Drug deal went bad for him, and he was desperate for cash—and I owed him money, and couldn't pay up."

But Sadler was in jail, when your wife disappeared, *the cops would say.*

"That's what Sadler thought you would think," he says. "The perfect alibi—but he had one of his 'homeys' do it for him."

And of course the police will believe him—in Pierce's mind, who wouldn't take the word of an upstanding white citizen over that of some black drug dealer?

But even dead, Lynn proves to be a pain in the ass—she pisses him off one last time, when he tries to slice through the pelvis, and the saw jams up in the bone, dragging the intestines out as he pulls the saw free. He feels foolish, for a moment, supposed expert at anatomy that he is.

But the moment passes, and before very long, he's finally finished down here. He cleans up the blood, making a thorough job of it, convinced he's left no traces for investigators to find. He loads up his SUV with his chain saw and his bags of "meat," hauls the saw and the bags over to Sadler's boat in the nearby storage shed, takes the boat out under the cover of darkness, onto Lake Mead, and rides around the rest of the night, dropping bags—and a chain saw, and maybe a gun—over the side.

The only thing Pierce misses is that one of the bags has a pinhole leak, dripping blood in the fishbox, on the deck, and on the gunnel before he finally gets it over the side. His subsequent thorough cleaning of the boat cannot remove these blood trails; but he does not know that.

Nor does the anatomy "expert" foresee the pelvic piece,

still filled with gas, breaking free from its weighted bag, starting for the surface only to be caught up in the anchor chain of the Fish and Wildlife worker, Jim Tilson.

All Owen Pierce knows is that he has one last thing to do: he must turn himself into a distraught husband unable to find his runaway wife.

Grissom wondered where the body had been when they were in the house that first night. Had Pierce already brought his wife's remains here? And where had Lynn's car been during all of this?

He asked Warrick, "You got pictures and scrapings?"

"Doing it now," Warrick said.

"Nick," Grissom said, "you help him in here. Also, check upstairs for scissors Pierce might have cut the curtain with. Take a sample of what's left of those curtains, too."

"On it," Nick said.

"Jim," Grissom said, "you want to come with me?"

"Where to?" Brass asked.

"Outside—one more thing I want to check."

Around behind the house, invisible from the street, sat a small clapboard shed of a garage, barely big enough for a car and a few tools. It had two old swing-out wooden doors held together with a chain and padlock.

"You have the key for this?" Grissom asked.

Using the key ring Sadler had provided, Brass tried one key after another until, on the fifth attempt, the lock gave. Each of them grabbed a door and tugged. Slowly, rusty hinges protesting, the doors swung open.

No car occupied the dirt floor and only a few tools hung on the wall around the place; seemed Sadler wasn't much of a handyman. In the far corner sat a rusted garbage can. Striding over to the dented receptacle, Grissom poured flashlight light down into it. Shiny glints winked back at him. "I think I just found the driver's-side window of Lynn Pierce's car."

"Anything else?" Brass asked as he joined Grissom at the trash can.

Bending over, Grissom withdrew a wadded-up piece of paper, which he carefully smoothed out in a latexed palm. "Receipt for a replacement window for a 'ninety-five Avalon." Grissom flashed a smile at the detective. "Paid cash at a U-Pull-a-Part junkyard."

Brass wasn't smiling, though, when he said, "You think he'll have cute answers for all of this?"

"Why don't we call on him, and see?"

14

AT THE START OF SHIFT, SARA SIDLE FELT SHE HAD drawn the short straw—Catherine was on her way to Showgirl World to serve the warrant on the dressing room, while Detective Conroy was heading back to Dream Dolls to reinterview Belinda Bountiful and the other strippers—again. That left Sara to supervise the lab work at HQ, in particular following up on anything Greg Sanders might have come up with. With Grissom, Warrick, and Nick all tied up with the Lynn Pierce case, she felt like a ghost haunting the blue-tinged halls of CSI.

In particular, she hoped to take care of one frustrating detail. They had been trying to track down the Dream Dolls private-dance cubicle carpeting ever since Jenna Patrick's body had been found. Ty Kapelos provided Sergeant O'Riley with the name of the cut-rate retailer who sold it to him. O'Riley'd been having difficulty getting in touch with the retailer, a guy named Monty Wayne, who ran a small discount business in the older part of downtown.

"Guy's been on vacation," O'Riley told Sara yesterday, "and his only other employee is this secretary whose English ain't so hot."

But this evening, upon getting to work, Sara found, on her computer monitor screen, a Post-it from O'Riley saying Wayne was back from his vacation. Even better, the retailer had provided his home number, saying it was okay to call up till midnight.

Sitting behind her desk and punching in the numbers, Sara tried to fight the feeling that she was spinning her wheels while everyone else on the CSI team was doing something really productive, not to mention more interesting. The phone rang twice before it was picked up.

"Wayne residence," a rough-edged male voice intoned.

"Mr. Wayne?"

"Yes."

"This is Sara Sidle, Las Vegas P.D. criminalistics. You spoke to Sergeant O'Riley, earlier?"

The voice brightened. "Ms. Sidle, yes . . . been expecting your call. How can I be of help to the police?"

"Sergeant O'Riley spoke to you about this carpeting in the back of Dream Dolls—"

But Wayne was all over that, wall to wall: "Oh yeah, I remember that shit. And it *was* shit—that Kapelos character got it cheap because I could barely give the stuff away."

"Why is that?"

"Came from this manufacturer in South Carolina—Denton, South Carolina. I used to buy a lot of stuff from them, but they been slipping. I took these two rolls as a sample."

"Would you know if anybody else locally carries it?"

"Hell, I doubt it. I happen to know I was their only Vegas client, even in their heyday. And now, hardly anybody buys from Denton anymore . . . might say they're hanging on by a thread."

He seemed to be waiting for her to laugh; so Sara forced a chuckle, and said, "Please go on, Mr. Wayne."

"I doubt if there's any more of that cut-rate crap in the state, let alone the city."

"Thanks, Mr. Wayne. Would you have the Denton manufacturer's number?"

"I already gave it to that Sgt. O'Riley, and I don't have it at home. Why don't you check with him? He and I went over pretty much the same ground."

Probably including the "hanging by a thread" gag, she thought; but she said, "Well, thank you, Mr. Wayne, you've been very cooperative," which was true.

He said it was his pleasure and they said goodbye and Sara hung up, quickly dialing O'Riley's desk; she got the message machine so she tried his cell, catching him in his car on his way to the aftermath of a convenience store robbery.

"Yeah, I talked to Goldenweave in Denton,"

O'Riley said. "They didn't sell that carpet to anybody else in Vegas, or even in the southwest. Is that helpful?"

"Could be," she said, thinking about it, the carpet suddenly seeming to Sara like the fabric version of DNA.

Finally feeling a little spring in her step, she bounced over to Greg Sanders in his lab, but found him sitting in a chair by a countertop, not working on anything, not even goofing off with a soft drink or video game or anything . . . just sort of sitting morosely.

"I was kind of hoping you might have something for me," Sara said from the doorway.

But the spiky-haired lab rat just sat there, as if he hadn't heard her.

She waited for a moment, then said, "Greg? Hello?"

He didn't move.

Finally, she went to him, placing a hand on a shoulder of his blue smock. "Greg, what is it?"

Shaking his head, he looked at her. "This stripper case of yours . . . I hate it."

"You hate it."

"Can you believe that? A case involving exotic dancers, and I'm longing for a decomposing corpse or maybe another skinned gorilla."

Sara pulled up a chair and sat beside him. "Be specific."

His sigh lifted his whole body and set it down hard. "Okay—you bring me enough raw evidence to fill a warehouse, and yet I get nothing from the prime suspect, but a ton of stuff from all the coworkers. I mean, they've all been in that room . . . but Lipton? Never. And there's enough DNA in that cubicle to start an entirely new species, only none of it belongs to him."

"What about the roommate?"

Greg turned to look at her, eyes narrowing. "Yeah, I was gonna ask about her."

"Why's that?"

"Well, first understand that there's carpet fibers on the clothes of all those Dream Dolls dancers—any of them, all of them could've been in that private dance cubicle at any time."

"We knew that. What's that got to do with the roommate? Tera Jameson?"

Greg offered her a palm, to accompany the only halfway interesting information he had: "She's got the carpet fibers on her stuff too."

"Hmmm. She's our other good suspect."

Greg brightened. "She is?"

"Yes . . . but she used to work at Dream Dolls, herself."

"Oh. Her DNA's in the mix, too, by the way."

"Could be the same reason. You get anything from the mattress or the sex toy?"

Another sigh. "Doing that next. I believe this is the first time you've brought me a vibrator."

She smiled a little but, heading for the door, said only, "Don't go there, Greg."

Sanders managed his own little smile, before his expression turned serious as he returned to his work.

Sara, on her way to the office, had the nagging feeling she'd missed something, that the puzzle pieces were all before her now, and she wasn't quite putting them together.

Detective Erin Conroy and Pat Hensley sat on metal folding chairs in the dressing room at Dream Dolls, a few of the dancers in various stages of undress milling about, applying expensive makeup and cheap perfume. Pat's alter ego, Belinda Bountiful, didn't go on for another half hour, and she was relaxing, enjoying a cup of coffee; so was Conroy, keeping it casual, not even taking notes.

Her back to the dressing table, almost plain without makeup, the garishly redheaded Hensley wore a low-cut lime top that shared much of her ample cleavage with the world; her jeans were funkily frayed and form-fitting, and she was barefoot, her toenails bloodred. But it was the Dolly Partonesque cleavage that kept attracting Conroy's attention.

Catching this, Belinda said good-naturedly, "If you got it, honey, flaunt it. I paid good money for these and I intend to get a whole lotta mileage out of 'em."

The refreshing bluntness of that made Conroy laugh. Then she said, "We were talking about Tera Jameson."

"Right. What else can I tell you?"

"Is Tera's sexual preference widely known in your circles?"

Hensley shrugged. "She don't advertise it, but she doesn't hide it, neither."

"What about Jenna?"

Hensley sipped her coffee. "She *didn't* advertise it."

"That she was a lesbian?"

"No. Anyway, like I told that other female dick, the other day—Jenna liked both flavors."

"She was bisexual, you mean."

"Yeah, I said that before. What are you getting at?"

Conroy chose her words carefully. "Another friend of hers claims Jenna was strictly straight."

Hensley smirked. "Couldn't have been somebody who knew Jenna very well."

Conroy sat forward conspiratorially. "What if I told you it was Tera Jameson herself who made that claim?"

"I don't care if Oprah told you: it's a crock. Tera's lying. Why, I have no idea."

"*Were* Tera and Jenna having an affair?"

"Well, they *did* have one . . ."

"Right up to the time of Jenna's murder?"

"No—it was over months ago. They still roomed together, but Jenna told me, in no uncertain terms, that she and Tera were history. Still friends! But history."

"Because of Ray Lipton."

Hensley nodded. "Jenna fell hard for the guy. . . . You mind if I start putting on my makeup?"

"Not at all."

Hensley turned her back to the detective, began

applying her makeup, and talking to Conroy in the mirror. "I can see why Tera didn't like Ray, though."

"Because he stole Jenna away?"

"Well, yeah, I guess, but . . ."

"Because he was a hothead?"

"That, too—though Lipton was mostly talk. I saw him do stuff like grab Jenna, by the wrists, y'know? But never hit her or anything."

Conroy kept trying. "What else didn't Tera like about Ray Lipton?"

"He looked down on Tera . . . he was very, what's the word? Provincial in his thinking. To him, it was perversion, girls with girls."

In the dressing room mirror, Pat Hensley was turning into the garishly attractive Belinda Bountiful. Conroy asked, "Pat . . . Belinda—this is important. Are you sure Jenna and Tera were involved, romantically? Sexually?"

A laugh bubbled out of the stripper. "Oh, yeah—I know for a fact!"

"Are you saying . . ."

Now the stripper turned and looked at the detective dead on. "Don't spread this around, okay? I got a husband, and two kids. But I work in a kinda bizarre line of business, you might have noticed, and I don't always see things, or do things that . . . conventional society would put their stamp of approval on."

Knowing the answer, Conroy asked, "How do you know Tera and Jenna were involved, Belinda?"

And Pat *was* Belinda now, when she said, "'Cause one horny drunken afternoon, girlfriend, I let the two of 'em make a Belinda Bountiful sandwich . . . that's *how* I know."

Taking a long swig from her coffee, Detective Erin Conroy smiled.

"You like our Dream Dolls coffee, huh? It's not bad, for a dive."

"Not bad at all," Conroy said, rising, placing the empty coffee cup on the dressing table. "Delicious, in fact."

Almost as good, Conroy thought, *as catching Tera Jameson in another lie.*

In the dimly lighted, smoke-swirling cathedral of skin that was Showgirl World, Catherine Willows—in a black leather coat, canary silk blouse and black leather pants—stood at the mirrored bar and waited, her silver field kit on the floor next to her.

The music pounded and a blonde pigtailed dancer in a schoolgirl micro-mini-skirt outfit was up on stage, toward the start of her set, and a few other girls in lingerie were meandering through the audience, even though the place was barely a quarter full, an early evening lull.

The bartender, a fiftyish guy in gray-rimmed glasses, came back from the telephone. "Mr. McGraw will be right out."

"Thanks."

A blade of light sliced into the darkness from the left, bouncing like a laser off the mirrors, and then as quickly disappeared. Stocky Rick McGraw—in a dark blue suit and lighter blue shirt without a tie—emerged from his office." "What can I do for you, Detective?"

"Crime scene investigator," she said, handing him the search warrant. "I'm here to search the dressing room."

The stocky club manager slipped the folded paper into the inside pocket of his suit without a glance. "Sure."

Catherine lifted one eyebrow and showed him half a smile. "You told Detective Conroy you wouldn't let her search the place without a warrant."

A small shrug. "And you brought one."

"Tera Jameson been in today?"

"Here now, but doesn't go on for a while. Wasn't scheduled—filling in for a sick girl." He gestured. "She's working private dances. You need her?"

"No. The night Jenna Patrick died, over at Dream Dolls—Tera worked that night, right?"

"Yeah. I told the cops all about it."

"Tell me again."

"Well, she was here, all right. We were kind of shorthanded, and she wound up doing sets at the top of every hour, for a while there."

"Do you have any kind of record of that? Is there a sheet that logs which dancers went on and came off when . . . that sort of thing?"

"What do you think? They sign in, they sign out; that's the extent of it."

"But you would testify she was here all night?"

McGraw nodded. "Six P.M. to three A.M."

Shaking her head, Catherine sighed and asked, "Dressing room in the back?"

"Yeah." He gestured toward the back with his head. "Don't you want me to round up Tera for you?"

Glancing this way and that, not seeing the Jameson woman anywhere, she shook her head. "Just the opposite. I wasn't planning on her being here. . . . Keep her out, while I'm in there, if you can."

"See what I can do. . . . No promises."

Only two dancers occupied the dressing room when Catherine—lugging the silver field kit—entered. Back here, the accommodations weren't much better than those of Dream Dolls. It didn't matter how nice a club was, the dressing rooms were all the same.

The nearest dancer was touching up her makeup. She gave Catherine a noncommittal nod in the mirror, her wide brown eyes sizing up the competition.

Catherine asked, "Tera Jameson's table?"

The dancer nodded toward the back. "She has the whole rear stall—she's a *star,* y'know." Turning from the mirror to look Catherine up and down, rather clinically, she added, "I didn't know she had a new squeeze."

Catherine said, "I'm with the police," and flashed the CSI I.D.

"And that makes you straight?"

Catherine arched an eyebrow. "The Jenna Patrick homicide?"

Now the woman got it, but she didn't seem to much care. "I didn't know her," she said, turning to herself in the mirror.

The other dancer had flopped onto one of the sofas, on her back, and was smoking a cigarette; she looked bored beyond belief.

At the far end, Tera had given herself some privacy by moving in a small clothes rack of her own, which she'd positioned as a wall between her and the next station. A window onto the rear parking lot was next to her table and obscured from view of the rest of the dressing room by that same clothing rack. Her makeup table and mirror was at right, while across the way—where there had once been another makeup station—another small rack of clothes was hanging with shoes below.

Tera's station itself was neatly organized. The chair was pushed in under the table, makeup case closed and sitting on the left side of the table, a box of tissues on the right corner nearest the mirror, a towel folded in quarters in front of it, another draped neatly over the back of the chair. The routine was readily apparent to someone who had once been in the life. Catherine eased into the latex gloves and went to work.

The makeup kit looked more like a jewelry box with a lid that flipped up and three drawers down the front. The top opened to reveal some small jars and brushes, and lipsticks laid in a neat row in a padded section on the right side.

But among the jars of nail polish and makeup, Catherine found a bottle of spirit gum.

Pleased, she bagged that and moved to the top drawer, where she found more lipsticks, rouges, bases, and powders. The second drawer contained much the same thing and Catherine wondered how much makeup one dancer needed. In the bottom drawer, she saw a stack of fashion magazines; she almost shut it again, then stopped and removed the magazines, and—crammed down under them—found a fake mustache and beard.

The beard/mustache combo looked as though it could match the rayon fibers they had found at Dream Dolls. With a satisfied sigh, Catherine bagged this major find and set it on the makeup table.

Catherine casually flipped through the garments on the rack nearest the station. She knew how it improbable it was that the Lipton Construction jacket would be hiding out here in plain sight, but she had to look. The circumstantial evidence was mounting, but she could already hear some lawyer saying Tera had decided to imitate her friend Jenna's old man act, and that's why she had spirit gum and blah blah blah.

But if that jacket turned up here, that would really sell a jury. . . .

She tried the other clothes rack and found nothing but stripper attire; however, when she checked down below, looking through the shoes, hoping to find a pair of man's boots, she noted a small suitcase and a matching train case. Pulling them out from where they'd been tucked away, Catherine snapped the suitcase open and found various street clothes; the train case held, among other things, the cosmetics that had been missing from Tera's bathroom this morning.

Suddenly Catherine knew this was Tera's final night at Showgirl World. The woman would gather her last night's wages—and this week's check, due tonight—and book it out the window to the parking lot.

Catherine punched Sara's number into her cell phone.

"Sara Sidle."

"It's me. I found spirit gum and the fake facial hair. There's even a damn window right by Tera's dressing table, for her to slip out of."

"Wow! Why did she keep that stuff around? Why didn't she dump it?"

"She's here now," Catherine said. "Maybe I'll ask her. You touch base with Conroy lately?"

"Yeah, I'm in the car with her now, heading your way. Conroy wants to question Jameson."

"What do *you* have that's new?"

"Greg's done with the tests on the evidence from the woman's apartment," Sara said. "Seems the sex toy has Jenna's DNA on it, and the menstrual blood stains from the mattress? They're from *both* women—Tera and Jenna, sharing a bed."

"So Tera's lover dumped her for a guy," Catherine said. "Ray Lipton, a homophobic hypocritical hothead. Tera decides to get even and kill her unfaithful lover, then frame the interloping boyfriend."

"She could have it all," Sara said.

"It's a motive," Catherine said, "but we still need something to tie her directly to the killing—beard isn't going to be enough."

"Look," Sara said, "keep Tera there till we get there."

"I had better," Catherine said. "She's a definite flight risk. Bags are packed here at the club . . . next to that window."

"Give us ten minutes. Oh yeah, one more thing Greg found—rug fibers from the lap-dance room at Dream Dolls turned up on jeans we took from Tera's apartment."

"Okay. I'll see you . . ." Catherine's voice trailed off. Then she said: "We've *got* her. She *did* it."

"Huh? How so?"

Catherine smiled into the cell phone. "If there were fibers from the private dance room at Dream Dolls, on Tera's clothes? She's guilty."

"But Tera worked there, too!"

"Yeah, she worked there *before* that carpeting was laid. Tera left Dream Dolls three months ago, and hadn't set foot in the place, since—or so she said."

"And the carpeting went in *two* months ago!"

"That's right. We've got her."

Sara spoke to Conroy, bringing her up to speed.

Suddenly Conroy was on the phone. "Keep Tera busy, if you can. Don't play cop: I'll make the arrest."

Cell phone back in her purse, Catherine returned to the makeup station to gather her things, but the plastic bag with the beard had slipped to the floor.

When Catherine bent to retrieve it, she looked under the table and saw a vent in the wall near the floor. Pulling out her Mini Maglite, she shone the beam at the screws and saw that the paint on them had been freshly chipped. From her field kit she got a small screw driver, and crawled under the table to unscrew the four screws; then she pulled off the grate.

Inside the vent lay a dark garbage bag. She pulled it out and allowed herself a little smile as she opened it. In the bottom of the bag were the Lipton Construction jacket and the men's boots Tera had worn that night.

And now Catherine could see it happening, in her mind's eye . . .

. . . back in her quiet corner of the dressing room, Tera tapes down her breasts and dresses in clothes similar to Lipton's. She shoves her hair up under a ball cap, glues on the fake beard and mustache and dons the dark glasses and the Lipton Construction jacket that she'd obtained from either one of his workers or a customer. She opens the window, watches for a quiet moment, drops into the parking lot where her car waits. Then, in drag, she drives to Dream Dolls, and somehow coaxes Jenna into the back room—either the disguise fooling the dancer in the dim lighting, or Jenna titillated by her former lover's masquerade.

Once in the lap-dance cubicle, Tera slips the electrical tie around Jenna's neck and yanks it tight. She watches the woman who betrayed her squirm in pain, then die.

Leaving the club, Tera returns—still in drag—and parks in the Showgirl World rear lot, waiting for the right moment to slip back through the window into the club, where she removes the disguise and hides the beard under some Vogue*'s and the jacket and boots in the vent. Soon she is to be back on stage, entertaining the masses, never having left the club.*

When the police come to her apartment, she puts on the act of the grieving former roommate, certain that the plot will work and Ray Lipton will spend the rest of his life in prison.

In building her alibi, Tera had run so tight a timetable that the damning evidence—the fake facial hair, the jacket, the boots—had been stowed away at Showgirls, for future disposal. But with cops coming in and out of the club, and all these eyes on her, Tera hadn't yet dared sneak them out.

Catherine bagged the jacket and the boots, and then she closed up her field kit and gathered everything—it was quite a haul—and set them on the floor next to Tera's station. Toward the front of the dressing room, the black dancer was about to go out in a silvery nightgown over silver bra and thong.

"Are you on next?" Catherine asked her.

"In about half an hour. I'm gonna go out and stir up some business, first."

Catherine showed her a five-dollar bill. "A favor?"

The dancer snatched the fivespot out of Catherine's fingers, then asked, "What?"

"Just go out there and see if Tera's occupied."

The dancer shrugged, went out, came back in less than a minute.

"She's giving a private dance. Way down on the end—it's a separate room, but no door. Slip out past the bar during a song, and she probably won't see you. Between songs, she might."

"Thanks."

Catherine lugged the evidence outside and locked it in the Tahoe. As long as Tera hadn't seen her, Catherine wasn't worried about the woman splitting—she was giving a private dance, and still had no idea that Catherine was even on the premises, let alone what evidence the CSI had found.

With the Tahoe locked, Catherine checked the magazine on her pistol and reholstered it. Maybe she wouldn't be making the arrest herself, but Catherine knew she was dealing with a killer. She glanced up the street, saw no sign of Conroy and Sara, and decided she better get back inside.

Inside again, she stopped at the bar where that fiftyish bartender was using a damp cloth on the countertop. She said to him, "Detective Conroy tells me you're an ex-cop."

The guy nodded.

"You know who I am?" she asked him.

"CSI."

"That's right. If there's trouble, what are you going to do?"

He eyeballed her for a long moment. "Call 911."

"Right answer."

He absently wiped his cloth over the bar. "Is there gonna be trouble?"

Shrugging elaborately, Catherine said, "Anything's possible."

"I've heard that theory."

Catherine instinctively liked this guy—not too excitable, no nonsense, just the sort of mentality needed in a place like this. "Detective Conroy and another CSI are on their way here now."

The bartender waited for the rest.

"When they arrive, tell them I'm in the private room." She pointed at the doorless doorway down on at the far end.

"No problem . . . Tera's in there now, y'know, with a couple patrons of the arts."

"Yeah."

"She in trouble?"

"Oh yeah."

Again he wiped the towel over the bar. "Wish I was surprised."

"But you aren't? Everybody else seems to like her."

He shook his head. "They're not paying attention. She's a wrong chick, and I'm not talkin' about her sexual inclination. It's just . . . her train don't run all the way to the station."

Catherine smiled. Cops never stopped being cops, retired or not. "Can you make something happen?"

"Try me."

"I don't want any other dancers and customers going in that room. Not till I come back out, or Detective Conroy goes in."

"I can do that."

Several moments later, Catherine slipped inside

the private-dance room, which was much bigger than the closet at Dream Dolls. It was actually more semi-private, able to accommodate two "private" dances at a time; the music in here was strictly from the outer club, leaching in through the doorless doorway—"I'm Not That Innocent," Britney Spears. Two black faux-leather booths without tables were in there, so a dancer could essentially enter the booth and entertain; mirrors covered the walls, and right now no one occupied the table nearest Catherine.

In a red jeweled g-string and nothing else, Tera danced in front of the other booth, though her image danced on all of the mirrored walls. Catherine stepped forward so that the two guys sitting at the table could see her. They were burly guys wearing cheap suits, blue-collar bozos at a bachelor party maybe, one with a buzz cut, the other with longish dark hair. Tera turned her backside to her audience, looked at Catherine, nothing registering on the exotic features, and kept dancing.

"You want to join in, honey?" the longhaired guy asked when he spotted Catherine.

"You're a little overdressed, ain't ya?" the buzz cut wondered, and laughed drunkenly.

The criminalist said nothing, just leaned against a mirrored wall and waited; Conroy would be here soon, and if Tera wanted to dance the time away, that was fine with her.

But Britney Spears had run out of protestations about her innocence, and as soon as the song finished, Tera stopped dancing, and smiled coolly at the guys. "More?" she asked them; she had numerous bills stuffed in the side of her g-string.

"What about your friend?" the buzz cut asked, nodding toward Catherine. "Get her to join in!"

That was enough: flashing her ID, Catherine walked over and said, "You two have had enough fun."

The two burly guys exchanged looks and decided she was right, and split, leaving Catherine and Tera alone, just as a new song came on.

"I'm working," Tera said, and flipped the greenbacks at the side of her g-string with a red-nailed finger.

"Not at the moment, you aren't."

Tera put her weight on one leg and smirked humorlessly at Catherine. "I have to get ready to go on. . . . I promised a guy . . ."

"How much is a table dance?"

"Twenty-five."

Catherine took a twenty and a five from her purse and held them out.

Tera's full lips pursed in a smile. "I *said* one of you three cops would be gay . . . didn't think it was you, though. . . . What's your name again?"

"Catherine."

Swaying seductively to the music, Tera asked, "Are you on duty, Catherine?"

"No," Catherine lied. "I just . . . had to see you again."

Still undulating, keeping time with her body, Tera smiled, and danced closer and closer to Catherine. Speculative. Unaware, and drawing closer, Tera leaned in, her lips almost close enough to Catherine to kiss her. Through the doorless doorway, Catherine could see the ex-cop bartender pointing the way, and Conroy (Sara just behind her) barreling through the club, a hand going to the pistol on her hip.

Just before their lips seemed about to touch, Catherine said, over the din of the throbbing music, "I know you did it."

Tera's eyes popped open, and she froze.

"I found the jacket in the vent, the beard under the *Vogue*s."

The stripper took two quick steps back, like she'd been punched. "No . . ."

"Yes. Fibers on your jeans prove you were at Dream Dolls that night. It's over, Tera."

On cue, Debbie Harry stopped singing, while Conroy stepped into the mirrored room, reaching behind her to pull out her cuffs; Sara Sidle entered and stepped up alongside the detective. Catherine saw Tera's eyes narrow, sensed the woman was about to act, and reached out . . .

. . . but the stripper was too fast for Catherine, and whirled to grab Sara by the wrist, and—showing surprising strength—flung Sara into Conroy, knocking the two women into the wall behind them, smashing into one of the mirror panels, shattering the glass.

In the outer club, the bartender was rounding up patrons and herding them out into the parking lot.

Just as the mirror broke, Sara's head careened off the wall; then she fell forward to the floor in a semiconscious heap, the deadly glass falling behind her like sheets of barely melting ice. Conroy stayed on her feet somehow, and was trying to pull her pistol. Neither woman seemed to have been cut, some part of Catherine's brain noted, even as she got to her feet and whipped the pistol off her hip, filling her hand, pointing it at Tera, who swiftly, nimbly snatched up a long shard of glass.

As Conroy turned to face her, the stripper—clutching the shard like a knife, unafraid of cutting her own hand—jammed the jagged glass into the detective's shoulder, and reflexively Conroy dropped her gun. Pain etched itself on Conroy's face, as she slumped to the floor, clutching her bleeding shoulder.

Sara Sidle pushed herself up to her hands and knees, fragments of glass sliding off her back, and looked up to see Tera grabbing Conroy's pistol off the floor. Still battling the pain reverberating in her skull, Sara reached for the pistol on her belt. Just as her fingers touched it, she felt something cold and metallic against her temple.

"Freeze."

Her back to the open doorway, Tera clamped onto a handful of Sara's hair and pulled the CSI to her feet. Sara opened her eyes to see Catherine standing directly before them, her pistol drawn and aimed at a spot just past Sara's head. *They had solved a murder,* Sara told herself; *they'd been so close to success and in just a few seconds, it had all gone so wrong. . . .*

That was when it dawned on Sara that these might be her last few seconds on Earth.

Catherine Willows pointed her automatic at the fierce-eyed woman holding Sara hostage. With

Conroy in the way before, Catherine hadn't been able to drop the hammer on the dancer. And now . . . now . . .

"Easy or hard, Tera," Catherine said, as matter of factly as possible. "Your choice."

The stripper held Sara in front of her, only a sliver of her face showing from behind Sara's skull. For all the confidence she was projecting, Catherine knew she didn't have a prayer to make this shot.

"Drop the gun, Catherine," Tera said, "and let me walk out of here . . . or this skinny bitch dies."

"I can't do that." Catherine glanced at Conroy who was on her knees to Tera's left. The injured detective slumped slightly forward, her good hand digging under her coat.

Tera pressed the gun harder into Sara's temple. "They say the second time is easier than the first . . . and the first time? Wasn't hard at all."

Slowly Catherine shook her head. "You know we can't just let you walk out of here."

"Sure you can, Catherine." Those exotic eyes were unblinking, and very, very cold. "Drop the gun—now."

Catherine swallowed thickly, sighed, and said, "All right, all right . . . you win."

"I thought I might."

Bending at the knees, Catherine held the gun slack in her hand, leaning toward the floor, about to put the weapon down. That was when Conroy's hand came out of her coat and she shouted, *"Tera!"*

The stripper spun, roughly dragging Sara with her. When Tera saw something metallic in Conroy's hand, she fired—not at Sara, but at Conroy, the bullet striking the detective in the chest, sending her sprawling backward, her hideaway spare pistol tumbling from her hand.

At the same instant, Sara had ducked to her left, the pistol explosion deafening her, the muzzle flash practically blinding her. But as she went down, she managed to jam her elbow into Tera's ribs, breaking the stripper's grip on her, creating a slice of daylight between them.

Catherine's pistol spoke.

Tera made a brief, strange cry as the bullet entered her chest, mist erupting from her torso, the shot straightening her, momentarily, before collapse came. The murderer of Jenna Patrick was dead before she hit the floor, leaving Catherine Willows—with a gun in hand—to look at her own dazed reflection in the wall of mirrors opposite.

After kicking the pistol away from Tera, Sara reached down and sought a pulse, but found nothing. She turned to see Catherine bending over Conroy, and moved to join them.

The detective opened her eyes, closed them, opened them again. "Well, *that* hurt!"

Nodding, Catherine said, "You gave me a scare . . . didn't know you were wearing your vest."

Wincing in pain, Conroy's good hand went to her chest. "The suspect?"

"Dead."

"Good." Conroy, helped to her feet by Catherine, added, "Politically incorrect as it may be . . . I say she deserves what she got . . . Sara, you okay?"

Sara, helping Catherine guide Conroy to a chair, said, "Fine—thanks to you two. How's your shoulder?"

"Not so good," Conroy said, the cloth around the wound blood-soaked. "Fingers are numb. You wanna call an ambulance?"

"Why don't I do that," Sara said and disappeared.

Catherine brushed a strand of hair out of Conroy's face. "Just sit there—stay quiet. Ambulance will be here soon."

"You know, I've been thinking about quitting . . . going back home to be closer to my folks?"

"You think now's a good time to be talking about this?"

Conroy shrugged with her one good shoulder. "I think maybe I'll visit my folks, and then come back to work a while. Before I decide."

"Good plan," Catherine said, humoring the woman, who was clearly already in shock.

Sara returned. "Bartender called nine-one-one when he heard the first shot. Ambulance and backup should be here any second."

Catherine rose and went over and knelt beside the sprawled-on-her-back lifeless body of the dancer.

Catherine Willows had rarely bothered wondering what her life would be like today, if she hadn't gotten out of these damn clubs and into college and CSI. But now, looking at Tera Jameson looking back at her with dark dead eyes, Catherine couldn't help but see herself there, on the floor, a lovely woman turned by a bullet into a piece of meat.

Or did places like Showgirl World and Dream Dolls turn women into pieces of meat, even without bullets?

She rose.

Sara asked, "You okay?"

"You know me—never doubt, never look back."

Nonetheless, inside of her, Catherine Willows wondered if she had just killed a part of herself.

15

THE MOON HAD TURNED THE EVENING AN IVORY-TINGED shade of blue; a few lights were on in the Pierce stronghold, both upstairs and down, the curtained windows emanating a yellowish glow.

Warrick Brown and Nick Stokes, in the Tahoe, drew up at the curb just as Jim Brass and Gil Grissom were getting out of the Taurus. Catching up with the detective and their supervisor, Nick carried his field kit, but Warrick—like Grissom—brought nothing but himself, as Brass led the way up the walk that curved across the gently sloping, perfect lawn. The detective rang the bell, the rest of them gathered on the front stoop like trick-or-treaters who'd arrived a bit early for Halloween.

The door opened on the first ring, as if they'd been anticipated; and Grissom—at Brass's side—found himself face-to-face with a young man he did not recognize. None of them did, in fact.

Brass tapped the badge on his suitcoat breast-pocket, saying to the kid, "Would you tell Mr. Pierce he has company?"

"I'm sorry, sir, but he's not here right now." He was a clean-cut, slender, tallish black-haired boy of sixteen or seventeen, in a green Weezer T-shirt, Levi's and black-and-white Reeboks. "Mr. Pierce has gone to pick up some carry-out."

"I see."

"But he should be back in a few minutes. . . . I don't know if I should let you in . . . but you could wait out front. . . ."

Grissom asked, "Who are you, son?"

An easygoing smile crossed the young man's pleasant face; the kid seemed familiar to Grissom, though he remained certain he'd never seen him before. The boy's response explained that: "Why, I'm Gary Blair."

Brass said, for the benefit of Nick and Warrick, "Your folks reported Mrs. Pierce's disappearance."

Gary nodded.

"And you've been dating Lori?"

"Yes." The kid looked from face to face of the crowded little group on the doorstep. "I guess it would be okay if you wanted to come in. . . . Like I said, Mr. Pierce'll be back in just a few minutes."

They flowed into the foyer, all of them standing around uneasily.

"Is Lori home?" Brass asked.

"She's upstairs changing her clothes. We're going out after dinner. She should be right down . . . why?"

Grissom could sense Brass's uneasiness. On the way over, the detective had mentioned that he didn't like the idea of arresting Pierce in front of his daughter, but saw no way around it.

With this in mind, Grissom suggested, "Maybe we can catch Mr. Pierce at the restaurant."

Picking up on that, Brass asked the boy, "Where did Mr. Pierce go to pick up the carry-out?"

Gary shrugged, shook his head. "All I know is, he's going for Chinese."

The muffled sound of the garage door opening ended this exchange, and Grissom and Brass traded glances—they knew the arrest would have to go down in front of the kids.

Her hair now a garish orange, as if her head was on fire, Lori came trotting down the circular stairs in gray sweat pants and a Fishbone T-shirt of which the bottom six inches had been cut haphazardly off to reveal her pierced navel and flat stomach. Though she looked less Goth, her blue eyes were again held prisoner within black chambers of mascara.

To Jim Brass it seemed that every time they visited this house, the daughter had taken another step away from the conservative religious beliefs of her late mother. He hoped she could find some sane middle ground, once they got her into foster care.

Lori and her boyfriend trailed after, as Brass led the CSI team into the kitchen, to meet Pierce as he came in from the garage, his arms laden with paper bags, his back to them as he shut the door, the unmistakable aroma of Chinese food accompanying him.

When he turned, the therapist's dismayed expression told them their presence in his kitchen was no surprise: he had seen the SUV and the unmarked car parked in front of his house . . . again.

Pierce, in a blue sweatshirt and black sweatpants, set the brown bags on the kitchen counter, and waited for what he knew would be coming.

And it came: "Owen Pierce," Captain Jim Brass said. "I'm placing you under arrest for the murder of Lynn Pierce."

"You're making a mistake," he said. "You're needlessly ruining lives, when you have nothing to go on but supposition."

Grissom said, "We've just been over at Kevin Sadler's house."

Pierce went ghostly, ghastly pale, and he leaned against the counter, as if to keep from collapsing.

Grissom continued: "The basement, the broken glass in the garage, the receipt, we have it all."

Lori ran to her father, and there was no accusation, just pained confusion in her voice, as she said, "Dad! What's he *talking* about?"

Pierce opened his arms and she filled them; he patted his daughter's head as she wrapped her arms around him, his eyes going to Brass, then Grissom. He seemed about to say something comforting to the child, but what came out was: "They're arresting me for killing your mother."

Gary Blair swallowed, and staggered over to a chair and sat at the kitchen table, slumping, leaning his elbows on the table and catching his face in his palms; his eyes were wide and hollow.

"It's not true," Lori said.

Slowly he shook his head. "It *is* true. . . . I hated her, Lori. I'm sorry."

His daughter drew away and stared at him, eyes huge within their black mascara casings, shaking her head. "You can't be serious. . . ."

"She kept pushing and pushing. Do I have to tell *you* how she was? Jesus this, Jesus that—I finally had enough of her. We loved her once, Lori, both of us . . . but you know as well as I that she was a different woman. . . . I shot her."

The girl drew away from her father's arms, and somehow her eyes grew even larger. "What?"

He reached out and took her by the arms and pulled her back to him, so he could look in her face. "You have to understand, Lori—*I shot her*. You have to accept that."

Brass, who had never before heard a more bizarre confession, looked sharply at Grissom, who seemed lost in thought.

Lori Pierce was shaking her head; across the room, at the kitchen table, her boyfriend was covering his face with one hand, as she said, "No, Daddy, no."

"Yes!" Pierce said. "You have to accept it. I shot her and—to protect myself—I did a terrible thing. I got rid of her body. . . . Don't make me say how."

Tears began to stream down the girl's cheeks, making a mess of her mascara; she was trembling as Pierce pulled her to him again, holding her, soothing her.

Brass got on his cell phone and called Social Services. Soon he clicked off, muttering, "Damnit," and turned to Grissom. "There's no field agent available now."

Grissom winced. "That means juvenile hall."

His daughter still weeping against his chest, Pierce—his eyes flaring—snapped, "I won't have you putting her in jail!"

"It's not jail," Brass began.

"Yes it is," Pierce said, biting off the words.

Brass did not argue; the father was right.

Gary spoke up. "She can stay at our house, in the guest room."

Brass thought about that, said, "What's your number, son?"

The boy gave it to him, Brass punched the numbers in, and soon had Mrs. Blair on the line.

"A social worker will be around in the morning," he told her, "first thing."

"We'll be glad to look after Lori till then," Mrs. Blair said.

With that settled, Nick accompanied the girl upstairs for her to pack an overnight bag.

With his daughter gone, Pierce—seeming strangely calm now, to Grissom . . . shock?—turned a penetrating gaze on the seated Gary Blair. "I need you to watch out for my daughter, Gary."

Gary said, "Yes, sir."

Grissom noted that the boy did not seem to have lost any respect for Pierce, upon learning the man had shot his wife and butchered her body for disposal.

Pierce was saying, "I know it's a lot to ask."

Gary rose, and when he spoke, his voice had surprising authority. "Don't worry, Mr. Pierce—I'll take care of her."

They all stood around awkwardly until Lori and Nick returned, Lori carrying a backpack and a small suitcase. Dropping the bags, the girl again ran to her father, throwing her arms around him, desperately. The pair hugged tightly, Pierce again telling his daughter that he loved her.

"It's going to be all right, Lori," he said. "I have to pay for my crime."

Nick accompanied Gary and Lori to the door, and Brass kept tabs through a window as the clean-cut boy and the Goth-punk girl walked hand-in-hand down the sidewalk, then crossed the street to a blue Honda Civic parked there, which soon pulled away.

Brass turned and faced Owen Pierce and gave him his rights. The therapist held out his hands, presenting his wrists.

"I'm supposed to cuff your hands behind your back," Brass said. "But if you're going to be cooperative . . ."

"When have I not been?" Pierce asked.

The guy had a point. Brass allowed Pierce to keep his hands in front of him for the cuffs, then led him out to the Taurus and put him in the backseat. Grissom climbed in front with Brass while Nick and Warrick got back into the Tahoe.

As they followed the Taurus back to CSI Division, a troubled Nick asked, "What the hell was that about?"

The normally unflappable Warrick, whose own

expression was dumbfounded, shook his head. "Weirdest confession I ever heard."

"In front of his damn *daughter!* Why would he do that?"

"I don't know," Warrick admitted. "Just being honest . . . better to hear it from him than somebody else. I guess."

"It's sick."

With a shrug, Warrick dismissed the subject. "Hey, can't ever tell what they're going to do or say, when they finally get busted."

Grissom joined Warrick and Nick behind the two-way mirror to watch as Brass led a low-key Pierce into the interrogation room. Brass turned on the tape recorder; a uniformed officer was in the corner manning the digital video camera.

Brass asked, "Your name is Owen Matthew Pierce?"

"Yes."

"And you've been advised of, and understand, your rights?"

"Yes."

"And do you wish to make a statement?"

"Yes." There was a long silence before Pierce spoke again. "My wife Lynn and I had an argument."

"Go on," Brass said.

"We'd been arguing a lot lately."

"I see."

"Her religion, it drove us apart. She almost died, or thought she almost died, anyway, and made some sort of . . . deal with God or Jesus." He shook his head, numbly. "When we were younger, she was great. Beautiful. Used to say she'd try anything once. The sex was unbelievably hot. . . . She'd do anything."

Nick and Warrick, behind the glass, exchanged glances; Pierce discussing his wife in these terms, during the confession of her murder, was both inappropriate and weird. Grissom, on the other hand, showed no reaction—a hand on his chin, he was studying Pierce like a bug.

"I mean *anything,*" Pierce was saying, and he was smiling now, reminiscing, "with *anybody.* We got into some wild shit over the years, and we both liked it."

"Is that where the drugs came in?"

Pierce pressed his hands flat on the table, sighed, the smile fading. "Yeah . . . back when we were swinging, we used to get high, grass, pills, but the most extreme thing we did was coke. In fact, it was the drugs that made Lynn get religion."

"You said before she got religion when she almost died."

"That was the drugs. She O.D.'d on some coke, had a seizure, I took her to the emergency room . . . it came out fine, but she freaked anyway. Next thing I know, she's going to church every twenty minutes and yammering about my almighty soul."

"Describe what happened on the day of your wife's death."

"We argued."

"Tell it in detail."

Another sigh. "Well . . . we argued. Lynn wanted

to send Lori to some private school, some religious institution, in Indiana. Lori didn't want to go, and I was against it, too. Lori could never stand up to her mother, so I was the one who took her on. Anyway . . . the argument escalated."

"Why did Mrs. Pierce want to send Lori away?"

Pierce shifted in his seat. "Before Gary Blair came along, Lori was pretty wild—Lynn found grass in her room, once, and she was dating some rough boys. That's when the talk started, about this Jesus school."

"This has been an issue for a while?"

"Yes. Maybe six months. Lori started going to church, dating Gary, to please her mother. But it wasn't enough: Lynn still wanted to ship her off to holy-roller class, to get her 'closer to God.' Lynn wanted to turn Lori into a goddamn clone of herself!"

"And you didn't buy that."

"Well, of course I didn't want my daughter to become the same uptight, judgmental asshole my wife had turned into."

"So—the argument escalated. Go on."

"We were yelling at each other, and Lynn went out to the garage, kind of . . . saying she didn't want to talk about it anymore. She'd made her mind up and that was that, and if I tried to stop Lynn, she'd . . . turn me in for my own drug use."

"Were you still using?"

He nodded.

"Please state that, Mr. Pierce."

"I was still using drugs."

"The argument moved into the garage?"

"Yes . . . yes. Lynn said she wanted to go for a drive to get away from me, but I wanted to settle the issue." Pierce closed his eyes, his head sagged forward. "I had a gun hidden in the garage . . . I felt I needed protection."

"Who from?"

"Kevin Sadler. Lil Moe, they call him. My connection, my dealer. I owed him money. That's why I had a gun."

"All right. Go on."

Pierce shrugged. "I went and got it from my toolbench, where I kept it. I pointed it at her, just to scare her, really. Told her not to leave or . . . She said I was a sinner and would go to hell. That's when I shot her."

"Where was Lynn, Mr. Pierce? Standing there in the garage, when you shot her?"

He shook his head. "No. Lynn had already gotten into the car and started it. I shot her through the driver's side window."

"Then what?"

Shrugging, Pierce said, "Well, hell—I panicked. I knew I had to get rid of the body. In my job, I know a little about anatomy; I'm not squeamish about anything to do with the human body. With Lil Moe in jail, I figured I could use his house, without anyone finding out."

"When did you do this?"

"That same night, late. As soon as I shot her, I put Lynn's body in the trunk, wrapped in an old tarp in the garage, and cleaned up the car, and drove it over to Lil Moe's. Put it in the garage, there. Then I walked to a commercial area and caught a cab and came back home, just before the Blairs showed up, pounding on my door, looking for Lynn. . . . See, I didn't want Lori to know what I'd done, obviously . . . and I'm always home for dinner. So I came home, and went back to Lil Moe's well after dark. I drove my SUV on that trip."

"Then what?"

"I carried Lynn inside the house, down into the basement and . . . cut her up with my chain saw." Finally Pierce's cool mask began to crack; tears started rolling down his face, though he didn't seem to notice. "I wrapped her up in the shower curtain, or anyway pieces of it, then put the . . . packages in garbage bags, along with the chain saw. I folded the bloody tarp up and put it in another bag. I used rocks from a garden nextdoor to Lil Moe's to weight them down. After that I spread more garbage bags on the floor of the SUV and put her in there. I picked up Lil Moe's boat . . . there's a trailer hitch on my SUV . . . and went to Lake Mead. I just rode around dropping bags into the lake until they were all gone. It was . . . peaceful. A beautiful night."

"Is that all?"

Pierce sagged. "Isn't that enough?"

Soon a uniformed officer came in to escort Pierce away, while Brass joined the CSIs in the adjacent observation room.

"How's that for chapter and verse?" Brass asked, pleased with himself.

Grissom said nothing, his face blank but for a tightness around his eyes.

"What's the matter, Gil?" Brass asked, a bit exasperated. "He copped to it! Life is good. We got the bad guy. Which is the point of the exercise, right?"

Grissom twitched something that was almost a smile. "We got *a* bad guy . . . but we don't have Lynn Pierce's murderer."

"What? Gimme a break! The son of a bitch confessed."

"The 'son of a bitch' lied," Grissom said.

Warrick stepped up. "That was one elaborate lie, then, Gris. . . ."

"Like all effective fiction, it had elements of truth. . . . For example, he cut up the body all right, that part of the confession was true. He just didn't kill his wife."

Nick's eyes were tight and he was smiling as he said, "You notice he didn't start crying, till he talked about cutting her up? Killing her, he was cool as a cuke."

Brass looked like somebody had poured water on him; of course he looked like that much of the time. Still, his aggravation was obvious as he said to Grissom, "Do you have any idea how much I hate it when you do this to me?"

Grissom smiled his awful angelic smile. "I hate to be the bearer of bad news, Jim . . . but the evidence doesn't lie."

"People do," Nick said.

"Pierce does," Warrick said.

Brass held up palms of surrender. "Okay—tell me why."

Grissom's expression turned somber. "Pierce said he stood outside the car and shot his wife through the car window, correct?"

"Yeah."

"We know from our tests that there was hardly any glass *inside* the car, and the blood was confined to the driver's seat. If Lynn Pierce had been shot from the outside, the glass would have blown in and her blood would have been splashed and spattered all over the passenger side of the car. And he said it happened in the garage. That garage was clean."

Brass's face managed to fall further. "So we still have a killer out there?"

"Yes," Grissom said with a nod. "But we know who it is."

"We do?" Brass asked.

Warrick's expression, and Nick's, asked the same question.

Grissom raised a lecturing forefinger. "You recall when we arrested Pierce, he made that drawn-out, unnatural confession to his daughter?"

"I'll say we recall," Warrick said. "Nick and I both thought that was way beyond weird."

Grissom asked, "And why would a father confess to murdering mommy, in front of darling daughter, unless . . . ?"

Nick's eyes popped and his head went back, as

he got it. "Unless they were getting their *stories* straight!

"Damn," Warrick said. "And right under our nose."

"We need to go back to the castle, one last time," Grissom said. "The queen is dead, and the king is covering up for the princess."

16

By this time, Catherine and Sara were back. Grissom took the two into his office, where they filled him in on the wrap-up of their own case. Both of them looked a little shell-shocked, and Grissom told them to take the rest of the night off.

"You'll talk to the psychologist tomorrow," he told Catherine.

"Great," she said with a humorless smirk.

"And then the shooting board."

"It was righteous," Sara said, shaking her head.

"I'm sure. Go home, you two, and get some rest."

Catherine was studying Grissom. "Well, what are you so excited about?"

"Me? Excited? I don't get excited."

"Sure you do . . . finding bugs at crime scenes, for example . . . or when you're coming down the home stretch of an investigation."

He owned that he, Brass, Warrick and Nick were about to search the Pierce homestead one last time.

"We're coming along," Catherine said.

"Absolutely, we're coming," Sara said.

"No. Go home, I said."

"Shift isn't over," Sara said.

"It's a big house," Catherine said. "Four more hands to find evidence. . . ."

Less than half an hour later, Brass and the night-shift CSIs again stood in the foyer of the Pierce home—all of them: Nick, Warrick and Grissom . . . Sara and Catherine, too.

Grissom was looking hard at Catherine, who stood there with field kit in hand. "Are you sure you're up to this?"

"No," Catherine said, "I'd rather sit at home thinking about what I'm going to say to the department shrink tomorrow."

"I'm going to take that as sarcasm," Grissom said.

"Why don't you," Catherine said. "Can we get started?"

Grissom led them into the living room, where everyone snapped on latex gloves, including Brass; all five CSIs had their field kits. With the family gone, the house was deathly quiet, almost tomb-like. Despite the high that accompanied what Catherine had described as "the home stretch," Grissom felt remorse slithering through his belly, regretting not only what had happened to Lynn Pierce, but for what would happen in the coming hours. . . .

Nick asked, "Do we think that .44 was the murder weapon?"

"A strong possibility," Grissom said.

"I'll tell you what's a strong possibility," Warrick

said. "Strong possibility that gun's in a garbage bag at the bottom of Lake Mead."

"Not if this family's concerns about Kevin Sadler were real," Grissom said.

"Which means it may still be here," Warrick said.

"Where?" Nick asked.

"Yeah," Sara said, mildly mocking, "just ask Grissom—he'll know."

But Grissom's expression had turned cagey. "Where is the one place in this house we haven't looked?"

"You kiddin', Gris?" Warrick asked. "We've turned this place upside down, like twelve times."

"Gil," Brass said, "I'm here more than I'm home."

"Remember that first night?" Grissom asked. "What was the one thing Pierce requested we do?"

"Not disturb his daughter," Nick said, not missing a beat. "She was too traumatized."

"That's right," Grissom said. "And which of us has searched Lori Pierce's room since then?"

Their looks traveled from one face to the next, none of them able to come up with an affirmative answer. The group followed Grissom quickly up the winding stairway, and soon they were crowded into the hallway, outside the daughter's room.

Plush pink carpeting covered the floor and a pink canopied bed dominated the left side of the room, half a dozen stuffed animals making the pink-and-red spread their jungle. Directly across from the door, a white student desk contained a monitor, keyboard, and mouse, with a single drawer in the center. The computer tower sat on the floor to the left of the desk. On the right side stood a four-drawer white chest, more stuffed animals herded on top. Along the right wall, a television and stereo perched on a small white entertainment stand with the closet door beyond that.

The Goth girl was still living in the little girl's room she'd grown up in.

After unloading their tools in the hall, they split up, doing their best not to trip over each other—it was actually a goodsized bedroom, but with six of them working there, the space seemed impossibly cramped. Catherine took the desk and dresser, Grissom the bed, Warrick the closet, Nick and Sara worked the components of the entertainment center. Using the RUVIS on the bed, Grissom was the first to sing out.

"Someone's been having sex on this bed," he said, like a bear finding signs of Goldilocks.

Everyone looked over at the multiple blossoms of white showing up under the ultraviolet.

"Lots of sex," Catherine said, raising an eyebrow.

Sara and Nick dismantled the television and stereo, finding nothing, reporting as much to Grissom.

Catherine pored over the dresser, found nothing on top or behind it, then went through the drawers one at a time. Except for a stash of condoms in the third drawer, she found nothing other than the girl's clothes. However . . .

"Traces of white powder on the desk," she said.

"Cocaine?" Brass asked.

"Greg will have to confirm, but take my word for it . . . that's coke."

No one argued with her. Their grave expressions indicated a mutual understanding that, despite the little-girl surroundings, Lori Pierce had grown up, and not in a good way.

The tower, monitor, and keyboard yielded nothing, but Catherine discovered a tiny bag inside of the mouse, the source of the white powder. Smaller than the bag they found in the vent in the basement, this one too carried the little red triangle that was Lil Moe's logo.

Catherine shared her discovery, then asked, "You suppose Pierce knows his daughter's buying drugs from his partner?"

"Remind me to ask Daddy," Brass said, "right after I present him with his Father of the Year award."

The top shelf of the closet contained boxes, books, and even more stuffed animals. Warrick leafed through the hanging clothes in the closet, a peculiar mix of the Goth girl and the preppier Lori; but again found nothing.

Not surprisingly, the closet floor was cluttered with shoeboxes; propped against the wall, behind the hanging clothes, leaned a tennis racket and softball bat, a glove nearby, and a pile of magazines—*Sassy, Spin, Sixteen*. After moving all this stuff out, Warrick went over the flooring, his flashlight beam illuminating his way.

In the corner, he found a tiny pile of dust. Loose floorboard, he thought, and pried at the board with a screwdriver. Slowly, one end came free and he eased the board free, then the one next to it, then one more. Craning his neck over the hole and shining his light down inside, he made a wonderful, terrible discovery.

Warrick felt a nausea burning a hole in his stomach as he realized what this meant. "*Got it*—I've got the gun."

Everyone traded looks of mixed emotion—no one had wanted this to come down this way.

Warrick bagged the .44, then went back into the hole, found the box of bullets, and two more bags of coke. "This just keeps getting better," he said glumly.

"Next stop the Blairs?" Grissom asked Brass.

Brass used Lori's phone book to get the number and punched it into his cell. ". . . Mrs. Blair, this is Captain Brass—would you check on your son, and Lori?"

"I don't understand. They're both in bed, asleep, Captain . . . Gary in his room, Lori in the guest—"

"Wake them, get them dressed, and . . . just sit with them, till we get there. Involve your husband, would you?"

"Captain Brass, I still don't understand."

Not wanting to alarm the woman, Brass said, "We just have some new questions that have come up, and it really can't wait."

". . . All right, then. Please hold."

Brass waited, everyone's eyes on him. Several endless minutes went by, when the woman's voice jumped into the detective's ear. "They're both gone! I can't find them anywhere in the house!"

"Calm down, Mrs. Blair. We'll handle it."

"But . . ."

"You and your husband just stay put. Someone will be around. We'll find your son and his girlfriend."

"Like you found Lynn? . . . I'm sorry. That was uncalled for, I . . ."

"Please, Mrs. Blair. You and your husband, stay put."

Brass pushed END and said to Grissom, "They're not there. Lori's gone missing—Gary, too."

"Where are they off to?" Sara asked.

"Are they on the run?" Nick asked.

"I don't think so," Grissom said. "I think they're coming here."

"Here?" Sara asked.

"Homeward bound," Brass said, nodding his agreement with Grissom's unstated thinking; he gestured to Warrick's findings. "Far as Lori knows, we're long gone, and Daddy's in lockup. But we might be back during the course of our investigation, and she's got drugs and the gun here."

"She'll want to ditch the gun," Warrick said.

"And use the drugs," Catherine said.

The detective pressed quickly on, urgency coloring his tone: "Let's pull the vehicles around the corner. If Lori is coming, let's not tip her off that we're here."

Warrick, Nick and Sara moved the cars; Grissom, Catherine and Brass put the room back together, but did not replace the evidence in its hiding places. When the car-parking trio returned, all six of them spread out through the house. Warrick and Nick took the basement, Grissom and Sara the first-floor rec room, and Brass and Catherine went upstairs to the master bedroom.

A few minutes later, the garage door whirred up, then down, and Grissom heard voices coming in through the kitchen.

A muffled voice, recognizable as Gary Blair's, said, "I'll wait here. . . . Hurry up."

And Lori Pierce's voice said: "You don't wanna go upstairs? Party a little?"

"No! I wanna get back before my parents miss us. Don't fool around, Lori!"

"I thought you liked to fool around . . ."

"Just get that stuff, and let's go!"

From their rec room post, Grissom and Sara heard her feet padding up the winding stairs.

Within seconds, Lori's reaction at realizing her stash had been discovered echoed through the house: *"Shit! Shit shit shit!"*

The girl came flying down the stairs, wild-eyed, just as Grissom and Sara came around to meet her. She froze on the stairs, a few steps from the bottom, then glanced over her shoulder—Catherine and Brass were just above and behind her. Warrick and Nick entered the foyer, the latter hauling a bewildered-looking Gary Blair by the arm.

"Lori Pierce," Brass said, in a neutral tone that was nonetheless chilling in the teenagers' ears, "you're under arrest for the murder of your mother, Lynn Pierce."

"What?" Gary Blair blurted. He shook himself free from Nick's grasp, but didn't go anywhere; his expression was that of a kid who'd just heard the truth about Santa Claus. "Her *father* did it—he confessed!" Gary looked around at the adults clustered in the foyer. "You heard him, you *all* heard him! *I* heard him."

Grissom's eyes weren't on Gary, but on Lori, as he said, "Mr. Pierce lied, son. . . . He lied to protect his daughter."

"My *father* killed my mother," Lori insisted, desperation edging her voice, her face, her gestures, animated. "Gary and me, we *heard* him confess—just like you did!"

Grissom walked up several stairs to face Lori, where she was caught between the two groups of grown-ups. "We heard him confess," Grissom acknowledged, "but we also heard him lie."

Lori's voice was filled with typically teenaged contempt. "How do *you* know?"

"We know because the evidence is at odds with what your father 'confessed'—your mother's murder couldn't have happened the way he said, Lori. And the fingerprints on the gun and the box of bullets are going to be ID'ed as yours."

"I didn't kill Mom," Lori said. "I loved her! *Daddy* hated her—that's why he killed her!"

Brass came down and took her gently by the arm and Grissom got out of the way, as the girl was read her rights and handcuffed.

The detective was about to escort the girl from the castle when Gary Blair said, to no one in particular, "I . . . I need to go home."

Lori swung her face toward the boy and gave him a withering look. "You suck," she said.

Brass walked the girl out, and Grissom answered the boy's question: "You're coming with us, Gary. You're a material witness."

Back at HQ, Brass chose to interview Gary Blair first. Grissom was in the interrogation room with them, the rest of the team watching through the two-way glass. The boy's parents had been called, and were on their way.

Brass and the Blair kid sat on opposite sides of the table. Tears rolled down the young man's cheeks and he was trembling.

"Do you want to wait till your parents get here, Gary, before we talk?"

"No . . . I'd . . . I'd rather talk without them here."

"Well, they're coming."

"You better ask your questions, then, 'cause once they're here, I'm zipping it."

"Okay, Gary. What happened that day?"

"Wh . . . what day?"

"What day do you think?"

The kid swallowed snot and tears, and tried to get his crying under control before answering. Finally, staring at the table, he said in a small, very young voice, "Her mom, Mrs. Pierce . . . her mom caught us in bed together, in Lori's room. She wasn't even supposed to come home until hours later, 'cause she had church . . . but her meeting was cancelled and she came home early and she caught us . . . doing it." He shuddered at the thought. "We'd been doin' some, you know, lines, too, and Mrs. Pierce, she found the coke on the desk. Boy, did *she* come unglued! I just shut up and tried to stay out of it, but they had this huge screaming match, Mrs. Pierce threatening to go to my mom and see that Lori and me were split up. Mrs. Pierce told Lori she was sending her to a special school, somewhere out of state, to repent and get tight with Jesus. Crazy stuff like that—but mostly, Mrs. Pierce was saying over and over that Lori and me could never see each other again."

Grissom asked, "Where was the gun, Gary? Somewhere in the garage?"

"No—in Lori's backpack."

Brass frowned. "Why there?"

He shrugged. "She'd started buying coke from this guy who was her father's connection, too."

"Did Mr. Pierce know about this?"

"No! Hell, no! But Lori met this guy at the house a couple times, when he came to do business with Mr. Pierce."

"The gun, Gary."

"I'm getting to that. Lori was afraid of this guy."

Frowning, Grissom said, "Lil Moe?"

"Yeah—Lori said he was hitting on her and she didn't want him to. She said that the next time he, you know, sexually harassed her, she was going to put a stop to it, and threaten him with the gun."

Frowning in thought, Grissom asked, "Where did this gun come from?"

Brass picked up on that. "Was it her father's gun, Gary?"

"Yes . . . she got it out of a drawer somewhere, and her dad didn't even miss it."

Brass took a deep breath, let it out, and said, "So,

Gary—what happened after Mrs. Pierce went ballistic?"

"Mrs. Pierce said she was going to drive straight over to my parents' house, and tell 'em what was going on."

"Your parents have no idea that you're sexually active? That you've used drugs?"

He shook his head.

Brass said, "Mrs. Pierce threatened to go your parents. What then?"

"Lori followed her to the garage, arguing all the way, but more . . . trying to reason with her now, and begging her and stuff. She got in the car with her mom, to try and talk her out of it. And they drove off, still yelling at each other."

"Did you know Lori had taken the gun with her?"

"No. It was in the kitchen, on the counter—the backpack?"

"What did you do then, Gary?"

He shrugged. "I just got my stuff and went home, praying that Mrs. Pierce didn't show up to blow my world apart. And then when Lori and her mom didn't show up, I figured Lori and her mom had worked it out—that she talked her mom out of telling my folks. Later that night, Lori called to say her mom had taken off somewhere. You know, needed time to think and stuff, after the shock of what she found out about Lori and me."

"You didn't know Mrs. Pierce was dead?"

"Oh, no. Lori told me that you people thought her mom was dead, but I didn't really know till I heard her father confess. I thought he was telling the truth. . . . Are you sure he wasn't?"

The interview continued a while, but nothing new was revealed; and then the Blairs were there, and Brass and Grissom left them alone with their son, after telling the young man to be frank with his folks.

"You tell them, Gary," Brass said, "or I will."

The interrogation with Lori Pierce did not go well, at first. Again Grissom accompanied Brass, while the rest of the CSIs looked on through two-way glass. The girl refused to budge off her father's story.

Watching the interrogation, Catherine said to Sara, "She's a smart kid. Knows if she keeps her mouth shut, her old man will take the rap."

"That's cold," Nick said.

Sara said, "So is killing your mother."

Grissom hadn't asked any questions yet; protocol gave that honor to Brass, but the detective was not getting anywhere, and was clearly frustrated, giving Grissom a wide-eyed look that granted the CSI supervisor permission to take a shot.

"Lori," Grissom said, "I'm a criminalist."

Lori Pierce looked up, her face haggard, years added to her features with each passing hour. She summoned some contempt for the adult: "And I care why?"

"Do you know what a criminalist is? What he does?"

The girl stared straight ahead, avoiding Grissom's casual but penetrating gaze.

"I work with evidence," he said. "Like finding your fingerprints on that gun."

Lori didn't seem to be paying any attention to this.

"Do you know what the evidence in this case is telling me?"

The girl gave him a patronizing look. "Don't talk to me like I'm twelve."

"The evidence tells me both you and your father are lying."

Within their mascara caverns, Lori's eyes seemed suddenly nervous.

With a smile that seemed friendly enough, Grissom said, "You're not going to tell me what really happened, are you, Lori?"

The girl showed him a middle finger and said, "Sit, and spin."

"How about I tell *you* what happened."

"Who told you, genius?"

"The evidence. The evidence says you argued with your mother over her catching you and Gary in bed and finding drugs."

She sneered at him. "You mean, Gary told you that. He is so ball-less."

Grissom continued: "Your mother was going to the Blairs to force Gary's parents into making Gary break up with you; then your mother was going to send you to private school."

"Gary. Again, Gary. *He's* not evidence. He's just a little weasel, and a *big* disappointment."

"You're right, Lori— that much Gary did give us. But after that, the evidence takes over the tale. You rode in the car with your mom. You were trying to calm her down, but she was in the grasp of religious fervor and there was no reasoning with her."

The first chink in her tough teenage armor appeared as a tear rolled down Lori's cheek, trailing mascara. "She didn't understand that I loved Gary . . . or thought I did."

"Your mother's religious beliefs were . . . unforgiving."

"Mom, she was like a Nazi, with all this religious junk. She was like Jim Jonesing my ass!"

"You tried to talk to her but she wouldn't listen. But there's something the evidence hasn't told us yet. . . . It will. But it hasn't yet. Where did you go, Lori? You never made it to the Blairs. Where *did* you go?"

She swallowed. Her lips were trembling, her eyes spilling tears. "The church."

Brass leaned forward. "The church?"

The girl nodded. "It's out past the Strip, on the outskirts of town . . . almost in the desert. It's got this big parking lot. I asked Mom if we could go there and . . . pray together."

Grissom said, "No one was around?"

"No other cars in the lot. Later that evening, there would be church stuff goin' on, but sorta over the supper hour . . . no. It was pretty deserted. But Mom had her own key; she was one of the church leaders, you know—we coulda gone in and prayed together."

"But you didn't go in and pray," Brass asked, "did you?"

"No. We sat in the car and I tried to talk to her, I really tried. Only she was so wrapped up in 'God's will' and how we're all sinners and need to be punished that . . . She was mental, she really was."

Grissom asked, "You grabbed the gun from your backpack on the kitchen counter, Lori, and took it with you, when you jumped in the car with your mother."

She nodded numbly. "Mom didn't see the gun. I had it wrapped in my jacket."

Brass looked like his head was about to explode. "You manipulated your mother into going to that church parking lot . . . so you could shoot her?"

"No! No . . ." Tears erupted full force now, long violent, racking sobs.

Catherine Willows, watching through the glass, could not bear any more of this; however hard-boiled a CSI she might be, Catherine was also a mother. She exited the observation booth and entered the interrogation room, glaring at the two men as she sat beside the girl, and comforted her.

After a while, Lori—Catherine holding her hand—said to them, "I didn't mean to shoot her, it was an accident. . . . I just couldn't bear to have Gary taken away. He was the only good thing in my life. He was all I had."

"Why did you have the gun with you?" Catherine asked.

"So I could threaten to kill myself. And that's exactly what I did: I told her I would kill myself right there, in front of her, if she didn't promise to let me finish high school here, and keep seeing Gary, and not tell his parents. I meant it, too! I even said I'd stop the drugs and Gary and I wouldn't have relations, anymore. Didn't do any good."

"How did your mother die, Lori?" Catherine asked, gently.

"It was an accident! She grabbed for the gun . . . I think she thought I was going to use it on myself, and . . . it just went off. The window blew out, and . . . it was awful. It was an awful nightmare!"

Grissom asked, "How did you get home?"

"I spread my jacket on the floor, on the rider's side? And I put mom down on the floor there, on the jacket, y'know? And I drove home. I don't know how. I wasn't crying or afraid or anything. It was like I was outside myself, watching."

"And then?" Grissom asked.

"Then I drove the car into the garage and got Daddy. Told him what happened, and . . . he took care of it. I know he went out to the church parking lot and kind of . . . cleaned up out there. Otherwise . . . he didn't tell me how or anything; all I knew was the car . . . and mom . . . were gone."

"Your father understood about the drugs, and you and Gary?"

"Actually, I . . . I never told Daddy about the coke. Just about the sex. . . . He said that was my business and Mom should have left me alone. He was great, really—perfect father, the best—never cared what I did."

"And with your mother gone," Grissom said, "the rules around the house loosened."

Brass asked, "How long had you been doing coke before your mom caught you?"

She shrugged. "A few months. Gary and I, we just fooled around with it, a little. But after Mom died, every time I went to sleep, I saw her face, her . . . bloody face. The coke made that easier to deal with. I could stay up for a long long time, then I'd pass out. And the good part was, I didn't have dreams."

Catherine sat with her arm around the girl, who again began to cry. Brass gestured to Grissom to step out into the hall.

Brass asked, "Is she telling the truth?"

"Her story and the evidence are compatible."

"I didn't ask you that, Gil."

"I can only tell you what the evidence tells me."

Brass was shaking his head. "That girl was ready to let her father take the fall for her. . . . She may have cold-bloodedly killed her mother, lured her to that church parking lot, and . . . Jesus!"

"We'll go out to that church and see what we can find," Grissom said. "We should find glass, and blood . . . but without the rest of Lynn Pierce's remains . . ." He shrugged.

Brass said, "I guess she's going to Juvenile Hall, after all."

Warrick, Nick and Sara exited the observation booth, joining Brass and Grissom.

"So Pierce walks?" Warrick asked, fire in his eyes. "He cuts up his wife with a chain saw, and *walks?"*

Brass shook his head. "Not hardly—accessory after the fact and possession. Don't forget his business arrangement with Kevin Sadler; Sadler will testify against his former silent partner. Pierce'll be gone a good long while."

"What about Lori?" Sara asked.

Brass said, "If they try her as an adult, she could get life."

Nick said, "I believe her story."

"So will a jury," Warrick opined.

"So she gets away with it?" Sara asked, vaguely disgusted.

"Lori Pierce has given herself a life sentence," Grissom said. "A life sentence of knowing she killed her own mother."

"All the coke in the world won't make that go away," Warrick said.

No one disagreed.

17

At the end of shift, Gil Grissom invited Catherine Willows to his townhouse, offering to fix her some breakfast. She accepted.

Sitting with her legs tucked under her on the small brown leather couch by a window whose closed blinds were keeping out the early morning sun, Catherine watched Grissom scramble eggs, standing in his sandaled feet on the hardwood floor in the open kitchen with its stainless-steel refrigerator and counterspace that spilled into the living room of the spacious, functional condo. Where they weren't lined with bookcases or stacked electronics, the white walls were home to framed displays of butterflies—beautiful dead things that Grissom could appreciate.

Catherine was sipping orange juice; actually, a screwdriver, the juice laced with vodka at her request.

"Like a bagel with this?" he asked, poised over the eggs with the same quiet intensity he brought to any of his experiments.

"That'd be fine—no butter, though."

He shuddered at that thought, but continued with his work.

"You know, I took this job because I like puzzles," she said.

"Me too."

"And I like the idea of finding out who is responsible for the senseless violence that seems to be all around us, chipping away at what we laughingly call civilization."

She was a little drunk.

Grissom said, "Again, we're on the same page." He, however, was not drunk; only orange juice in his glass.

"I never expected," she said, "in a job where I only carry a gun 'cause it's part of the job description . . . where I'm investigating the *aftermath* of crimes, not out on the streets like so many cops are . . . I never . . . never . . . never mind."

He lifted his head from the eggs and looked over at her. "You saved Sara's life . . . and Conroy's. You should feel good about yourself."

"Would you feel good about killing someone?"

". . . No." He used a spatula to fill a plate with eggs. Half a bagel—unbuttered, lightly toasted—was already deposited there.

Sighing, she pulled her legs out from under her and sat up on the couch. "You didn't do me any favor, you know, sending me back into that world."

Grissom walked over, her plate in one hand, utensils and napkin for her, in the other. "You mean, those strip clubs?"

"Those strip clubs. That young woman I shot . . ." And the tears came, and Catherine covered her face with a hand.

Grissom, stunned, sat down next to her, but gave her plenty of space, her plate of eggs in one of his hands. He waited patiently for her crying to cease, then when she looked at him, handed the plate toward her.

She took it, but he left his hand there for a long moment, and for that moment they held the plate, together; their eyes met and finally they both smiled a little . . . friends.

Soon he'd gone to fetch his own plate of eggs, and his own bagel—buttered, untoasted—and sat next to her on the couch, where they ate in silence, other than an occasional compliment from Catherine on his cooking, which he did not acknowledge.

"This guy Pierce," she said, and sipped her drink.

"What about him?"

"I don't know, I just can't wrap my mind around the guy. . . . He's not a monster. I mean, he must love his daughter—he tried to take the blame for her. But he also coldbloodedly cut up his wife with a chain saw."

"*We* look at dead people dispassionately," Grissom said. "Bodies become evidence, to us. Some would consider us coldblooded."

"Maybe. But that man loved that woman once . . . Lynn Pierce used to be a vibrant, happy woman who Owen Pierce loved. How could even a coldblooded bastard like him learn to live with what he's done? And that his daughter murdered her own mother? His wife, a woman he must have once adored? How can he handle it? How can he *deal* with it?"

"Oh I don't know," Grissom said, and took a bite of bagel. He chewed, swallowed, and—conferring Catherine his angelic smile—added, "Maybe in prison, he'll get religion."

Author's Note

I would again like to acknowledge the contribution of Matthew V. Clemens.

Matt—who has collaborated with me on numerous published short stories—is an accomplished true crime writer, as well as a knowledgeable fan of *C.S.I.* He helped me develop the plot of this novel, and worked up a lengthy story treatment, which included all of his considerable forensic research, for me to expand my novel upon.

The real-life C.S.I. to whom Matt and I have dedicated this book—Criminalist Sergeant Chris Kaufmann CLPE, Bettendorf (Iowa) Police Department—provided comments, insights and information that were invaluable to this project. Books consulted include two works by Vernon J. Gerberth: *Practical Homicide Investigation Checklist and Field Guide* (1997) and *Practical Homicide Investigation: Tactics, Procedures and Forensic Investigation* (1996). Also helpful was *Scene of the Crime: A Writer's Guide to Crime-Scene Investigations* (1992), Anne Wingate, Ph.D. Any inaccuracies, however, are my own. Also drawn upon was *Dead Water* (1995), Pat Gipple and Matthew V.

Clemens, a nonfiction account of a torso slaying and a pioneering genetic trial.

Again, Jessica McGivney at Pocket Books provided support, suggestions and guidance. The producers of *C.S.I.* were gracious in providing scripts, background material and episode tapes, without which this novel would have been impossible.

Finally, the inventive Anthony E. Zuiker must be singled out as creator of this concept and these characters. Thank you to him and other *C.S.I.* writers, whose imaginative and well-documented scripts inspired this novel and have done much toward making the series such a success both commercially and artistically.

MAX ALLAN COLLINS has earned an unprecedented eleven Private Eye Writers of America "Shamus" nominations for his historical thrillers, winning twice for his Nathan Heller novels, *True Detective* (1983) and *Stolen Away* (1991).

A Mystery Writers of America "Edgar" nominee in both fiction and nonfiction categories, Collins has been hailed as "the Renaissance man of mystery fiction." His credits include five suspense-novel series, film criticism, short fiction, songwriting, trading-card sets and movie/TV tie-in novels, including *In the Line of Fire, Air Force One* and the *New York Times* bestselling *Saving Private Ryan.*

He scripted the internationally syndicated comic strip *Dick Tracy* from 1977 to 1993, is cocreator of the comic-book features *Ms. Tree, Wild Dog,* and *Mike Danger,* has written the *Batman* comic book and newspaper strip, and the mini-series *Johnny Dynamite: Underworld.* His graphic novel, *Road To Perdition,* has been made into a DreamWorks feature film starring Tom Hanks and Paul Newman, directed by Sam Mendes.

As an independent filmmaker in his native Iowa, he wrote and directed the suspense film *Mommy,*starring Patty McCormack, premiering on Lifetime in 1996, and a 1997 sequel, *Mommy's Day.* The recipient of a record six Iowa Motion Picture Awards for screenplays, he wrote *The Expert,* a 1995 HBO World Premiere; and wrote and directed the award-winning documentary *Mike Hammer's Mickey Spillane* (1999) and the innovative *Real Time: Siege at Lucas Street Market* (2001).

Collins lives in Muscatine, Iowa, with his wife, writer Barbara Collins, and their teenage son, Nathan.

CSI: 1102